The
Summer
House by
the Sea

JENNY OLIVER

ONE PLACE. MANY STORIES

HarperCollins
PUBLISHERS
Since 1817

HQ
An imprint of HarperCollins*Publishers* Ltd.
1 London Bridge Street
London SE1 9GF

This edition 2017

3
First published in Great Britain by
HQ, an imprint of HarperCollins*Publishers* Ltd. 2017

ISBN:
PB: 9780008217945
e-Book: 9780008217969

Printed and bound by
CPI Group, Croydon CR0 4YY

For Waldo and Woody

CHAPTER 1

Ava was standing at the crossing when her phone beeped. She took it from her pocket at the same time as glancing left for traffic.

Instead of looking right, Ava opened the WhatsApp message from her brother, Rory: *Gran in hospital*, it read. She frowned down at her phone and wondered how Rory could ever think that was enough information. But then the horn of the 281 bus stopped all other conscious thought.

The shriek of the brakes filled the air as she saw the huge windscreen, the wipers. The face of the driver in slow motion, mouth open. Her whole body tensed. She felt her hand drop the phone. Time paused.

There was a fleeting thought that this was actually really embarrassing.

And then – smack – she didn't think anything else. Just felt the hard pain in her hip, then the thwack of her head as she was thrown down on to the tarmac, and an overriding sense of unfairness because she wasn't yet ready to die.

CHAPTER 2

The nurse waited patiently as Ava tried once more to get through to her brother.

'It's voicemail,' Ava said, apologetic. 'Everyone's on voicemail. No one's answering their phone, I've tried everyone. I'm really sorry.' All her friends were in meetings or on the tube or at lunch, unreachable.

'It's fine.' The nurse's nametag read Julie Stork. Ava wondered if using her name might aid familiarity – she found it a bit creepy when the man at Starbucks called her Ava because he'd written it on a cup every day, but she could do with an ally. The alternative was another nurse, Tina, who Julie was talking quietly with now. Tina was terrifying. Her uniform stretched tight over her solid figure, hair scraped back in a ponytail, all-seeing eyes like hungry jackdaws. She'd been the one to inform Ava that she couldn't go home without someone to watch over her for twenty-four hours, while making it very clear that they needed the bed back as soon as possible.

Without the pressure of having no one to come and get her, Ava might have quite enjoyed her hospital stay. Starched white sheets, lamb chops and green beans, sponge pudding and custard, and a tatty out-of-date copy of *OK!* magazine. But her eyes hovered distractedly to her phone the whole time, her fingers scrolling through her contacts every few seconds, texting, WhatsApping, refreshing.

She felt her cheeks flush with embarrassment as she heard Nurse Tina mutter, 'There must be someone.'

So when her phone beeped she pounced on it. A text from Rory: *Can't get away. Jonathon coming to get you.*

Ava put her hand over her mouth. How could her brother send her ex-boyfriend, of all people? Send his PA, one of the runners on set, anyone. Not the guy he'd set her up with and who she'd split from three months ago.

She sat up quickly to get dressed and out of the stupid hospital gown that did up at the back, the magazine clattering to the floor. She tried to check her reflection in anything she could find: a knife from her plate. She scrunched her flat hair. She felt dizzy. She paused on the side of the bed and looked up just in time to see Jonathon sauntering up the hospital aisle with a sardonic grin on his face.

'Hi, Jonathon,' she said with an embarrassed half-smile as he stopped, hands on hips, at the end of her bed.

'Hit by a bus, eh?'

She nodded. Tried to stand up but felt faint and sat down again. He swooped round the side of the bed to help her. 'Thanks,' she mumbled.

'It's fine. Take your time.'

She remembered how familiar his face had been. The wide brown eyes and ruddy cheeks. The frustrated look he'd given her when she'd told him that she didn't think they were going to work as a couple. That she wasn't very good at relationships and she didn't think that she was what he was looking for. That she was good at being on her own. And the wide eyes narrowing as he said, *'Yes you are.*

The Summerhouse by the Sea 11

You're going to have to be. Because honestly, I don't think I know you at all.'

Now he looked all bright and breezy, the collar of his navy striped rugby shirt turned up, jolly eyes sparkling, while Ava was struggling to stand in her open-backed gown. She shuffled on bare feet to close the curtain, a task which Nurse Tina took over, drawing it with a quick flick of her wrist, hustling the exit process forwards.

'You need any help?' Jonathon asked, picking up the magazine from the floor and having a flick through.

Ava shook her head.

Jonathon went to stand outside the cubicle as she picked up her socks. The effort of pulling one on was like clambering over a brick wall. Waves of tiredness made her want to snuggle back down into the pillow. She tried to undo her gown but couldn't reach the strings at the back. Limbs heavy and useless. She tried again.

In the end she sat, hands either side of her, and shutting her eyes said, 'Jonathon.'

'Yep,' his head poked through the curtain.

'I think I'm going to need some help.'

She saw the raised brow, the slight quirk of his lips. Then he walked in and carefully undid the back of her gown. She held it to her front as she took out one arm at a time and he handed her her T-shirt. She felt him watching with veiled amusement as she tried to get her top on without exposing any more of her body. But when it came to her skinny jeans she finally had to relent, her toes lost somewhere in the tight denim and the waistband halfway up her thighs. 'Could you help me pull them up, please?' she said, cursing Topshop. If she wasn't so completely shattered the humiliation would have been unbearable.

Finally dressed, Ava had to take a second to sit on the bed and get her breath back. She realised the window behind the bed made the perfect mirror as she saw her flat hair and white face staring back at her.

Jonathon gave her his arm and she took it reluctantly to stand up.

'You know, this is the most vulnerable I've ever seen you,' he said, chuckling at her obvious displeasure at needing help.

They walked out slowly, Nurse Julie watching with an expression that presumed they were a sweet young couple heading home to eat chicken soup and curl up in front of *Homes Under the Hammer*. Nurse Tina glanced up from her desk with a satisfied nod and handed Ava a leaflet on concussion and signs to look out for.

Ava just wanted to curl up and sleep, but Jonathon was still talking. 'That's pretty crazy, isn't it? Given we went out for more than six months.' He paused as he held open the door and added with a grin, 'I'm still a pretty good catch, you know, Ava . . .'

She managed a smile.

As he bundled her into the soft leather seats of his Volvo, the vulnerable, mildly concussed side of her realised how easy it would be to cosy on down with him in front of some daytime TV. To slip back into the warm, comforting familiarity. But she knew it wasn't right. Her litmus test was to imagine introducing him to her mother, had she been alive. The three of them sitting down to afternoon tea and her mother's attention drifting as Jonathon talked politely about his job, his hobbies, his military fitness training. Her mother immediately sizing him up as average. Ava imagined herself cutting in with his achievements, with the fun they had, and her mother with an expression that questioned who she was trying to convince.

Jonathon turned to look at her as he cruised down the main road. 'I'll drop you at Rory's and then head straight off, got to get back to work, OK?'

And Ava realised that the 'good catch' statement was just that, a statement, to show her what she'd missed. There was no *Homes Under the Hammer* option available to her, even if she wanted it. 'Yes, absolutely fine.'

When they pulled up outside Rory and his wife Claire's Victorian semi, Jonathon came round to open Ava's door, but she'd opened it on her own. He shut it after her instead.

'Got all your stuff?' he asked, as he followed her to the pavement.

Ava nodded. 'Thank you. You know, for . . .' She gestured to her clothes and the car. 'Everything.'

'It was my pleasure, Ava,' Jonathon smirked, leaning in to give her a quick peck on the cheek, then waving to Claire who had just opened the front door. As he slipped back into his heated leather seat, he added, 'It was actually quite enlightening. Getting to see beneath the . . .' He made a gesture to her face and body, then coughed and said, 'Not literally. You know what I mean?' Then shook his head and with an awkward wave pulled the car door shut.

Ava watched him drive away, the grey sky merging with the road and the pavement. She didn't have time to dwell on what he'd said because her ten-year-old nephew Max came bounding to her side.

'Aunty Ava! Where's your bandage? Mum said you'd been hit by a bus. Wow! That's so cool. It must have *really* hurt!'

Claire appeared behind him. 'Sorry I couldn't pick you up, I was getting Max from football. You OK?'

Ava rubbed her head, felt the tears of the day pushing behind her eyes. She shook her head. 'Not really,' she said.

Claire reached out and put her arms around her, enveloping Ava in the kind of hug mums give on TV adverts, that make everything better and smell of fabric softener and strawberries. Ava was momentarily jealous of little Max standing next to her on the drive, eating chocolate digestives and watching YouTube on a laptop balanced precariously on his arm.

Ava stepped out of the hug, brushing her hair back, wincing as she felt the huge bump on the side of her head. 'Thanks,' she said to Claire, who nodded in understanding and ushered her inside, into the bright kitchen diner where she sat down on a battered club chair at the far end, next to the bifold doors that opened out on to the decking and the neatly mown lawn.

'What do we need to do?' Claire asked as she put the kettle on. Ava handed her the hospital leaflet, momentarily relieved to pass all responsibility over to someone else. Someone who was just innately caring, practical and kind. Who got a bag of frozen peas out of the freezer, wrapped them in a tea towel and put them carefully on her head, who made her a cup of tea and put sugar in for the shock, and went and found a blanket for her shoulders even though the house was completely warm enough.

Claire ruffled Max's hair as she walked past him, and once again Ava thought how lucky he was.

Her phone started beeping with replies from her friends, finally out of all-day meetings and finished at the gym, asking if she was OK, whether she needed anything. Ava closed her eyes.

Max plodded over with his laptop and the packet of digestives. 'Do you think anyone filmed it, Aunty Ava? We should try and find out,' he said through a mouthful of biscuit crumbs. 'Because you could send it into Ultimate Fails and they'd put you on YouTube.'

The front door slammed and a man's voice said, 'That's enough, thank you, Max.'

Max rolled his eyes. 'Hi, Dad,' he said, perching himself on the armrest of Ava's chair and disappearing back into his laptop.

Rory strode into the kitchen like a businessman might in a film. Cool and confident, a little distracted, emanating stress. He looked like he always did, just older. Top button on his shirt undone, blond hair a fraction ruffled, sleeves rolled up. He looked at Ava.

She felt like a fool with peas on her head and a blanket round her shoulders.

'You alright?' he asked, leaning up against the duck-egg kitchen unit.

She nodded.

'Nothing broken?' He poured himself a glass of water.

Ava shook her head.

'Good,' he said, downing the drink in one.

She was about to tell him how annoyed she was that he'd sent Jonathon to get her when he asked, 'Up to travelling?'

Ava narrowed her eyes. 'Why?'

Rory rolled his lips together, ran his hand through his hair. Glanced at his wife who had paused in the doorway. 'Not good news, I'm afraid.'

'What?' Ava asked. She suddenly remembered the WhatsApp she'd read before the bus hit.

'She's died,' he said, typically matter-of-fact. 'Gran's died.'

Ava felt her whole body shrink.

'All very natural. Peaceful,' he said, refilling his glass. 'And they don't waste any time in Spain. Funeral's tomorrow.'

Ava sat very still, trying to stop her bottom lip from wobbling, not wanting to cry in front of Rory, hugging the frozen peas absently to her chest. Wishing that today and every other day to come was yesterday.

CHAPTER 3

'Get off your phone, Rory, this is a wake.'

'I'm not on my phone. I'm just checking something.'

The room was cool and dark compared to the scorching Spanish heat outside. It smelt of furniture polish, clouds of heady sweet perfume and the waxy candles that burnt bright next to bunches of fake flowers on every surface.

'That's being on your phone,' Ava hissed in a whisper.

'It's not. Anyway, they're all on their phones.' Rory gestured to the group of men in the corner of the little room where their grandmother's body was laid out behind a pane of glass, resplendent in all her finery – a shocking turquoise silk kaftan, pink velvet trousers, jewelled sandals, her sparrow-like wrists bedecked with chunky plastic bracelets, and around her neck three or four Bakelite necklaces – an outfit she'd had waiting in the back of the wardrobe for this very occasion.

Ava looked over and sure enough, half of the mourners who'd come to pay their respects were chatting away on their beaten-up old phones. Two men played dominos, while a group of women were knitting as they talked animatedly to the deceased.

'Just put it away,' Ava sighed, trying to ignore the remains of yesterday's headache.

'You're very self-righteous for someone who got hit by a bus while on their phone,' Rory said, as he did another quick refresh of his emails before slipping it in his pocket. 'What do you think they're saying to her?' he added, nodding towards the knitting women nattering away to the body.

Ava shrugged. 'I have no idea. But whatever it is, it's very passionate. I'm feeling really British.' She looked down at her outfit. They were both dressed starkly in black, crumpled from the flight and a hot taxi ride from Barcelona airport. Behind them were men who'd come straight from work in overalls, another in a three-piece white suit, and women in rainbow colours, chatting, wiping their eyes. The crying around them was free and open, but Ava held hers painfully tight in her chest, not quite able to let herself go in front of her dry-eyed brother and all these strangers. 'I don't know what I'm going to say.'

Rory shook his head. 'No, me neither. I'm terrible at this kind of thing. I'm only just getting over the fact that we can see the body.' He glanced backwards towards the door as if looking for a quick escape.

'You want to sit?' One of the knitting women turned, her face as wrinkled as a raisin, a touch of smudged mascara on her grooved cheek that she patted away with a neatly folded handkerchief. Beside her she had a little pug dog, his lame back legs propped up on a harness with wheels.

'Oh no, it's fine. Fine. You stay,' Ava insisted.

Ava and Rory had been hovering awkwardly since they'd arrived. If their father had been there, he'd no doubt have taken charge and said something meaningful about how valuable she had been to them all. But as he was in China, cruising the Yangtze River, he wasn't there to take charge.

'I have said enough,' the woman replied, standing so that Ava could take her place and ushering the women next to her to do the same. The candles all around them flickered.

Rory nudged Ava forwards. 'I'm not really sure what to say,' she laughed nervously as she felt the eyes in the room watching.

'Say whatever you like.' The woman raised her hands as if to encompass the world. 'You are here to keep her company.'

'To remind her of how greatly she was loved,' another woman with bright dyed-red hair added as she went past. 'Although we all know how much she liked a bit of gossip.'

Ava and Rory took the seats, staring at the figure laid out in front of them, her rouged cheeks and pink lipstick, her costume jewellery glistening in the dull spotlights, her beads, her velvet, her tiny shiny shoes.

Ava looked at Rory.

'We flew out Ryanair, Gran,' he said. 'You'd have hated it. No leg room.' Then he made a face like he didn't know what else to say and beckoned for Ava to continue.

Ava swallowed. 'You look amazing, really great outfit,' she said. It felt as though the whole room was listening, so she stood up to talk a little quieter, her mouth close up to the glass, eyes staring at the fabric of her grandmother's kaftan. 'It feels like we haven't been out here for ages. I'm sorry about that. I wish I'd seen you.'

Not knowing what else to say she glanced down at the floor, at her black shoes. 'I've worn really boring shoes,' she added, looking back up, this time at the

face she knew so well, now lifeless and powdery.
'Oh God,' she put her hand to her mouth, 'I'm going
to *really* miss you.' Her voice caught. 'I'm sorry.
Everyone's watching me.' She closed her eyes, stared
into the darkness of her eyelids and said, 'I suppose
I just want to say thank you.' She opened her eyes.
'Thank you, for everything. I feel like you're going to
ring me and tell me that this all went really well.' She
half-laughed, then stopped, because as she stood there
her eyes suddenly saw her own reflection in the glass
rather than what was behind it. The black of her dress
made her body disappear and she saw her face overlaid
on to her grandmother's. Her bobbed brown hair over
shocking white curls, open blue eyes overlaid on closed
tanned eyelids shaded with a stripe of bright hot pink.

At the same time a group of people bustled in
through the door, as more of her grandmother's friends
arrived together, all wild gesticulations and a tumble
of easy words, clutching tissues and holding hands.
The space around them thronged. Rory stood up, their
chairs now odd little empty islands as the number of
people standing amassed.

A man in a slick black suit walked to the front and
started to sing. Ava's breath caught in her throat as the
sound of this lone deep voice echoed around the room.

She stared at her face merging with her gran's. With
Valentina Brown – Val – her wonderful, opinionated,
feisty grandmother, aged eighty-four, her outfit and her
funeral preparations ready, her life lived like a peach
so ripe it was ready to burst. Died at the same moment
as Ava had lived. Like a deal had been struck with the
universe to save her.

Ava could almost hear her voice. *'You stupid girl.
Me, I'm ready. You. You are not ready. You have more*

to give than this! You could have anything you like. Babies, husbands. I know, I know, I'm old-fashioned. Anything, Ava. Life is precious and time is not your friend. This is fate. Don't sigh. I can hear a sigh down the phone. No respect – just like your mother. Just think for a moment, if this was it, Ava, would you be happy with what you've achieved?'

Ava stared transfixed at the glass. Was her life something to be proud of? Had it really been lived as well as it could? If someone had stood at the lectern to speak, what would they have said about her?

Then, just as the haunting song was reaching its peak, Rory's phone started to ring.

'Oh man.' Ava rolled her eyes.

'Sorry!' Rory held up his hand. 'Sorry,' he said, as he fumbled to turn it off.

Then the coffin lid shut. Ava blinked. The curtain drew around the glass and the reflection popped.

'Are you alright?' Rory nudged her on the arm.

'Yes.' Ava tucked her hair behind her ears. They followed as everyone in the room headed towards the door.

'Sure?' He narrowed his gaze.

She nodded, sliding her sunglasses down as they stepped out into the dazzling bright sunshine of the little Spanish town, a place familiar from holidays – a fifteen-minute drive from their grandmother's beachside house – visited for the supermarket, the nightclub and a day trip whenever it rained.

The mass of people spewed out into the road, the noise in the air like starlings. And when the procession began it was like burying royalty. People came out of shops to nod their heads, stood in the doorways of the little tapas bars, leaned against the gnarled trunks of the orange trees to watch. The air was perfumed with the hint of late blossom and exhaust smoke, while the sun baked them all like an oven.

There was a band made up of three old guys with a trumpet, an accordion and a tambourine, led by the singer from the wake. The music and the chatting followed the coffin all the way to the cemetery, loud and lively, the wobbling mass of people like jelly through the streets.

All exactly to Valentina Brown's specifications.

Ava allowed herself a moment of morbid self-absorption to imagine, had it been her, the rainy, grey afternoon, people shaking out their umbrellas and wrapping their black macs tight, complaining about the terrible summer they were having, her father standing quietly in the front pew while Rory gave the eulogy. She glanced at him surreptitiously checking his emails. Great.

At the cemetery the sun flickered through giant fir trees, welcome shade as the group paused in front of a big white wall of little black doors. Behind these niches were the coffins of the people in the gilt-framed, sun-bleached photographs screwed above each door. Faded artificial flowers and alabaster Virgin Marys watched mournfully over the proceedings as rays of sun dappled like fingers of dusty light.

Words were said in Spanish, a blessing Ava couldn't understand. So she remembered instead her first taste of chorizo and chickpeas, and the sound of Padrón peppers sizzling in the pan, so incongruous in the little Ealing bungalow where her grandparents lived, the crazy-paved outside wall and the gnomes in the garden. Remembered the piping hot doughnutty churros and the pots of warm melted chocolate for breakfast that they ate in their sleeping bags in the front room on swirly brown carpet in front of the two-bar electric fire. And then summer holiday trips in the car, driving endless miles through France and across Spain to Mariposa, the beach town where Valentina Brown grew up. Home of the Summerhouse. Once a ramshackle fisherman's hut – a place where their great-grandfather hauled his boats to store them for the winter and mend his nets – transformed into a little haven on the cusp of the sea by Eric Brown, Val's husband, his pale English skin and dislike of sand keeping him happily indoors with his Black & Decker and PG Tips. Summer after summer the roof was tiled, the walls plastered, the bathroom and kitchen refitted, a little terrace added and a first-floor bedroom built into the wooden-beamed eaves. Ava remembered standing in the shade of the palm trees, handing her grandfather nails and spirit levels, while Rory mixed thick cement with a trowel and they both got told off for flicking each other with white paint. And as Eric carefully laid the pebbles for the front path, Ava wrote the words 'Summerhouse' in shells and a great discussion ensued as to whether there should have been a space between the words, Rory rolling his eyes at her stupidity and Val appearing to clip him round the ear before bending down and writing 'Our' in shells in the wet cement above.

It was the perfect summer hideaway. And when Eric passed away, Val decamped from Ealing to Mariposa full-time, and the Summerhouse became her everyday house. But for Ava and Rory it was still the place that holidays were made of.

'She had a bloody good innings,' Rory whispered as Val's coffin was lifted.

Ava turned to look at him, snapped out of her memories. 'It's not a cricket match, Rory.'

He snorted under his breath. Ava looked away, out across the sea of mourners, to the hats and the white hair, the smiles, the open tears, the handkerchiefs, the cigarettes, the hipflasks, the veils and the bright pops of corsage colour.

She saw the fullness of a life take shape in the people come to mourn it and was struck by the single thought: *I have been given a second chance.*

She turned back to see the coffin carried towards its final resting place, waves of sunlight dancing on the carved wood while glitter-edged artificial flowers shone pink around the niche in the wall like a welcoming cocoon. And as the coffin slid inside the chamber, Ava reached up to wipe the first tear from her cheek.

CHAPTER 4

The little tapas bar was heaving with people, Barcelona warming up for the night. Ava and Rory had been dropped off by their taxi on the way from the cemetery to the airport after Ava persuaded Rory they had enough time for a quick drink. Rory had huffed, reluctant. He didn't like leaving the airport to chance.

The evening sun was hovering on the cusp of the rooftops. Sparrows jumped in the dust. A guy in the square opposite the bar was playing the guitar, tapping his foot gently, a cap for change at his feet. Ava leant forwards on the little barrel table she was sitting at to watch. Behind the guitar player a couple on a bench were arguing, while across the square little children yelped and shouted on a climbing frame. The coloured lights strung between the plane trees glowed fairground bright.

'Bloody hell, it's carnage in here.' Rory appeared, balancing little plates of tapas on top of two sherry glasses, elbows out like chicken wings from battling his way through the crowd. His phone was ringing. 'Take these,' he thrust the drinks at her as he fumbled for his phone. 'I have to take this. It's work.'

Ava sat for a second, sipping her sherry, then, with nothing else to do, checked her own phone. Before she'd flown to Spain she'd sent an email to her friends about a dinner next week, the subject line:

I'm alive!! Everyone had immediately said they could come. But now her friend Louise, who was thirteen weeks pregnant, was asking for it to be postponed because the date clashed with a midwife appointment. Someone else had agreed, relieved because they had a work do they'd forgotten about; another cited arrangements their partner had made without telling them. Ava scrolled through the emails, mocked by the *I'm alive!!* subject header on every decline.

She didn't want to be upset. But this was starting to happen more often: the casual cancel. All she could think was that she rarely said no to an invite. Normally she would have been scrolling through her diary right now to try and find other dates that might work, might pull the group together, write some extra jolly response to keep the momentum going. Ava was constantly rearranging, juggling, to make sure that she could see everyone, do everything, make sure everyone was happy, and she hated the part of herself that wondered why, when she most needed it, they couldn't do the same for her. Because she knew it was fruitless. They weren't being callous – it was just the older they got, the harder it was to mesh their lives. They weren't at university any more, nor loafing about in their first jobs, free and easy. Her friend Louise was expecting twins, for goodness' sake.

And she wanted Louise to have babies. It was exciting. It would be lovely. But it put paid to Ava's secret wish that Louise and Barnaby, her husband, might realise they hated each other, divorce, and then Louise would move back in with Ava, and all the fun they used to have would commence once more. Twins made the wish a lot less practical.

Rory reappeared, chucking his phone down on the table. 'Bloody work. They're completely incompetent.

How long have we been gone? Twelve hours max and they manage to balls it up in my absence.' He raked a hand through his hair. 'I can literally feel the stress in my veins.' Exhaling dramatically, he took a big swig of his drink.

Ava watched him take his seat again, barely pausing to appreciate the warm evening air, the buzz of the square, the sharp, cool sherry. It always amazed her to think of him as someone's boss, as some bigwig revered documentary-maker, because really he was just her annoying brother who she remembered videoing himself doing embarrassing David Attenborough impressions in the back garden. Now though he was tipped for a BAFTA and was invited for dinners at No. 10. She'd never seen her father look so taken aback as the moment one Christmas when Rory announced that he had been invited to a bash at the Prime Minister's. Their dad had absolutely no understanding of television bar the *Ten O'Clock News*, and seemed quite stunned that it could lead to something he would deem a serious accolade. He took himself off to his study, shaking his head with bemusement.

'Shall we have a toast to Gran?' Ava said, raising her glass.

'Yes absolutely, nice idea.' Rory clinked his glass to hers. They both took a sip.

The dry crispness of the sherry flamed her throat and nose as though she'd inhaled the scent. It tasted of Spain. Of nights sitting on her grandmother's veranda, bare feet up on the railing, looking out over the little courtyard garden, the man in the house opposite watering the flowerpots on his wall with a tin can on a long bit of bamboo, the rustle of the palm leaves in the wind, the hoot of the gecko, the sweet ripe perfume of fat purple figs and the fresh-river tang of red geraniums.

The bar filled up around them, bodies squishing to get through, and Rory and Ava talked for a while about the ceremony, polite musings about how nice it had been, how much their grandmother would be missed. Then Rory said, 'So . . . Gran's house,' fishing a small drowning fly out of his drink. 'I'm thinking we get someone in to clear the place out, put it on the market as soon as possible.' He looked up as he was ushering the fly off his finger on to the barrel table to check Ava was listening. 'I could do with some cash at the moment. Our mortgage has skyrocketed and Max's school fees just seem to completely ignore inflation. Yeah?' He was still in work mode. Used to people doing exactly what he told them.

Ava had the fleeting thought, as he spoke, of how nice it would be to come back to Spain and sort out the Summerhouse herself. She wondered if any of her friends might want to come with her. The list of declines to a simple meal made it seem unlikely. That was the problem with getting older, there were fewer and fewer people to go on holiday with. She imagined herself in the future, resorting to coach trips for company. She didn't actually mind a coach trip – apart from the fact that everyone watched you get up to walk to the toilet – she just wanted to go on one out of choice rather than desperation.

The alternative would be to come out here on her own. To really grasp the idea of a second chance and head off into the sunset to find herself. But the thought made her uneasy. She wasn't sure she had the courage for so much aloneness. She had no trouble curling up on her sofa at home watching Netflix by herself all evening, but that was generally because she always knew that the next night or the next lunchtime or the next breakfast she was meeting someone, whether it was a client or a friend or even her dad. There was always someone. Always a dinner, always a drink. And if one person cancelled she invariably found another. Aside from her close friends she had a little black book of acquaintances, an intricate network of possibilities. There was always a dot on her iPhone calendar. She made sure she wasn't lonely by rarely being alone.

Across from the bar the guitar player paused for a beer, nodding when a couple of people clapped. The mood of the playground opposite morphed as the little kids ran off for dinner and a group of loping teenagers took over the swings.

Ava's phone buzzed with a text message.

It was from Caroline, a girl she hadn't spoken to in ages who she'd seemingly called in desperation from the hospital. They'd done work experience together at Peregrine Fox Antiques – which predominantly meant walking Peregrine's dog and popping out to buy espressos. Caroline had left for a job at an auction house and was now senior press officer. Ava realised she must have underestimated her concussion because she couldn't actually believe she'd called Caroline for help, given their lack of recent contact and Caroline's ability to always make her feel as though, while everyone else was leaning in, Ava was lying back taking a nap.

Ava! Great to hear from you! Sorry taken so long to reply – we're in the middle of a HUGE forgery scandal. All super stressful and not something I should even mention on text. LOL. Will probably be indicted. How's things?? Your LinkedIn says you're still working at Peregrine's btw – need to update.

Ava exhaled, blowing her hair up out of her face, the curl landing back in the same place. She almost laughed. The world itself was conspiring to spotlight her every failing.

Exactly as her LinkedIn profile suggested, Ava *was* still working at Peregrine Fox Antiques. She loved her job. She sourced antiques for rich clients at the tiny company run by the brilliant, very camp Peregrine Fox. She was good at it. People trusted her. They sold her things for nothing and bought things from her for a fortune while Peregrine drank copious espressos and did the same thing, just more flamboyantly. Ava had an eye for quality that came from trailing round after her mother, who only felt like she'd truly made it in life when the very best became her everyday default. Her eye for a bargain came from trailing round after her grandmother, who had a self-patented technique for elbowing to the front at jumble sales. Ava's greatest success to date was unearthing a Chippendale blanket trunk in the back room of a Sussex farmhouse that was being used to store muddy boots and dog food.

But now, seen through Caroline's eyes, it made her feel as though she was still twenty-one and doing the filing.

It felt like a sign.

Ava turned her phone over on the table, didn't reply to the text. She watched the fly Rory had saved still making its way dozily to the edge of the table.

Rory had taken the opportunity to read his emails again. 'Going to have to drink up so we can get to the airport,' he said, eyes glued to his screen.

Ava checked her watch. There was acres of time. 'You know, Rory,' she said, swallowing, her mouth suddenly dry, talking before her brain had fully formulated a plan, 'maybe I might come out here for the summer.'

Rory took a quick slug of sherry. 'What do you mean? What – to Spain?'

'Yeah,' Ava nodded. 'Maybe I could pack up the Summerhouse. You know, take some time off work. Live in it for a bit?' He was watching her and that made her carry on, uncomfortable. 'Maybe this might be a good opportunity for a . . .' She tried to find the right word. He was still looking at her, dubious. 'A restart. A re-evaluation.'

The guitar player had started up again. The teenagers on the swings were rolling cigarettes, tinny music from their phones clashing with the guitar. The bar heaved with people, knocking their chairs as they pushed past, hands full, carrying drinks out into the square. It was still warm, but the air around Ava suddenly felt hotter under Rory's scrutiny.

'Don't you think you'd be better off maybe buying a house with the inheritance? Or,' he paused, tapped the table with his index finger, 'not running out on perfectly good relationships. How was Jonathon by the way?' When Ava rolled her eyes in response, he stretched his shoulders back, as though his shirt, or her life, was an annoying discomfort. 'Those are the kind of things that would lead to your future, Ava.'

She studied him. Noticed how age made him look harder. Like all his edges had squared off. 'You sound like Dad.'

Rory shrugged. 'No bad thing. Look, thing is, Ava, I think it's better that we just sell. I can't sit on that money while you take a holiday. I'm sorry, I know that sounds harsh. But it's going to have to be a no. OK?'

She didn't say anything, knew from experience that it was pointless arguing with her brother, he was like a brick wall. It was the same as when they were kids, his bedroom door always tight shut, Ava desperately guessing the password that might let her in, too naively exuberant to realise that the game was endless because there never was one.

But Ava's interest was piqued. The idea of a second chance, a different way of living, a change, wouldn't go away.

She picked up her glass and took another sip. She knew the bus accident wasn't fate, just a bad combination of WhatsApp and the Green Cross Code. She knew there were no deals with the universe or cosmic signs. But it felt like she had somehow been handed this possibility by her grandmother, and she couldn't allow it to slip through her fingers.

She imagined sitting by herself on that Spanish veranda, with the view of the courtyard garden and the sweet-scented close night air. And Ava knew suddenly that if her grandmother could do it alone, so could she.

Rory was still talking. 'It was funny, wasn't it, when that guy said he felt sorry for Grandad. No more peace in heaven for him.'

Ava laughed. 'Yeah, it was.'

'God, I'd have had to say something about you, wouldn't I? If that bus had got you.'

'That's a nice way of putting it, Rory.'

Rory sniggered into his sherry. Then he looked at his watch. 'Come on, drink up, we've got a plane to catch.'

She realised she was suddenly itching to know what he would have said about her if the bus had indeed got her. Intrigued by a possible heartfelt truth, she crossed her arms, glass dangling from her fingertips, and with feigned nonchalance so as not to appear too eager, said, 'Go on then, what would you have said?'

Rory frowned as he considered the question. Then he downed his drink and grinned. He had a habit of picking up on when she wanted something, and her silent patience was a huge giveaway. 'I'd say that you were a real pain in the arse growing up but sometimes you can be quite funny now.'

Ava made a face. 'You wouldn't have said that,' she huffed. 'Come on, what would you actually have said?'

Rory laughed. 'I'm not telling you what I would have said.'

'Why not?'

'Because people don't say what they think about you until after you die. That's the bitch. You never get to know.'

Ava frowned. 'Here they know,' she said, pointing towards the bustling Spanish street, the air filled with life lived richly. 'They tell each other stuff like that here. Like, Gran knew by the end that, yes, there'd been bad bits but overall she'd lived a great life. People loved her. All they went on about was how adored she was, how great she was. She knew she'd aced it.'

Rory tipped his head and swirled the dregs round in his empty glass. 'Well, lucky her, that's all I can say.' He got his phone out again and refreshed his emails. 'Come on, we've really got to go,' he said, standing up, slinging his suit jacket over his arm.

Ava checked her phone. It was piling up with more messages: new dates suggested for the *I'm alive!!* dinner. The sweetness of friendship that she hadn't factored on. It made her waver on the decision building inside her to defy Rory and come out to Spain anyway.

The man playing the guitar came round, proffering a hat for change. The waiter swept past, clearing their glasses from the table like magic, the teenagers blew smoke rings up at the sky, the arguing couple stood silently fuming. Ava put a euro in the hat. Rory didn't.

'Do you ever think that there's still time?' Ava asked, hand clutching her phone as they started to walk in the direction of the main road.

'Sorry, what was that?' Rory said, distractedly searching for a taxi, pushing his hair back from his face. 'God, it's so hot here.'

'I said do you ever think there's still time?' she repeated, looking straight at him.

'Still time for what?'

'To ace your life.'

'Me?' he said, looking confused, 'I *am* aceing it.'

Ava stared after him, amazed at his unwavering certainty as he strode away to flag down a cab. Then she looked down at the emails on her phone, everyone raring to go for the new date – *I'm alive!!* – and she knew that returning here on her own would disrupt the steady predictability of her life. Would answer back to all the faults in her life that had been disconcertingly exposed since the bus crash. She imagined her mother would have done it simply for the adventure. It was the very definition of *I'm alive!!*

And she knew she couldn't let her brother be the reason she didn't do it. Nor for that matter the safety of her friends. She opened a new email.

Thanks guys, for trying to rearrange, but I'm not going to make it. I'm going to be in Spain for the summer!

CHAPTER 5

It was pouring with rain. Ceaseless, monotonous, Armageddon-type rain. The sky was like concrete, the horizon a mesh of cranes, half-built tower blocks and jagged scaffolding. Rory was standing in the middle of an industrial estate in East London, on the set of his current documentary project, filming the life of a mute swan and a Canada goose who had set up home in an abandoned Tesco trolley next to a small, dank excuse for a pond. The birds found fame when one of the office workers set up an Instagram and Twitter account for them – #SwanLovesGoose – and across the globe people fell for the hopelessly devoted mismatched duo.

Almost overnight the birds became a symbol of love, peace and acceptance. National treasures, they were mentioned on *X Factor* and the fun bit at the end of the BBC news. The horrible pond became a conservation area. And Rory snapped up all the rights immediately. As well as the documentary, there was a book written from the point of view of the female swan scheduled for release at Christmas.

'God, why can't they just mate? Why can't they do something?' Rory was dressed in his blue waterproof, the rain dripping from the peak of the hood on to his nose and into his cold Styrofoam coffee cup.

He could see the money racking up every time he glanced from his camera crew to the two overfed birds sitting on the depressingly grey water doing absolutely nothing. The old shopping trolley sat empty.

Rory used to have a lot of patience when it came to nature. He'd built his living on his ability to wait it out. After critical acclaim for his degree show film about the Michelin-starred beach café next to his grandmother's house in Spain, he'd followed up with a documentary about the *Fête de l'Escargot* in France and the traditions around snail-hunting season, which shot him to prominence as one of the youngest BAFTA documentary nominees. He hadn't won, but his name had been on people's lips and he'd dined at No. 10, chortling with the PM over canapés. At just twenty-one his star was on the rise, but that same year his son Max had been born. Plagued by reflux, the baby hadn't slept, the cries echoing round the flat twenty-four-seven. His wife Claire struggling and Rory exhausted, at his worst when he hadn't had any sleep, his brain frazzled as he tried to work, money painfully tight. It was a ten-month black hole in his life. And when things started to get back to normal the wave of success seemed to have rolled on without him. No longer riding out front, he was paddling to keep up at the back, always a step out of sync. He spent ten months driving across America in search of the quintessential diner, only to find a bigger budget version of the same idea scheduled for release two months before his quiet little film. He worked harder and harder. Obsessively. And yet never bettered the French snail success. More recently, in the relentless quest for the BAFTA, he had taken on more commercial projects which he hated. He'd spent last spring on tour with a controversial young indie rock band, filming a supposed warts-and-all behind-the-scenes exposé that, while highly praised, had been a frustrating six months watching lazy teenagers sleeping, playing videogames and refusing to rehearse. To make matters worse, the BAFTA that year was nabbed by a quirky little film by a virtually unknown director who'd sprung to fame via YouTube, setting off to record the 300 different types of snow that the Eskimos were reputed to have words for.

All Rory's hopes were now pinned on this swan and goose, which he counted on having just the right amount of commercial whimsy to bag the gong. But not only were the birds doing absolutely nothing, Rory was stressed and tired. The plane home from Spain had been delayed for hours on the runway and he still didn't feel like he'd caught up on sleep.

He huffed back to his Portakabin, past the catering van. Larry, the chef, nodded towards the fat birds and said, 'Not much going on, is there?'

'No,' Rory replied. 'Absolutely bugger all.'

'I'll go home and get my rifle if you want, shoot one of them!' Larry laughed. 'That'd boost the ratings.'

Rory paused. That wasn't actually a bad idea. He didn't want to shoot one, of course, but maybe they could do something to chivvy it up a bit. He called to his assistant, 'Petra, meeting in my office, five minutes. Get the team.'

The Portakabin was cold but dry, except for the trail of muddy footprints and the dripping of six wet jackets on the backs of a hastily assembled group of chairs. Two of the team were perched on the side of Rory's desk. A packet of custard creams was doing the rounds.

'Do you think this is what it's going to be like the whole summer?' Petra stared out the window at the rain.

George, the assistant producer, shook his head. 'We don't have summer in Britain any more. Global warming. We're just going to be grey and bland forever.'

Petra made a face.

'OK, listen,' Rory clapped his hands together then rubbed them to warm up. 'We need these birds to do something, pronto. And they aren't doing it themselves. I don't want to put them in danger, as such, I just want to spice things up. Ideas?'

The only noise was the crinkle of the custard cream packet.

'Come on, you lot!' Rory sat back in his swivel chair, hands behind his head. 'This is what I pay you for. Think. What can we do with them?'

George shrugged, mouth full of biscuit. 'We could kidnap one. Goose could handle it, I reckon.'

Petra made a sad face. 'That would be really mean, though.'

'Petra,' Rory glared at her, 'it's not real. If we kidnap him he'll be in this bloody Portakabin, probably eating all my biscuits, if you lot leave me any.'

Rupert, a foppish researcher, nudged the one remaining custard cream still in the packet on to the edge of Rory's desk.

'I used to live near a farm, actually, one of those ones open to the public that kids go to,' said George. 'Just before Christmas some people broke in and stole all the rabbits and ducks and chickens. They think it was for Christmas dinner.'

Rory smacked the table with his hand. 'I like it. Now we're talking.'

'Really?' said Petra to George. 'They ate them?'

George nodded.

'That's terrible,' she said. 'Some people.'

Rory ignored her. 'So, OK, this is good. We kidnap Goose. Petra, I want you to look into logistics. Get the police in – and what? We spin it that he's been taken for Sunday lunch? It's a real shame it's summer not Christmas. George, can we get someone from that farm on camera? Just having that as a story will get the idea into people's minds. I like it.'

Foppish Rupert added, 'My parents have a farm in Hampshire. Goose could stay there for a while.'

Petra looked out the window again at the dank, rainy industrial estate. 'Probably never want to come back.'

Rory nodded. 'Well that would be even better. A post-kidnapping lovers' tiff.'

George laughed.

Petra looked back at them all, expression pained. 'This is really mean.'

Rory sighed. 'Yes, we know it's mean, Petra. But if we don't do it then nothing happens, the film's a flop, everyone forgets about the bloody birds and some fox'll probably eat them or the council will evict them. We're actually doing them a favour – in a roundabout sort of way. Right,' Rory stood up, grabbed the biscuit packet, and popping out the last custard cream said, 'Action that, people. Let's get back to work.'

CHAPTER 6

Later that day, Rory was sitting at the kitchen table opposite Max, drinking a cup of tea and impatiently refreshing his Twitter feed, waiting for a scheduled announcement about the Eskimo-snow BAFTA winner's latest project. Feeling confident about his own #SwanLovesGoose kidnapping plan, he'd picked Max up straight from the set in a great mood, then cooked an amazing risotto that Max had picked all the peas out of and said was a bit smelly. They had had a row and weren't speaking when his wife came home from work.

'Have you seen your sister's Instagram?' Claire said, as she walked into the kitchen. She threw her bag down on to the leather club chair by the window and gave both Rory and Max a kiss.

'No.' Rory immediately opened up his Instagram app. 'What is it?'

'She's on her way back to Spain,' said Claire, pouring herself a glass of water while surveying the mess in the kitchen.

'She's what?' Rory scrolled through Instagram in search of Ava's post.

Max was now forking up all the bits of chorizo from the risotto while simultaneously watching a Minecraft video on his laptop.

'You're not allowed the laptop at the table,' said Claire.

'Dad's on his phone.'

'I'm not eating anything,' said Rory, his tone exceedingly similar to his son's.

'Rory, get off your phone. Max, get off your laptop.' Claire shut the dishwasher.

'You just told me to look at this picture!' said Rory, incredulous.

Max huffed. 'I need to watch this.'

Claire gave Rory the kind of look they'd shared for the last ten years. A we're-meant-to-be-in-this-together look that made him roll his eyes then lean forwards and snap the laptop shut.

'Oh, what?' said Max.

'Just eat your dinner,' said Rory, his tone still reflective of the earlier risotto argument.

Max glowered at him. 'What about you?'

Rory had to tear himself away from the photo Ava had posted of the sun rising over a plane wing to make a show of clicking his phone off. Max looked smug.

Claire ate a spoonful of the leftover risotto from the pan. 'You're getting closer to that spot on *MasterChef*, Ror,' she said with a laugh.

Despite the distraction of Ava on her way to Spain, Rory felt a little flush of pride that someone appreciated his cooking, and raised a brow at Max to show how wrong he'd been. Then he was straight back to the subject of the Instagram photo. 'I can't believe she's gone back already! She's unbelievable.'

Max looked up. 'What's wrong with Aunty Ava?'

Claire bit down on a smile. 'Nothing. She's just not your father.'

Rory took a slug of his tea and shook his head as if he was being hard done by. 'That's not what I'm saying at all. Although if she were like me I doubt she'd have been hit by a bloody bus and have zero direction in life. You know what she's like, Max.' He looked at his ten-year-old son as if he were thirty-five and didn't just judge his aunt by the presents she bought him. 'I've never met anyone less able to settle down. Aside from my own mother. Talk about thinking the grass is greener. She thinks it's bloody fluorescent anywhere she isn't.'

'She's got FOMO,' said Max, standing up to get some ketchup from the fridge.

'Yes, no – I'm sorry, I have no idea what that means,' said Rory.

'Fear of missing out.'

Rory sat back. 'You're quite right, she has exactly that. FOMO. I like that.'

'Where have you been, Dad? Everyone knows FOMO.'

Rory raised a brow. 'Earning money so that you can know words like FOMO.'

'It's not actually a word,' said Max, 'it's an acronym.'

'There you go.' Rory raised his hand as if that were the case in point. 'I've been earning money so you know words like acronym. Please don't put ketchup on that risotto.'

Max squirted red sauce all over the remaining rice. Rory drank his tea to stop himself from saying anything, his fingers itching to get back to his phone and the Eskimo-snow director's Twitter announcement.

'At least he's eating it,' Claire said, in an attempt to keep the peace, having another spoonful from the pan herself before taking it to the sink to wash up.

Rory stood up, surreptitiously swiping his phone into his pocket so he could go into the living room, check Twitter, and leave the pair of them to their tomato ketchup. But as he started to walk towards the door he paused, a thought suddenly occurring to him. 'You don't happen to know where Ava's staying, do you?' he asked.

'Yeah, at your gran's, I spoke to her earlier. She popped by the office actually to pick up the spare key for her flat – she's rented it to an airbnb tenant while she's away. That's a good idea, isn't it?'

'She did what?' Rory felt his jaw drop in disbelief.

Claire was filling the sink with hot water, distracted, not really listening. 'Rented her flat to airbnb. I'd like to live in Spain for the summer, wouldn't you? The beach, the sea, fresh figs, and little coffees and tapas. It'd be amazing. Imagine that rather than having to go upstairs to write a stupid, pointless presentation for a job interview I shouldn't be having because they should be promoting me rather than interviewing me.'

Rory had completely forgotten about Claire's impending job interview. 'It'll be fine. If it's got your name on it, you'll get it,' he said. 'Now tell me about Ava.'

Claire raised a brow at him. 'I *will* get it, Rory, I would just like to be rewarded for the work I've done rather than humiliated by being pitted against people massively junior to me whose only qualifications seem to be their social media followings.'

If he wasn't so furious at his sister's blatant disregard, he would have reminded Claire that he'd told her a year ago to work on her social media presence, but Claire's attention had drifted back to the idea of a summer in Spain. 'Do you remember when we sat at Café Estrella till nearly sunrise drinking that orange Spanish drink? What was it called?'

'Licor 43,' Rory said quickly. 'I said she couldn't go.'

Claire was still daydreaming. 'Shall we quit our jobs and go and live in Spain?'

'No,' Rory shook his head. 'You're not listening. I told her she couldn't go.'

Claire made a face. 'Why?'

'Don't look at me like that. Because we've got to sell the house. I can't just sit on a chunk of inheritance while my sister fannies about doing flamenco or whatever it is she wants to do. And knowing her, she'll go for a week, get bored and come back again. Look at what happened to poor Jonathon. I thought maybe the bash on the head might have made her see sense when he picked her up from the hospital.'

'Oh God, Rory, you can't force someone to be with someone they don't want to be with. Just because you thought they were right for each other, doesn't mean she had to.' Claire rolled her eyes then turned away from him towards the sink and started washing up. 'Can you dry?'

Rory hated drying up, he couldn't see the point, but Claire was holding a tea towel out for him and it wasn't worth an argument. 'OK,' he said, reaching for the cloth. 'And there's nothing wrong with Jonathon. He's a perfectly decent bloke, she was just being too picky. Sometimes you just need to fix on a path through life and get on with it. It worked for us.'

He knew immediately that he'd said the wrong thing. Claire washed the dish she was holding very slowly. She started to say something then stopped herself.

Rory waited. He swallowed. He dried the saucepan, wishing he could suck the words back into his mouth.

Max, sensing something was about to kick off, picked his plate up from the table, squeezed between them to put it next to the sink, then disappeared with his laptop.

'Look, I didn't mean it quite like that. I just meant . . .' Rory paused. What had he meant? To all intents and purposes, they had had to just plough on with a course in life. They had been twenty-one. Claire had been pregnant. Of course they were going to get married.

Claire was still focused on the now very clean dish.

'Anyway,' Rory ran a hand frustratedly through his hair, trying to divert the subject away from his faux pas, 'we've got to sell Gran's house. It's the only answer. My life is stressful enough without knowing there's a veritable goldmine sitting across the Channel that could pay off a whack of our mortgage. Have you seen that area? It's not a sleepy little village any more. Even the bloody hipsters have moved in. I saw them with their beards and their trendy restaurants. You know a place is up and coming when there are lime green single-speed bikes chained to the lampposts.'

'We have enough money, Rory.'

'We could have more.'

'Everyone could have more. We do OK.'

'Claire, if you saw how much money goes out of my account every month to pay for all this, you'd be saying sell the Spanish place as well, believe me.'

She put the dish down on the draining board. 'I know how much money goes out, Rory, because the same percentage goes out of mine. You don't earn that much more than me.'

'I didn't mean it like that,' Rory sighed, shaking his head, his tone implying he couldn't say anything right. Then, after a pause, as they silently washed and dried, he started to feel a little hard done by. He knew he shouldn't say anything else, but as the feeling grew he found himself unable not to, and added, 'I think actually it's fair to say that I do earn quite a lot more than you.'

Claire smacked a saucepan down on the counter and turned around. 'Are you serious?'

'Yes,' he said. Then, a little less certain, 'I think so.'

'Oh my God. You are so frustrating. Why say it? Why do you always have to have the last word? Does it ever occur to you why you earn so much more? Because you got to trot off around the globe to build your career while I stayed here to bring up our child. I was basically your live-in babysitter, Rory. And I'm well aware that it was a choice that I made, but it would be nice if you could recognise it every now and then.' Claire exhaled, rubbed her forehead, forgetting she had rubber gloves on, and then had to wipe the suds away with her sleeve. 'I don't earn as much as you, Rory, one because my industry doesn't pay as much, but two because it took me twice as long to get where I am because I had a child to look after. Our child. And maybe, if you paid me the amount that childcare costs these days, I *would* have as much money as you.'

'I don't want to have an argument, Claire.'

'That's such an infuriating answer.' She put her hands on the sides of the sink and looked up at the ceiling in exasperation. 'Who *wants* to have an argument? If you don't want an argument, why say it in the first place?'

Rory was starting to feel out of his depth. He wanted it to end, but the stubborn feeling that his point hadn't yet been recognised made him soldier on. 'Because the fact is, the majority of the money worries in this family fall on my shoulders.'

'Oh my God!' Claire's cheeks had flushed red with annoyance.

Rory's phone buzzed. He put his hand into his pocket.

'Don't you dare get your phone out.'

Rory stopped, but when he found he didn't want to let go of the phone in his pocket he was suddenly reminded of the dirty old comforter Max had had as a baby.

Claire sighed. 'Sometimes it would be really nice not to have to compete for your attention with that thing.'

He could see frustrated tears start to build in her eyes. He knew how annoyed she'd be that she was crying. He wanted to call a little pause, to reach out and touch her arm or something, but equally he couldn't back down. He felt like pointing out that everyone wants time alone in a relationship and he chose to spend his on his phone – would she prefer it if he started getting the newspaper delivered like his father and disappearing off to read that every evening?

The thought that the Eskimo-snow director's announcement would have been made on Twitter by now flitted into his mind.

Again Claire started to say something but then stopped, shook her head, as if it were all pointless. 'Well, as far as I know, we're not destitute. I think we have enough money for your sister, who nearly died last week, to spend a summer by the beach in Spain. Don't you?' She moved away from the sink, pulling her rubber gloves off, and walked over to the fridge to get the white wine. As she poured herself a glass she looked up at Rory and said, 'I know you work hard, but not everything is about money. I think sometimes you treat us like we work for you. But we're your family. You can't just bulldoze over people, because one day they'll stop suddenly and realise that they are just "ploughing forward on a fixed path in life".' She raised her brows as she repeated his words. Rory looked down at the floor. 'If you can't see the problem in you saying no to Ava then you're not the person I thought you were.' She left the kitchen and disappeared into the hallway, clearly unable to be in the same room as him.

Rory exhaled. He shut his eyes for a second then reached into his pocket and got his phone out. He didn't want to think about anything that had just happened. He wanted to ignore it all, read the text that had come through, focus back on a world he understood: his BAFTA nemesis's project reveal and the all-consuming race for the top prize.

But at the foot of the stairs Claire paused and turned. 'You need to make sure Max has done his homework,' she said, her eyes widening in surprise when she saw his phone. 'You know, Rory, I wonder sometimes if it were between me and that sodding phone, who would win.'

'I got a text.'

'What does it say?' she asked, coming back towards him.

Rory opened it, then said, a little sheepish, 'My parcel will be delivered tomorrow between ten and twelve.' Then he paused, his mouth curving up into a half-smile. 'Will you be in?'

'You've got some nerve, Rory,' she said, shaking her head. 'Don't give me that look. Don't think you can get away with it with that look.'

'You love that look,' he said. Knowing he'd got her now. It would all be alright.

She glanced down at the rug, straightening the tassels with her foot, to pretend she wasn't smiling, but he could see that she was. 'You need to make sure Max gets off that computer and does his homework.'

'Aye aye, Captain.'

She shook her head. 'You're really annoying.'

'And that's why you love me.' He stepped forwards, about to put his arms around her but his phone rang. 'Oh God, this is work, I have to take it.'

Claire looked up, completely dumbfounded. 'Don't you dare take it.'

'I have to take it.' Pressing *Answer*, he said, 'Hello, hi, yeah, Bruce, what's happened? What? How?'

But before he could say any more he felt the phone plucked from his fingers. He tried to tighten his grip but he'd realised too late and could only scrabble for the shiny surface. 'What the hell? Claire, what are you doing? Hang on, Bruce,' he shouted.

With the aim of the county netballer that she had been until they'd had Max, Claire took a few paces backwards and hurled his phone into the downstairs toilet.

'What the hell have you just done?' Rory ran into the bathroom to see his mid-contract iPhone sitting at the base of the loo. He had his sleeve rolled up and his arm in the water before he could even tune into her reply.

'I'm trying to make you look at me, for Christ's sake. I'm trying to make you exist right now with me and with Max. You're never here any more, Rory. You're never present. It's like you're always distracted. And Max is growing up and this bit is meant to be easier. Our life should be getting more fun but it's not. It feels like it's getting worse. I don't want you to feel like you're stuck with us, with this life. Because to me it's precious. It's all I have.'

'I didn't say I was stuck with you,' he said, distracted, hauling the dripping iPhone out of the toilet, trying to get it to switch on, vaguely seeing an expression on her face and a tremor in her hands he hadn't seen before, and feeling in the pit of his stomach that this was serious, that the ground beneath him wasn't as stable as he'd presumed it to be, but the call from Bruce was, in that moment, more serious. 'I've got to get a phone!' Chucking the useless iPhone on top of the loo, he moved Claire to one side, hands on her shoulders.

She pushed him away with a stunned, 'What are you doing?'

Rory wasn't listening. 'Max!' he shouted. 'Max, give me your laptop!' He barged into the living room and commandeered the whizzy new laptop that he had no idea how to use. Rory was an Apple man – all the touch-screen shenanigans on Windows 10 was out of his jurisdiction. He handed it back. 'Get me on Twitter.' When Max paused he shouted, 'Now!'

Max did as he was told.

And there it was.

BREAKING: *Rory Fisher to eat #SwanLovesGoose for Sunday dinner!*

CHAPTER 7

The little village of Mariposa was exactly as Ava remembered it as a kid. A hidden treasure at the bottom of a winding path off the main road, it was a curl of golden sandy beach and turquoise sea. Houses lined the coast like Neapolitan ice cream: pink sandwiched between vanilla and chocolate, tall to the sky, their shuttered windows like eyes staring out to the bright blue of the Mediterranean. Ava wheeled her bag past the Café Estrella, keeper of so many of her family memories, its terracotta roof tiles speckled with moss, the awning a little wonky, tables spilling out on to a cracked concrete terrace, the sun radiating from the pavement in tentacles. As she'd walked down the slope to the tiny beach town she'd passed a new restaurant, Nino's, heaving with lunch trade. In comparison, Café Estrella looked worryingly closed.

She paused to look back at the bustling restaurant, wondering for a second about the change, but then found her gaze distracted by the familiar view ahead of her – postcard perfect and etched on her brain for imaginary visits on cold winter days. The pale glinting sea receding to dark navy and melting into ice-blue sky. White fishing boats like gulls bobbing on the water. A line of yellow buoys marking a path for the watersports speedboat. Swimmers diving off orange pedalos, while sunbathers basked on golden sand. Blue and white sunshades with matching loungers. Dripping lollies, barking dogs, the rat-a-tat of bat and ball. The hiss of the shower. The gentle curl of the waves. The birds stalking up and down in the sand.

She pulled her bag further along the path and shielded her eyes to get her first glimpse of her grandmother's house across the square, the small white villa visible through a rusting black wrought-iron fence. Behind it, like pastel footsteps, more ice cream houses climbed the hill. Their arched windows, geranium-strewn terraces and zigzags of washing lines leading the eye up and up till it reached a large house at the top – stone-coloured brick, shaded by huge sweeping pines, their branches like blackened clouds – and then across from that to the rows and rows of vines that marked the hillside like lines on paper.

Down on the beach, the air smelled of the orange trees in pots around Café Estrella, their leaves shiny as plastic, and the drunken fig that had crushed the wall and lay draped half across the path, its ripening fruit sweetening the air with a perfume so heady, so addictive that the more Ava inhaled the more she needed, as if all the breaths in the world wouldn't satisfy the craving. Light-headed from all the sniffing, she bounced her case across the cobbles of the square in the direction of the rusty black gates. On the wall above the letterbox was a bell with a little light and the words *Valentina Brown (Mrs)*.

She couldn't quite believe she was here.

She had wavered slightly when she'd touched down in the UK. Wondered whether to back track and relegate the whole idea to a conversation topic about how her big bad brother had denied her this chance of a lifetime. She had actually half-presumed that her boss Peregrine would be the one to put the kybosh on it – unable to manage without her – but instead he'd been nothing but supportive, waffling on about her loyalty to the company. He could think of nothing more worthwhile than taking a break to find oneself and wished he had done it himself at her age. He and their intern – a dashing young up-start, Hugo, the incredibly self-assured son of Peregrine's best friend – would hold the fort in her absence. If she was honest, she'd been a little put out by Peregrine's blasé belief that the company could manage perfectly well without her, secretly wishing herself indispensable. But he clearly wasn't worried, coming back from lunch with a travel diary, still in the Paperchase bag with the receipt, as a parting gift to seal the deal.

So here she was, unzipping the pocket in her bag for the key, still on the familiar little black bull keyring, a miniature version of the huge cut-outs that loomed high above the roadside on her taxi journey from the airport, reminding her that this was Spain.

She looked across at the Café Estrella. In the darkness a TV flickered. Two old men played chess on a table in the shade. The blackboards were tired and smudged. There was no one there that she recognised. The waiter was drying the cups, his glance flicking between the TV and his few customers. She remembered nights when they'd danced on the tables.

She turned the key in the iron gate lock and walked up the dusty path, past the bougainvillea trailing unchecked over the fence and the pots of plump green succulents. Her fingers were shaking slightly and at the front door she fumbled the key, dropping it on the threshold. Bending down to pick it up she saw the shells. Pressed into the cement by her and Val: *Our Summerhouse*. She paused and rubbed one of the little shells with her thumb before taking a deep breath, picking up the keys and going inside.

The corridor was dark. The shutters closed. It was stranger than she'd imagined, being there alone. No smells of cooking. No vacuuming or absent-minded flower-arranging or kettle boiling. No stray cats purring. No telephone ringing or swearing at the TV, no diary scribbling or wild gesticulations about making no noise and coming to the window to look at what was going on in the street outside.

Nothing, Ava noted as she pushed the door open, just some junk mail on the mat and dusty dried lavender in a vase.

It was empty, unlived in, musty.

She walked straight through to the living room and opened the windows, the air instantly filling with the salty breath of the sea. She stood with her hands on the sill, looking out at the beach, at the rows of bronze-limbed sun-worshippers and children digging holes in the sand. Then she turned her back to the window and took in the familiar sight of a million old Spanish paintings wonkily filling every inch of the magnolia walls. The sofa, threadbare, spilling with cushions. The coffee table stacked high with big art books, stains on the glass from coffee cups. The shelves toppling with family photographs. The desk by the window covered with papers. Everything exactly as she remembered it but coated with a thin layer of sticky dust.

In the kitchen she tore off a bin bag and went through the fridge, chucking everything out. Then did the same in the avocado bathroom, binning the half-used bottles of shampoo, the night creams and the flattened toothpaste tube. The little half-bar of soap by the bathroom sink, heartbreaking but unusable, too closely tied to the once living.

As she looked, Ava did her best to ignore the growing weight pressing down on her, trying not to dwell on the life that had gone. She blinked away the vision of someone finding her own half-bars of soap, immediately glad that she'd chucked everything out for the airbnb tenant.

Her friends were WhatsApping. *So jealous of your weather. How's it going?*

She paused in the corridor to reply, leaning up against the cool geometric tiles. *Great. Amazing. It's the kind of heat that makes you have to move slower. So relaxed.*

It was sort of true. It was hot, sticky limbs weather.

No one replied. She checked the time. They were all at work, stressed and manic and attempting to double-screen in meetings. All of them jealous of her holiday, not realising that she was a little bit jealous of them.

She looked up and caught sight of the coat hanging by the front door: bright red brocade with a faux leopard fur collar, ankle length, cylindrical. It had swamped Ava as a kid in the same way it swamped Val in old age. She remembered it being tucked around her on the plane as she slept on the way back from visiting her mother in New York. She glanced to the right, almost to check no one was watching, then leant forwards so her nose was just touching the material and inhaled the scent of citrus, sandalwood and juniper. *'The thing about men, Ava, is that they like the smell of power. Always wear cologne.'*

And she realised, suddenly, that there would be no more such skew-whiff wisdom in her life. Unwanted at the time, unbearably poignant in retrospect.

She took a step back, turned and found herself staring up to the bedroom. The open door at the top of the stairs, the big gilt mirror on the wall, the dusky pink walls. Val's room. The steps creaked as she walked. It was a lethal staircase, a flimsy banister with no spindles, and steps with open risers. As kids they would lie on their backs to slip through the gaps between each step and see how high they could go and still be able to cope with the drop to the floor. When Val caught them she banned the game, which of course didn't stop them, but, as usual, it was Ava who got hurt when it all went wrong.

Now she paused on the top step, hand on the wobbly banister, and watched the sun battling its way through a gap in the curtain. There were velvet slippers tucked neatly under the bed waiting for feet. Faded ribbons tied on the gold, scrolled bed frame. A huge canvas of a black and white flamenco dancer leant against a shelf above the bedhead next to the window. Whirlpools of sun and dust eddied in the air.

Ava walked inside. She could see her reflection in the mottled mirror of the neat little Victorian wardrobe. She swallowed. She wanted to scoop everything up in her arms and walk holding it forever.

This was her family. Her stability. One of life's guarantees. Like Christmas at Rory and Claire's; the Starbucks next to Peregrine's shop; Louise trying to be funny on WhatsApp. It was safe here. There was love here. Wonky advice and unending gossip, but a home whenever she needed it. And of course, someone who would talk, unendingly, about her mother; hours they had spent together remembering the stage lights, the smell of backstage at the theatre, the heat of the dressing room, the taste of make-up in the air.

Ava's eyes trailed across to the carved wooden cabinet and a mirror above it draped with jewels; necklaces glimmered in the sunlight, bowls of rings shone on the surface next to a cluster of little ornaments and glass bottles. Shoe boxes snaked ladders up the wall.

Next to the wardrobe there was a door to a room in the eaves that she presumed housed things like the Hoover and ironing board. Walking over the tread-worn Indian rug, the sounds outside of beach playing and bells ringing, she went to turn the handle but the door didn't open. The paint had almost melted it shut. She tugged a couple of times, about to give up, when it pulled free to the sound of splitting paint.

It wasn't a room for the Hoover. It was a dressing room. Ava narrowed her eyes but just saw outlines in the darkness. She searched the wall for the light and when she finally found it, a tatty bit of too-short string, she clicked and a million sequins shone as the little ante-room lit up.

'Bloo-dy hell.' She put her hand up to her mouth.

A rail, filled with furs and rhinestone jackets, afghan coats and sequinned ballgowns, bowed under the weight. Pairs of shoes – patent, velvet, some with diamanté buckles – were crammed into every nook and cranny. Black-and-white-striped hat boxes were pushed on to too-small shelves next to baskets of silk scarves and belts curled like sleeping snakes. On a peg hung a fox fur, still with its little face and tiny claws, and next to him an open jewellery box filled with sunglasses. Everywhere she looked there was something: a lipstick that had rolled from its basket, a homeless brooch on a ledge, a bulging make-up bag with a zip that wouldn't close, a teetering stack of glossy programmes.

Ava stared with her hands on both sides of her face. These weren't her grandmother's things but her mother's. Things she had thought lost, gone, given away forever.

The smell in here was different. No more cologne but sweet, dark perfume. Guerlain's Shalimar. The grooved glass bottle with its golden seal such a familiar sight in her youth. And lipstick, chalky and red. And the remnants of decadence: money and fur, couture still in dry cleaning plastic, expensive shoes once so carefully protected in soft white bags.

Ava could barely breathe.

It all suddenly felt completely different. No longer just the bittersweet task of packing away her grandmother's long, beautifully lived life, but of being handed back her mother. As though she was standing there in the poky little room with her, hat shading one eye, lips slicked red, selfish, unreachable, magnetic, magnificent.

Ava backed out of the room, her hand gently closing the paint-cracked door. She walked fast, almost a trot, towards the staircase, the hallway and the front door, and seconds later was outside. Out into the bright heat of the sun, out into the noise of the beach and the shimmer of the wide blue sea, out where time kept moving and she could breathe like a normal person again.

CHAPTER 8

Rory was heartbroken.

It had taken less than an hour for the tweet and linking article to go viral.

Executive producer, Bruce Haslen, had arrived in his Range Rover, where they sat, rain hammering the windscreen.

'I know you didn't mean it, mate. But it wasn't one of your brightest ideas.' Bruce tapped the cream leather steering wheel.

Rory felt utterly sick. His whole career was being shredded before his eyes. People were questioning all his past work, sending him #VileRory hate messages, mocking up pictures of his face on a Christmas dinner goose. People were tweeting and retweeting faster than he could refresh Bruce's iPad. All this was happening and he didn't even have his own smartphone.

'Can't I just send out some kind of apology? Draft something with PR?' Rory said, and even to his ears it sounded lame.

Bruce sat back and exhaled, staring up to where the rain battered the sunroof, then turned to look Rory's way. 'Too late for that, I'm afraid. They're already placarding. One lot have made a human wall of protection around the nest.'

Rory put his head back against the plush leather and shut his eyes. 'Well at least something's happening, I suppose.'

Bruce gave a half-hearted attempt at a laugh. The rain thrashed around them in the darkness.

'I'm sorry, mate,' said Bruce.

'Not your fault,' Rory said. 'Bloody Petra though – who tells their *Daily Mail* boyfriend about something like this? Why didn't I know she was shacked up with a journo?'

'New romance, evidently.' Bruce shrugged.

Claire ran out of the house with a brolly and tapped on the window. 'Are you all OK?' she asked. 'Anyone want a cup of tea? Glass of wine?'

Rory shook his head. 'No, I'm just coming back in.' He barely looked at Claire as he opened the door, part of him still annoyed with her for throwing his phone down the toilet, which, given the escalation of events, he knew wasn't healthy or fair but he couldn't help it.

Bruce started the engine. 'We'll reconvene in a week and see where we're at. I think you're off the swans for good, but I'm sure you'll be fine for the jellyfish.'

Rory couldn't see how he'd be fine for the upcoming *Jellyfish Apocalypse* documentary. People remembered. They'd say that he'd somehow warmed up the ocean and bred them himself to create the epidemic.

Once inside he disappeared to the bedroom and sat refreshing his Twitter feed on his laptop. The Eskimo-snow documentary-maker had refrained from commenting on Rory directly, but when tweeting about his exciting new project – which it transpired was a voyage across the Pacific Ocean in search of Plastic Island – he added the hashtag #honestwork, which made Rory cover his face with his hands and shout with frustration.

'You should go to sleep,' he heard Claire say as she came into the bedroom.

He ignored her. Refreshed the app again. His Twitter feed couldn't even register the number of retweets and comments about him there were so many. He also had Ava's Instagram feed open in another window and he stared at a picture of their grandmother's house. 'I can't believe she went anyway, even though we agreed she wouldn't. How could she?'

'You need to turn it off, Rory, it's driving you mad.' Claire got into bed and turned her sidelight off, casting the room into gloomy darkness. Rory's face was lit only by the blue glow of the laptop.

'I won't be able to sleep.'

'You haven't tried.'

'I know I won't be able to.'

Claire shuffled up the bed a bit. 'They say that blue glow stops the melatonin that helps you sleep.'

Rory gave her a look.

Claire breathed in through her nose and out again. 'It'll be OK, Rory. I mean, maybe it's not a bad thing? Maybe it's a chance to do something new?'

Rory felt his jaw clench. 'I don't want to do something new. This was my dream. I was living my dream and I just wanted to keep on living it. Forever. And ever. Till I died or got so old that I couldn't physically manage to do it, but even then would know that I could do it if some new technology was created to keep me alive. Jesus.' He bunched his hands into fists. 'I don't want it taken away from me.'

Claire was looking up at him from her half-sitting position. 'We've got to find a bright side to this.'

He stared at the pattern on the curtain, just visible in the black. 'There is no sodding bright side. My life is basically ruined.'

'Well why did you plan to kidnap the bloody goose?' Claire bashed the duvet with her hand then immediately sighed, as if she hadn't meant to say what she'd said. Like she'd been holding it in. After a pause she said, 'The way you talk about it, it's like you have no acknowledgement of the fact you still have us, you still have your home. This is *one* part of your life, Rory, and we'll fix it.'

They both stared straight ahead at the curtains, the only noise the sound of rain tapping on the window.

'And Rory,' Claire said a little softer, turning to look at him while he stayed staunchly turned away, 'what use is a BAFTA if it's for something you've faked? Surely it would ruin everything about accepting it. You'd stand there and do some speech and know you'd packed the stupid goose off in a black bag in the middle of the night.' She shook her head in disbelief at the very idea. 'Christ,' she said, 'I don't even know who you're doing it for any more, because it isn't for me or Max. I don't think it's for you because you don't seem to be particularly enjoying it. You used to love your job, Rory. And that made all the sacrifices we made OK. But look at you . . . You're tired and stressed and angry. You're not even making films you like any more. And God, if any of this is to impress your father then, do you know what? You could just go and buy one of those cheap knock-off statues and tell him you won. He wouldn't know the difference.'

Rory didn't reply.

Claire huffed a frustrated breath and slid back down the bed, rolling away from him to go to sleep.

Rory listened to her breathing in the quiet. He could tell she was faking the slowness of her breaths to make it seem like she was asleep. He wondered if maybe she was crying.

Usually he'd lean over and see, but this time he didn't. He went back to refreshing. Over and over. Watching the tweets tumble down his feed, vitriol and hatred all directed at him.

He felt like he was outside his body, looking down on himself sitting in bed, lit blue, with his wife silently crying beside him. He was suddenly overwhelmed by a feeling that he hadn't had since he'd sat on the floor in the corner of his bedroom after learning that his mum was leaving. He felt the same hot, wet tears of shame. Of utter, overwhelming helplessness.

He felt Claire stir.

Tears were now rolling uncontrollably down his cheeks, hitting the computer, the sheets, his T-shirt. He tried to wipe them away but it was physically impossible, there were more than he could feasibly hide.

'Rory?'

He looked away.

'Rory?' Claire sat up, her voice concerned.

He shook his head.

He felt her arms snake round his shoulders and move down around his upper arms as she hugged his back and he tried to pretend that he wasn't crying and her hands weren't getting soaking wet.

CHAPTER 9

Ava had caught the bus into town and spent the afternoon trying to escape the scorching sun. Immersing herself in little tourist shops and the swanky new department store, trying on clothes she didn't need and drinking too much coffee. The thought of going back to her grandmother's house was so overwhelming that she considered booking into a hotel, but the practicality of her suitcase still being there made her get the bus back to the little beach town again.

She walked down the path to see paddle-boarders gliding out into the dusk on ice-flat sea, barely leaving a mark on the water. It was late and Nino's, the new restaurant, was still going strong. Couples queued for tables while the heat enveloped them like candyfloss.

She took a seat at the run-down Café Estrella, where in contrast she was one of the only people at a table. The old men who'd been playing chess earlier now sat in the corner smoking cigars, while a couple of guys propped up the bar.

Ava was just Googling Nino's reviews when a voice said, 'Ava? Darling, is that you?'

'Flora!' Ava turned in the direction of the woman wandering up from the beach. Her hair wet from the sea, an old black sarong with faded pink flowers tied across her chest, ratty old plastic sliders on her feet.

'May I?' she asked when she reached Ava's table, pointing to a chair.

'Of course,' Ava nodded. 'It's your café,' she added with a laugh, surreptitiously closing the TripAdvisor page of glowing reviews for Nino's.

'I barely saw you at the funeral,' Flora said, squeezing the water from her hair.

Ava remembered spotting Flora in a veiled black hat and waving across the throng of mourners. Now though, she had to suppress her shock at how much Flora had changed. This was a woman who Ava had seen reduce grown men to gibbering wrecks. Her own brother had spent a summer filming the café for his degree show and followed Flora around like a puppy.

A British food writer, Flora was famed for her looks. Her figure. Her glossy blonde hair and perfect pout. But instead of the voluptuous glamourpuss, sitting in front of Ava was a really tired-looking middle-aged woman with weathered skin and hair in need of a retouch.

'How are you?' Ava asked.

'Hot,' Flora said, crossing her legs and sitting back in her chair, fanning herself with the menu. 'Old.'

Ava shook her head as if she didn't know what she was talking about.

Flora called to the waiter to bring over some drinks. 'Sherry?' she said to Ava, who nodded.

Ava was struggling to work out what Flora was doing late-night swimming while her café slowly faded away, losing all its trade to the place on the opposite side of the path. 'They're new,' she said tentatively, gesturing towards the heaving restaurant.

Flora didn't turn to look. 'There's three of them who run it. City boys. Came from Barcelona. Stole my business.'

'Oh,' said Ava.

'Yes,' said Flora. Then she sighed. 'No. Who am I kidding? It hasn't been the same since Ricardo left and now I'm stuck with the bloody place.'

Ava did a sort of half-neutral, half-sympathetic face. While it was public knowledge that Flora Foxton had fallen head over heels for up-and-coming Spanish chef Ricardo Garcia on a cookery show she'd filmed across the Mediterranean, Ava wasn't sure how much she was meant to know about events leading up to Ricardo's departure. It was safe to say she knew every single minute detail, as relayed by her grandmother in unnecessary whispers over the phone, as if Flora might hear them through the wall, across the path and all the way over at the café.

Valentina Brown had never trusted Ricardo. She had scoffed on the phone when he had presented Flora with a knot of turquoise thread instead of an engagement ring. Ava had said that she thought it was quite romantic. As had Flora, clearly, as she proceeded to solely finance the set-up of the very successful Café Estrella from the profits of her once-bestselling cookery books, to allow Ricardo to show off his modern take on classic tapas. The critics mocked the location but Ricardo drawled in interviews that 'People will travel for the best' and refused to budge from his little beachside idyll. It was this same arrogant passion that had made Rory's graduation film such a success. And Ricardo had been right. People had come. The café had garnered a coveted Michelin star. But while whipping up his fancy new tapas and proclaiming himself the saviour of Spanish cuisine, Ricardo's growing reputation had put him in the spotlight of the rich and famous, who whisked him off to prepare birthday feasts on mega yachts and cater weddings in the Hollywood Hills – all a world away from Flora and their little beach café.

When Flora told Val that Ricardo had left her for a very young American underwear model who he was now living with in Chicago, Val had whispered on the phone to Ava that she was not surprised one little bit, and added with quiet confidence, '*Never trust a man who gives you a piece of string instead of a ring.*'

Now, as Ava sat opposite Flora, she saw the heartbreaking reality of what had previously just been idle gossip. 'I'm really sorry,' she said.

'Well, what are you going to do?' Flora sat back in her chair, piling her damp blonde curls on top of her head and wrapping them with an elastic band from her wrist. 'People came here for him and, well, he's not here, is he!' She looked round at the empty café tables. 'And that lot, they're young.' She nodded her head backwards towards Nino's. 'They've got the energy to triple fry their chips and serve their oysters in shot glasses. Which frankly, to me, sounds disgusting anyway, but people seem to like it. They talk about it a lot.' She gave Ava a wry little look and then, glancing out to the sea, said, 'I just hide in the back nowadays, ghost-writing cookery books for skinny celebrities and avoiding my accountant.'

Ava laughed.

Flora smiled. 'But it's OK. How are you doing? Missing Val? She was bloody annoying half the time but it's not the same without her.'

'I know.' Ava nodded. The sherries arrived, the waiter setting them down on little paper coasters, half an eye on the beach, studiously ignoring them. 'Thanks,' Ava said. He didn't reply. Flora rolled her eyes as if there was nothing she could do about him.

Ava smiled into her sherry, then waited until they were alone again to say, 'It's harder than I thought, being in the house. There are just so many memories.'

Flora took a sip of her drink. 'And she had a lot of crap.'

Ava, who had been expecting sympathetic words of advice, snorted into her drink. Flora laughed, as if she'd taken herself by surprise.

'She does have a *lot* of crap,' Ava agreed, liberated. She didn't mention her mother's room; like stepping through the wardrobe into Narnia, it was her precious secret to keep.

Flora smiled. 'Just go in, ruthless, and chuck it away. I think it's the only way. Val wouldn't want you poring over her stuff. She knew it was tat, half of it. I was with her at the boot sales when she bought it. Bag it up, bin it and enjoy the sunshine. That's what she'd have said. Don't you do this kind of thing for a living?'

Ava thought about her job. She tried to compare Val's house, with all its knick-knacks, to the palatial New York townhouses and cliff-top ancestral piles in the Scottish Highlands where she would pitch up for valuations and contents auctions. Places where she was handed plastic shoe covers at the door and white gloves to wear when inspecting the art or browsing the library. While she did think about who had sat in the pair of French Louis XIII armchairs she was bidding ten grand on, or who had lit the £20,000 Italian Baroque candelabras, their lives were more often than not secondary to the wealth. What they left behind was more valuable than their memory. Whereas with Val, every item was a manifestation of her self. Every chipped vase and tacky flea market print seemed to carry her voice. '*There's no more room in my house. But I like it. You like it? Not fancy enough for your lot of course. I'm going to have it. Where I'll put it? But I'm going to have it.*'

And then there were her mother's things. Ava could price a regency giltwood mirror or mid-century Murano chandelier with her eyes shut, but that little room was beyond value.

Flora took another sip of her sherry, flumped her wet hair with her hand and, glancing around said, 'I'll tell you who does have some interesting stuff, have you met Tom yet? Bought the vineyard on the hill. He's poured some money into that house. It was practically derelict when he bought it. You wouldn't recognise it now.'

Ava shook her head. 'I've never met him,' she said, but she'd heard all about Tom-On-The-Hill as well. Retired actor. Kept Val up with all the drilling and banging during the renovation, but made up for it with a bottle of expensive brandy when she climbed the steps to complain. They'd smoked cigars on his terrace together apparently, and Ava had always wondered if they were having an affair.

'He's over there by the bar,' Flora said, nodding towards the people drinking inside. 'Tom!' she shouted. 'Come over here, darling.'

Ava sat up in surprise when the guy at the bar turned at the sound of his name.

Oh my God! She tried to act completely natural.

'He was very famous once,' Flora said in a conspiratorial whisper. 'But I'd never seen anything he'd been in.'

Ava couldn't quite believe what she was seeing.

This was Tom-On-The-Hill.

Walking towards her was not the eighty-year-old retired actor that Ava had imagined having brandy with her grandmother on his terrace, the two of them perhaps holding hands.

Tom-On-The-Hill was none other than Thomas King. Probably the biggest television star of Ava's teenage years. The fresh-faced, chocolate-box heart-throb who had shot to fame on *Love-Struck High*. She could remember the recording of the final episode being passed around their school like gold dust. Everyone impatiently waiting their turn, and secretly praying that their VCR wouldn't be the one to chew up the tape. She and Louise had queued to see him at the National Television Awards, but Louise had started hyperventilating when he'd walked past and had to be taken off by the St John's Ambulance crew for a cup of tea and a Hobnob.

Now as he stood in front of her, all faded shorts and crisp white shirt, his hand held out for her to shake, looking pretty damn perfect and far too pleased with himself, Ava could barely get the words together to say, 'Nice to meet you, I'm Ava'. She didn't want to shake his hand, her palm suddenly a little clammy from the proximity to fame, his rough and cool in comparison.

'Tom,' he said.

And Ava filled the silence by saying, 'Thomas King,' as if he might need reminding of his own name, and immediately regretted it.

'I am indeed.'

Flora put her hand on Tom's arm and said, 'Val was Ava's grandmother. She's here to pack up the house.'

Ava nodded, mute. Wishing she'd been able to play it cooler. Her brain chastising her for even admitting that she knew who he was. How cool would it have been to have had no idea who he was, or at least manage to carry out a pretence as such.

Tom was talking, saying how sorry he was about Val and that he'd been away for the funeral. 'It's all done so quickly in Spain,' he said, and Ava nodded, shamefully distracted from his respectful sympathy, trying to work out whether he was wearing tortoiseshell glasses and had grown his hair a bit long to try and hide the heart-throb jaw and eyes.

He seemed to be able to sense her distraction and paused, his mouth twitching into a smile. His whole demeanour switched to predatory with just a roll of his shoulders and a lean against one of the awning pillars. 'So how long are you staying?' he asked.

Flora cut in, saying, 'I should go.' A couple of tourists were inspecting the menu on one of the far tables. She stood up, but as she did she leant forwards and added in a conspiratorial whisper, 'The problem is I've started to hope they don't sit down at all. I want them to just leave me alone.'

Tom raised a brow. 'Not a good thing for a café owner.'

'I know! It's no win,' Flora said, hoisting her sarong up where it had slipped down over her boobs and making her way through the network of chairs to chat up her potential customers with a lacklustre smile.

Ava wasn't sure whether to answer Tom's question or if too much time had now passed. She hated that she was agonising over such trivia, so readily trying to impress him.

'May I?' he asked, pointing to the seat Flora had vacated.

'Yeah, sure.'

'So,' he said, reclining, hands in his pockets, all cool and relaxed like he owned the place, his beer bottle half-drunk on the table in front of him. 'How are you enjoying it?'

'Good thanks,' Ava said quickly.

He nodded.

She started to say more – pleasantries about her trip into town – but realised his attention had been diverted by a woman in a skin-tight red dress and glossy brown hair heading into Nino's.

'Sorry, what was that?' he asked, glancing back.

Ava shook her head. 'Nothing.'

The silence gnawed.

Tom looked out towards the beach. Ava looked too, at the long shadows of the palm tree leaves on the sand, at the dangerously lilting fig tree and the potted orange trees, their perfume intensifying with the evening.

Unable to bear the silence any longer, she said, 'So, *Love-Struck High* . . .', not really sure where she was going with the comment.

Tom took a swig of beer. 'You were a fan?' he asked, wiping his mouth with the back of his hand, smug half-grin on his face.

'I watched it,' she said, a little dismissive. 'If I was home and it was on.' Given his expression she was hardly going to admit to the *Love-Struck High* parties at Louise's house, where they watched their favourite episodes back to back, his face emblazoned on Louise's spare bed duvet set. Or the countless school trip games of Shag, Marry or Dump that had seen the whole minibus shacked up with Thomas King.

The two other guys at the bar finished their drinks and stood up. One of them shouted over to Tom that they were leaving.

He waved a hand in acknowledgement, downed the rest of his beer and said, 'Well, it was a pleasure to meet you, Ava.'

Ava nodded. 'You too.' Although she wasn't quite sure that she meant it.

He stood up, then paused, hands resting on the back of his chair. 'You staying at the house?' he asked, nodding towards her grandmother's place across the little square.

'Yes.'

He shuddered slightly. 'Spooky.'

Ava glanced over at the dark windows of the house that seemed to loom in the twilight. 'I'm trying not to think about it too much,' she said, once again feeling the tendrils of fear that had been itching all afternoon at the prospect of going to bed alone in the house.

'Not worried it might be haunted?' he asked, almost as if deliberately trying to wind her up. His friends had headed out of the bar and were starting to walk towards the path leading up to the car park.

'It's not haunted.'

He backed away, seeming to contemplate something for a second, then shrugging one shoulder said, 'Well, if it all gets a bit too scary you're welcome to come and stay at my place.' He gestured back towards his own house on the hill. 'Anytime,' he added, with a slight narrowing of his eyes. A flash of blue. His gaze steady. The hint of a smile.

And she finally understood what he'd been driving at. She almost laughed. Thomas King was living up to exactly what the papers always said about him.

'No, you're alright,' she said, her tone incredulous but amused. 'I'm a big girl, I'll be fine. But thanks for the offer,' she added, finishing her drink.

Tom laughed. 'Well, if you change your mind . . .' he said, hands outstretched before turning to join his mates.

'I think I'll be OK,' Ava replied, but he was out of earshot.

She got up to leave, shaking her head with disbelief, laughing to herself as she walked away past the orange trees and the fig. The tension of going back inside popped, her attention diverted from the possibility of ghosts, from the blast of memory waiting in the little room, from the sadness of the scrap of soap.

Lying on the living room sofa, all the lights blazing, she spent the next hour Googling Thomas King and WhatsApping Louise.

Louise is typing . . . *Not surprised he owns a vineyard – he was a pretty terrible actor. Did you know he has a daughter? At college in Barcelona apparently.*

Ava is typing . . . *COLLEGE! How old is she?*

Louise is typing . . . *16. It was while he was still doing Love-Struck High. God I loved that show. Do you remember crying when his girlfriend died on the beach? It was so sad. I'd forgotten how OBSESSED with him I was! If you sleep with him my teenage self might stab you through the heart.*

Ava laughed out loud. Having been afraid that she would be lying in the dark in hopeless panic, she suddenly found the familiar links to her childhood – the Google images of *Love-Struck*, her mother's possessions, her grandmother's knick-knacks – strangely comforting, coupled with the gentle lull of the waves, the scent of warm dust and juniper and the heat pressing down like a blanket as she curled up around her phone.

CHAPTER 10

'You'll be alright on your own?' Rory said, putting the last bag in the car and closing the boot. It had stopped raining and the sun was somewhere behind the fog of early morning cloud, making the air smell like a greenhouse, warm and muggy like wet grass.

Claire nodded. 'I'll be alright. You're sure you'll be alright?' she asked, her hands on Max's shoulders, stroking the tips of his too-long hair, her son just on the cusp of an age that he would allow it.

They had decided at three a.m. that Rory would go to Spain for a couple of weeks, or however long it would take for all this to die down. And given that Max was due to break up in just over a week he would go too. It didn't seem healthy for him to weather the Twitter storm alone at school. And it felt like a good bonding opportunity.

Claire would stay for the time being. She had her interview coming up and *Home Style* magazine, where she was currently deputy editor, was so busy this time of year that taking a last-minute holiday would crucify her chances.

They also both seemed to know instinctively that this was something Rory needed to do alone. That somehow being together wasn't delivering their most successful selves at the moment.

Max picked up his battered old school rucksack.

'Hang on,' said Claire, taking the bag from him.

Max looked confused as she rested his hand luggage on the wall and unzipped it. As she pulled out his laptop, his little face fell. 'What?' he said with a whine. 'No way.'

'You're going to go on a digital detox,' she said.

Max kicked the wall. 'I don't want to go on a digital detox. I like digital. What am I going to do without my laptop? What am I going to do on the plane?'

Claire ruffled his hair as he sulked. 'Get your dad to buy you a book at the airport.'

'I don't want a book. I want my laptop.'

Claire shook her head.

'This is so unfair,' Max said. 'This is so unfair.' He turned to look at his dad, but the deathly paleness of Rory's face and the aura of holding-it-together-hopelessness meant Max didn't repeat his protest for the third time.

Rory opened the passenger door. 'Come on, mate. In the car.'

Max tried Claire one last time. 'Please let me take it, Mum?'

'No.'

Rory had an inkling the laptop ban was as much for his benefit as Max's. To stop the obsessive Twitter refreshing. Rory himself had reverted to an old Nokia that could do nothing more whizzy than send and receive black and white texts of 160 characters.

Max stuck his bottom lip out.

Rory saw Claire hold back a smile as she bent down to hug him. Reluctant at first, he rolled himself round into her arms and Rory heard her whisper in his ear something along the lines of, 'Be good, look after your father, and I love you,' as she gave him a huge, bone-crushing hug. Then she stood up, face to face with Rory.

'Take care of yourself,' Claire said, pushing her hair back behind her ears, then clearly not knowing what to do with her hands, folding her arms across her chest.

It started to rain slightly. Just the odd tap-tap on the pavement.

Rory nodded.

'Be nice to your sister,' Claire said.

Rory nodded again.

'Have you told her you're coming?' she asked.

'No.'

'Rory!'

'I will.'

Claire rolled her eyes.

The rain tap-tapped heavier.

Rory stepped forwards. 'We'd better kiss so I don't leave on an eye-roll,' he said.

She smiled.

He bent down, a bit nervous, and kissed her on the corner of her mouth. Claire reached up and held his face, kissed him square on the lips, quickly. Then she put her arms around his neck and hugged him.

Rory could smell the Chanel and Max's shampoo because she'd run out of her flash stuff. He thought he might cry again. *Hold it together, you pussy*, he told himself.

'Have fun,' Claire said brightly as she stood back.

'I'd have more fun with my laptop,' said Max, cheeky this time.

Claire swiped his hair.

'I love you,' she said as they both went round to their respective sides of the car, and Rory wondered how much of it was for him.

CHAPTER 11

The café was almost unrecognisable in the morning. Ava had woken early, the air humming with oppressive heat and the sound of car horns, street sweeping and bells ringing. From the window she could see the café tables full of people, hear the scraping of chairs, see the hands waving in greeting. A completely opposite atmosphere to the previous evening.

Showered and dressed in denim shorts and a white T-shirt, she tried to do her make-up and sort out the kink in her hair, but the gradual pooling of heat in the room got the better of her and she left the house, rubbing the line in her cheek from the pillow and trying to ruffle up her hair. As she went to shut the front door she caught a last glimpse of her indent on the living room sofa cushions where she'd slept, and remembered waking at three o'clock in the pitch-dark morning. She had felt exactly as Tom had suggested she might. Spooked and afraid, absence filling the space with the same intensity as the heat. She had felt the same unease as she had at her grandmother's funeral. That of having a life not quite lived right. But lying there she found herself perplexed as to what one did with a second chance. She was still Ava, just Ava in Spain. The problem was that she had taken herself with her on her adventure. Afraid still of her aloneness. Afraid of everyone pairing off and moving on. Afraid that her closest next of kin was Rory. Who was right this minute ringing, presumably to have a go at her for coming back to Spain. She looked at his name flashing on her phone screen and made the instant decision to silence the call. Remembering that she'd had the courage to defy him by coming out here, and the unfamiliar frisson of power that decision had given her, was enough to make her shut the door on the view of her night and go and find out why Café Estrella was suddenly doing such a roaring trade.

The air outside was still as glass. Electric fans whirred on the bar, ineffectual against the mirage of heat. Ava took a table in the shade of the ripped awning. The café was less packed than she'd thought when looking down from the window, but there were definitely more bums on seats. All of them pensioners' bums, dressed in polyester trousers, drip-dry powder-blue skirts and opaque tights, brown tweed slacks and polished black lace-up shoes. She recognised faces from the funeral. There was knitting. There was chatter. The sound of newspaper pages turning. The scents of warm bread, cigar smoke and strong coffee merged with the salty sea air. Everyone, it seemed, over the age of seventy-five descended on Café Estrella for breakfast.

As she was staring intrigued at the colourful array of customers, a figure plonked itself down in the seat opposite.

'Hello.' Thomas King pulled off his sunglasses.

'Er, hello,' Ava said, surprised at his arrival.

He looked terrible.

She surreptitiously ran her hand through her hair all the same, still under the spell of wanting to impress simply because he'd been famous.

'I had the worst night's sleep I've had in years,' he said, reaching forwards to toy with the menu, tapping the laminated corner on the table. 'You kept me awake.'

Ava almost snorted. 'Me?'

'Yes.' He tried to catch the waiter's eye. 'God I need a coffee. You need a coffee?' He turned back to Ava who said, 'Yes,' still unsure what he was doing at her table. Tom signalled to the waiter then sat back, rubbing his neck as he thought about what to say. 'I think that maybe yesterday I wasn't quite as supportive as I could have been.'

She raised a brow.

Tom shook his head. 'And I don't think Val would have been impressed.'

'No,' she said.

'No,' he agreed. 'She'd have killed me. I felt pretty bad. All night. That's what kept me up. I think she was haunting me,' he said, his expression giving the sense of a smile just lurking below the surface. 'So. Well . . .' He held his arms wide. 'Sorry.'

'That's OK,' Ava said, a touch more dismissive than she might normally be, just for the satisfaction of being so casual in the face of what seemed like an act – all doleful eyes and messy hair, like he was still on set somewhere.

The waiter came over with the coffees, a third of the cup slopped into the saucer, and two pastries, both apricot.

Tom yawned as he poured the spilt liquid back into the cup. 'He's the worst waiter,' he said, then picked up one of the pastries and took a huge bite.

Ava glanced around the café, not sure if the second pastry was for her and, even though it was petty, not wanting to give him even the smallest satisfaction of being able to say no if she asked. 'Who are all these people?' she said instead, gesturing towards the other customers. The old women knitting and doing the crossword. The wispy-haired men chatting across tables in their Fair Isle socks and woollen tank tops, unfazed by the heat. The newspapers being frowned at, the chess moves being scoffed at, the cards being counted, all with a healthy side order of gossip.

Tom looked to where she pointed and smiled as he chewed. 'They come for Everardo,' he said, cryptically.

Ava looked around, puzzled. The little café seemed to pulse in the sunshine. 'Is that a thing?' she asked. 'Like Zumba?'

Tom laughed. 'No. It's a person. Everardo. The baker.' He tilted his head towards the man, head bent over, drinking thick black coffee next to the now-half-empty huge woven bread baskets on the counter. 'Starts work at four in the morning and comes down here at the end of his shift from town, only person he'll deliver to is Flora. And he's the best. Brings her everything, always has, and no one here misses it.'

'Really?' Ava couldn't quite believe it. She stared at the tall, unassuming man sipping his drink, his hooked nose and sad, drooping eyes. Then she looked again at all the people and saw this time the plates on their tables. The glossy buns topped with tiny cubes of crystallised sugar, the sticky glazed croissants being dunked into milky coffee, the buttery soft *magdalenas* the shape of half-avocados resting on saucers. There was warm bread and jam and *pan con tomate* – thick slices of toasted sourdough rubbed with garlic, drizzled with olive oil and served with little glass jugs of tomato pulp to spread over the bread.

'Why does he only deliver here?' she asked.

Flora wafted past in a bright canary-yellow sundress and matching flip flops, carrying a plate of *magdalenas* for the neighbouring table. She paused with her hand on the back of Ava's chair and whispered, 'Because he's madly in love with me. Oh yes, a hundred percent,' she nodded conspiratorially. 'They all are, that's the trouble, but he's not my type at all.'

Ava looked up and caught Tom's eye as he hid his smile behind the rim of his coffee.

'And do they all stay for lunch?' Ava asked.

Flora scoffed, 'Of course not. Tight old buggers. They go home for lunch. They can cook lunch. But no one can bake like Everardo.'

'Try one,' said Tom, pushing the plate with the second pastry her way.

As he did, the sun shone through a crack in the awning, turning the apricot in the centre gold, and Ava took a snap with her phone to post on Instagram. It looked so totally delicious and seemed the perfect innocuous subject with which to showcase the immediate success of her trip to the outside world without having to delve into anything personal. Something that made this real without being too real.

As she was trying to come up with a caption better than '*Yum, Yum*', the woman with bright red curly hair, who she recognized from the funeral, put down her knitting and said, 'Are you photographing your croissant?', looking perplexed through giant glasses.

Ava glanced up from her phone, sheepish.

'Why are you doing that? Why is she doing that?' the woman asked an old man with a huge grey walrus moustache and a pale blue suit and loafers, lacquered walking stick leaning up against his chair. He shrugged and said, 'I have no idea, Rosa.'

'It's just for erm . . .' Ava started, not quite sure how to explain something that would seem completely stupid and inane if said out loud.

Tom laughed through his nose, his expression a little pitying as he held his coffee cup with both hands and sat back, legs stretched in front of him, crossed at the ankle.

She was saved from her explanation by a woman to the red-haired woman's right, her deep, wrinkled, raisin-tanned face also familiar from the funeral, her sparkling jewellery clattering as she pointed Ava's way and said, 'You are Val's, yes?'

Ava sat up straight and nodded. 'Yes.'

The woman studied her, beady eyes narrowed. Under her table was the lame pug dog with the wheeled contraption. 'In this light you look like your mother.'

Her red-haired companion exhaled as though she didn't wholly agree. They were all staring at Ava now.

The man with the walrus moustache crossed his arms in front of him. 'Now there was one very fine lady.'

Ava smiled his way.

He winked.

The raisin-tanned woman scoffed. 'She was a walking pain in the neck.'

Ava was about to jump to her mother's defence when she heard the sudden thundering of footsteps and a breathless little voice next to her say, 'Dad's-been-Twitter-shamed-and-we're-all-on-a-digital-detox,' as Max practically careered into her chair.

All eyes and ears in the café perked to attention. Ava could see the raisin-tanned woman mouth 'Twitter shamed?' at her red-haired friend.

Ava stood up, completely taken aback by the sight of Max, and, with her hand on his shoulder, looked to where he was pointing. Rory was dragging their cases across the concourse, his short blond hair dirty and flat, skin tired, eyes black. 'Oh my God,' she said, her hand over her mouth.

'All got a bit much at home,' Rory said by way of jokey explanation as he drew level, then added, 'Hi, Flora.' And to Tom, 'Hang on, aren't you Thomas King?'

Tom stood up, all casual cool. 'I am, mate.'

'I thought so.' Rory was nodding at him as he might a Madame Tussauds' waxwork he'd recognised without having to read the placard. 'Ava had a poster of you on her wall when we were growing up.'

'I did not!' Ava gasped.

Tom smirked.

'Yes you did,' said Rory, emphatic. 'I remember it.'

'I didn't.' Ava shook her head, then looking to Tom said, 'I really didn't.'

Rory sighed as if it were all too much. 'She did, honestly. Trust me. Anyway, here we are,' he said, slumping down in one of the vacant chairs. 'I could murder a coffee,' he added, dragging Ava's untouched cup towards him.

'I'll get you a coffee,' Flora said, while Rory muttered his way through the whole #VileRory saga – 'I'm being what's known as shamed on Twitter. I didn't even know it had a name at the beginning of the week. Now I'm an expert' – his bravado so cling-film thin that he was having trouble sustaining it.

Max sat in the other chair and asked, 'Can I have your croissant, please?'

Ava nodded, her attention now on her phone and the cascades of #SwanLovesGoose #VileRory tweets. She was gobsmacked. It would have almost been funny if he wasn't sitting opposite her looking like death warmed up.

'Do you want to know something weird, Aunty Ava?' Max said, clearly bored by the whole thing, pushing her phone to one side, his mouth full of apricot croissant.

'OK,' she said, distracted, glancing worriedly at her brother who had slipped into a glassy daze next to her, his eyes focused on the phone that Max had made her put down on the table as she listened to him.

'Well,' Max started, taking a deep breath, 'I forgot to pack my toothbrush and on the way here I saw two toothbrushes on the pavement and then, just there on the slope, I saw another one in the road. Don't you think that's weird?'

Ava nodded. 'That's weird.'

'I thought so,' Max agreed. 'I'm digital detoxing,' he added. 'I think it's making me see more.'

Tom snorted a laugh. 'How old are you?'

'I'm ten,' said Max.

'And you're digital detoxing?' said Tom, his tone half-impressed, half-incredulous.

'That's the world we live in,' Max said, all serious.

Rory shrugged at the whole notion of a digital detox. 'It's for my benefit. Claire's way of stopping me being online,' he said, voice wavering as he tried for indifference.

Max popped the last of the croissant in his mouth and added, 'Except he checked on the airport computers at Heathrow and Barcelona. Naughty Daddy!' he said, giving his dad a look that was, Ava thought, strangely reminiscent of Rory himself.

Rory sighed, ran a hand through his greasy hair. 'I'm going down to the beach,' he said, and standing up, sloped off down to the water's edge.

Max was still rabbiting on about detoxing and toothbrushes as Ava glanced at Tom. They'd both seen Rory's hand as it swiped her phone off the table.

The sun was unrelenting. Ava fanned herself with a menu. She could sense Rory's desperation in his every move. Even from behind he looked shattered. Like he hadn't slept for a month. Damp patches of sweat on his grey T-shirt.

All the oldies were unashamedly earwigging. Flora came over with a chocolate milk for Max, and they watched Rory as he stood hunched over on the beach, completely ignoring the view as he disappeared into a Twitter wormhole.

'Where's your phone?' said Max's little voice suddenly, as he cut his own monologue short to reach for the chocolate milk and followed their eyes to where Rory was standing.

Ava winced. 'Your dad has it.'

'Aunty Ava! That's not allowed!' Max looked at her with abject disappointment.

'I know,' she said. 'I know, I see now.'

Tom said, 'Maybe you need to digital detox too. Help him out.'

'Me?' Ava said. The idea of it filled her with horror. Her phone was her lifeline. 'No, I can't detox.'

'Why not?'

'I need my phone.'

Tom laughed. 'No one *needs* a phone.'

'I do.'

'What, to take pictures of croissants?' He looked at her. 'You can't do it, can you?'

She scoffed. 'That's not going to work. Of course I can do it. If I wanted to.'

'Go on then. Get it back, turn it off, hide it somewhere.'

'No,' she said, feeling like she was getting backed into a corner. 'You turn yours off.'

'I don't have one.'

'Oh of course you don't.' Ava rolled her eyes.

Tom grinned.

'Go on, Aunty Ava,' said Max. 'If I can do it, you can.'

'Spoken like a true ten-year-old,' said Tom.

Ava thought back to the middle of the night when she'd stared at Instagram photos of her friends at a rained-off barbecue, drinking bottles of beer while squashed under a plastic B&Q gazebo, and wished she was there. When she'd comforted herself with dots on her calendar for the annual Halloween party at Peregrine's, fireworks on the common with her friends, Midnight Mass at the church near Rory's, New Year's lunch at her dad's house. The constants – signs that normal life would resume.

One second she'd been lonely, she thought, looking out at the glare of the sun, the next she had too much.

Rory swore loudly from the shoreline and they all watched him flop to the sand and sit with his head in his hands.

A new chap arrived with a chess board under his arm and called over to the raisin-tanned woman, but he was shut down with a sharp, 'Not now,' while Rosa clicked her knitting needles together furiously as they all stared straight ahead at their new beach cinema.

Ava felt Max's warm little hand creep into her own. The feel of it surprised her. Caught her off guard. 'Do you think my dad's having a nervous breakdown?' he asked, huge eyes staring across at her like a goldfish.

Ava swallowed. It was all very odd, this role reversal. Her brother distracted, dishevelled, unsettled. She suddenly the designated grown-up Max was looking to for help, when she was usually the one making funny faces at him during boring speeches at weddings or Midnight Mass. Rory fit the role of adult so brilliantly that it was almost necessary to rebel, just to add some contrast. He couldn't have a nervous breakdown. That wasn't the way the dynamic worked.

She could feel Tom watching her. She could feel the whole place watching her.

'No,' she said, squeezing Max's small hand. 'No, he's not having a nervous breakdown. Not if we can help it.'

Standing up, Max's hand still in hers, Ava marched across the sand to where Rory was sitting. She looked much more confident than she felt. All the eyes from the café boring into her back. She picked up her phone before Rory's hand shot out to grab it. 'I think we could all do with a bit of a digital detox,' she said. 'Everyone's doing it? Aren't they?' She looked down at Max. 'It's very on-trend.'

Max giggled.

Rory sighed.

She looked down at her phone and felt a pang of desire to quickly WhatsApp Louise with an update – her brother was trending on Twitter for goodness' sake, that needed discussing – but she turned it off, fully off. Not just on standby.

Max let go of her hand and went to sit on the sand next to his dad, who barely acknowledged he was there.

'What shall we do now?' Max asked.

Rory was staring straight ahead, shattered. He turned to look vacantly at Ava. Two pairs of goldfish eyes on her now. Ava swallowed down a rising sense of panic. This had never happened before.

'Well,' she said, as brightly as she could. But then found herself lost for what to say next. She was usually great at making things OK, but with Rory it was different, he was always the one who took charge. Everything she thought to offer seemed immediately ridiculous. 'We could all go back to the Summerhouse, have a cold drink, start packing things up. No, Max, you won't want to do that. Erm. Go for a walk. Go for a drive. No, I don't have a car. A cycle. Or we could get the bus into town. Let's do that, let's go for some sightseeing.'

Then a voice next to her said, 'Why don't you just go back up to the café? Rory, mate, there's a beer waiting for you. Max, I know the guy who runs the watersports if you fancy a go on anything. He's got a little boy about your age. See over there,' he pointed in the direction of the pontoon that bobbed in the water at the end of the peninsula. 'We could go over, say hi?'

Max jumped up with a definite yes.

'That OK, Rory?' Tom asked, as Rory heaved himself to standing, brushing the sand from his trousers.

'What? Yes, yes, fine. Fine.'

Ava looked at Tom as he put his hand on Max's back and steered him towards the watersports pontoon. She hadn't expected him to follow them down to the beach. She'd expected him to have watched with vague interest for a minute or two and then go in search of someone in a bikini. He hadn't looked at her at all, just cut through her waffling with the most simple, obvious plan.

Maybe he sympathised with Rory? Recognised what he was going through – both the unwanted fame and the pressure of fatherhood? See, this was why she needed a phone. All this minutiae needed to be recounted, analysed and explained.

Flora was waiting for them at the table with a tray of little beers, along with the all-seeing wrinkled eyes of the breakfast lot, their hands engrossed in their tasks – their knitting, their chess, their newspapers – mouths deathly silent, ears pricked up for the next instalment.

CHAPTER 12

In the distance, Rory could just see Max's head poking out of the top of a lifejacket as he plopped backwards into a giant rubber ring, a shaggy-haired blond kid in the one next to him and a real dude at the helm of the speedboat. At least Max was in paradise.

Ava wasn't saying anything, he could feel her watching.

Flora was sitting at the adjacent table, going through a list of prices, half with them, half not.

He took a moment just to sit in the dappled shade of the orange trees and drink his beer. Served in a glass smaller than a half-pint with condensation dripping down the side and a frothy white head sliced to the side with a palette knife. He reached forwards to pick it up. Felt the warmth of the foam and the ice cool of the beer on his lips. He shut his eyes, felt the sun flicker yellow on his face through the awning, heard the white noise of cicadas. Felt the familiar patterns of the plastic chair and inhaled the drifting smoke of an old man's cigar.

Memories of holidays here: of his mum dressed up to the nines for dinner, mesmerising the collective gaze of Café Estrella; of card games he was itching to win, with Val needing constant reminders of the rules and Ava cheating while his mum languidly turned a blind eye and a cigar of his dad's burnt to a stump in the ash tray. Moments in the sun where, under Val's beady-eyed gaze, their mother behaved herself, slipped into her rightful role. Where to Rory's delight she sat legs outstretched on the beach building sandcastles with them, moving every time the shade obstructed her tan, as Val watched from her deckchair, her newspaper untouched as she maintained order, her skin the colour of treacle, her swimming hat dotted with purple plastic flowers.

The university summers, just him and Ava. No one talking of anything other than what the first drink was going to be. Thinking he was the bee's knees. Taking a canoe out on the sea and paddling miles, coming back sweaty and tanned and chatting up the waitresses.

More than halcyon days. Days when the future was as wide open as a Wild West prairie.

'It'll blow over, you know,' Ava said. 'You just have to make it matter less. In the end, no one cares about these things.'

'She's right,' Flora said, without looking up. 'They have their own dramas to deal with. Except this lot,' she added with a little smirk, pointing towards the breakfast gang.

Rory gave a half-hearted laugh. He wanted to say that he couldn't make it matter less. That, without him having realised, his job had come to define him. That he'd thought he had life buttoned up nice and tight and now it seemed all the toggles were in the wrong holes. But he didn't say things like that, so he nodded, noncommittal, then opened his mouth to ask Ava what she'd done since she'd been here, but found himself saying instead, 'I think it's all over. I think I might be losing my marriage as well.'

'What?' Ava said, surprised. 'But you and Claire are . . .' she seemed lost for the right word, then just said, 'you and Claire,' as she might about other guaranteed pairings like Marmite and toast.

Rory took another sip of his beer, unable to quite believe that he'd said what he'd said out loud. But he had to tell someone. Since iPhonegate, since Claire had looked at him like she might actually walk away, it was like a large balloon had been sitting, expanding, in his chest. He wondered whether, if he looked down, he might see that he'd risen from his chair as it floated away.

He realised fleetingly that this must be why people ask if you 'need to talk'. He imagined his father rolling his eyes. Then wondered how many balloons were weighing him down.

He glanced at Ava. 'You know that time I came out here to film Flora and Ricardo? That's probably the last time in my life that I felt like I was me. Like I had time.' He looked around him.

'But you were twenty, Rory,' Ava said. 'Everyone feels like that at twenty.'

Dots of light coming through the ripped awning were dancing on Ava's face. She looked like she had that same holiday. Carefree. Ava always looked carefree.

'It's not being twenty. It's just not being relied on. It's having no responsibility. No pressure. Look at this lot . . .' He pointed to the chess players. 'They have all the time in the world.'

'That's dangerous talk, young man,' the raisin-tanned woman said, lowering her newspaper, the pug asleep in her lap getting a shock. 'Just think what your grandmother would have to say about that. Why do you think we've got all the time? We've got all the time because we're running out of time. Never wish your life away. Never.'

'Listen to Gabriela.' The man in the pale blue suit with the moustache agreed. 'You don't want to be old, trust me,' he said, none of them with even a hint of remorse at their blatant eavesdropping.

Rory ran his hands over his face. 'I'm just so tired.'

Ava was staring at him. He could tell she didn't know what to say. She had the same stricken look on her face as when their dad had told them that their mum wasn't coming home. He'd told them in the morning and then taken them shopping for a treat in an attempt to counteract the news. Rory had bought a pair of red and black Nike Air Max trainers that he'd been begging for for months. He distinctly remembered the joy of the orange box and the smell of the new leather and feeling a bit guilty that he'd got them, because he'd known their mum wasn't coming back to live with them for a while and part of him knew it would make life much less stressful. Ava hadn't been quite the same. Unable to find anything she wanted to buy, she'd had a massive meltdown in House of Fraser, and they'd all had to go and have a cup of tea and a cake in the depressing café that smelt of jacket potatoes and vegetable soup. In the end their dad had folded up five ten-pound notes and told her that she should buy what she wanted when she saw it.

It occurred to Rory now that he had no idea what she'd bought. He just remembered her having to always sleep with the light on and spending hours begging their dad to call New York, almost without fail to be told that their mother had just gone out.

It wasn't lost on Rory that the age he'd been when he'd got those trainers was only a few years older than Max was now. Yet he didn't feel man enough to manage the response if he and Claire split. To say with the same absolute certainty as his father that life would move forwards and they would all be just fine.

'You've got to go back,' said Ava, wide-eyed and panicky. 'You've got to go home and talk to Claire. You have to. You can't stay here. You need to sort it out.'

Rory felt suddenly like he could push back his chair, start walking and never stop.

The decision to keep his bum on his seat was made for him by Flora. Big, buxom, blowsy Flora, who had captured a nation with her warm, no-fuss cookery and a pair of breasts the subject of 165 complaints to the BBC when she'd appeared in a very low-cut velvet top on a Christmas special. Flora may have been a good twenty years older than him, but Rory had spent a lot of time behind his camera while filming his documentary about her and Ricardo, staring at that satin-clad figure.

Today, however, like Rory, Flora looked a little more world-weary, but when she smiled at him she was still a confusing cross between what he'd wished his mum had been like and a hormone-spinning boyhood crush. 'You can't go back. Not while you feel like this,' she said, peering at him over the top of her pearlised pink reading glasses.

'Oh I really think he should,' said Ava.

Flora shook her head. 'No. You have to let it settle. Everything is out of place. You have to let it settle before you make any decisions. Like the sea here after a big storm. Just take some time, sit on a sun lounger, do some fishing.'

'I don't like fishing,' said Rory. The idea of doing nothing was abhorrent to him. He never did nothing. If he lay in bed for too long in the morning he got restless legs. He needed to be doing something.

Flora laughed. 'Have another beer.'

'If you insist!' Tom appeared from between the orange trees, grinning. He took a seat in the sun and, pointing back towards the pontoon said, 'Rory, your son is a speed demon.'

'He is?' This was news to Rory.

Tom nodded. 'He wants to go for a spin along the coast in the speedboat with Alessandro and his kid, Emilio. That OK with you?'

'No, he should probably come back,' Rory said, turning round in his chair to see Max waving at him, hair wet, massive smile on his face.

'Nah mate, he's fine, he's enjoying himself,' said Tom. 'Relax.'

Rory stiffened in his chair. He was a terrible relaxer, especially when told to. But as he looked at his grinning son, he realised that he spent an awful lot of time at home trying to get Max to do something – to eat, get dressed, get off the damn computer – and here he was desperate to get out into the wide blue yonder. Why did Rory think he should come back anyway? Because he didn't want him to be a nuisance? Because it was nearly lunchtime and Max should have something to eat? Because . . . He didn't know. It was all in chaos, what difference did it make what time they ate? Rory wished he could be ten years old and in a speedboat. He did a thumbs up towards the pontoon and Max whooped.

'You alright?' Tom asked, legs outstretched in front of him.

Rory was immediately envious of Tom's casual ease with life – his unironed shirt and unkempt, undefinable facial hair that was too short for a beard and too long for stubble. His ability to seemingly kick back and do nothing.

Rory nodded. 'Yes. Thank you. Apologies for earlier on the beach.'

'Fine with me,' Tom said. 'I know what it's like to have the papers twist your words,' he added, before his attention was diverted to the tray of little beers Flora put down on the table.

Rory wanted to disappear. To fast-forward life till it was back to normal. He missed his phone. Not for Twitter but for everything it held. All the articles, all the nuggets of information. Its ability to transport him somewhere, anywhere, for however long he wanted. If he had his phone now he could take himself away.

Ava seemed to be the one trying to keep it all normal. 'Shall we have some lunch?' she said, grabbing the waiter's attention as he passed and asking, 'Can I order some tapas?'

He shrugged and flipped his pad to a new page.

'The chickpeas and chorizo . . .' she started.

'No.' He shook his head. 'We don't have that.'

Flora shifted uncomfortably in her seat, feigning deep interest in the accounts she was working on.

'OK, the calamari?' said Ava.

'No.'

Ava frowned. 'What do you have?'

He thought for a moment. 'Tortilla.'

'OK,' she said. 'Tortilla and olives.'

'No. No olives.'

'How can you not have olives?' she said, pointing to the hillside dotted with olive trees.

The waiter chuckled to himself. '*Si*, we have olives,' he said, walking off, sniggering at his little joke.

Across the path the early lunch crowd were all starting to drift from the beach and into Nino's, a queue already forming.

At Estrella the tables were still cluttered with finished coffee cups, wasps buzzing around empty breakfast plates.

On the table in front of Rory was a pile of croissant crumbs. He pushed one of them with his finger, a triangle shape, and sat it on a square. It made a house. Then he pulled the others into a line to make a road and then a tree. By the time he'd finished the second beer there was an aeroplane in the sky and he'd poured a line of sugar out from his leftover sachet to make the clouds and rays of sun while the others chatted in the background.

His glass empty, he looked up to see if anyone was having another to find them all watching him.

'That's quite a scene you've made there,' said Tom, looking impressed at the crumb and sugar picture.

'I, erm . . .' Rory frowned. 'I'm not terribly good at doing nothing,' he said.

'I think you're going to have to, Rory. You need time to think,' said Ava.

'Give the guy a break,' Tom laughed. 'He's hardly going to sit at a table and think about his life all day. Doing nothing is a pretty daunting thing.'

'You seem very good at it,' Ava said, brows raised as she looked at him.

Tom laughed. 'I own a bloody vineyard.'

'Well shouldn't you be there, tending your grapes?' Ava asked, a little confused.

Tom shook his head. 'This is not my favourite stage.'

Ava made a face. 'What does that mean?'

'We're in the ripening phase,' he said. Ava still looked clueless. 'It's too stressful. Too much is in the hands of the weather. I'm more about the harvesting. The doing.'

'Exactly,' said Rory. 'I need to do.' He sat up, brushing his crumb scene on to the floor much to everyone's horror. 'I need to be doing. I can't sit here just getting drunk. I need a project. When's picking time?' he asked Tom.

Tom shook his head. 'Not for a month or so, I'm afraid.'

The waiter brought over a plate of tortilla cut into diamonds and a little bowl of purple black olives.

They all peered at the slightly dry-looking omelette, the lines of the plastic packet still in grooves on the surface.

Rory remembered the fluffy white tortilla that Flora used to bring out straight from the pan, served in great wedges with garlic mayonnaise. He remembered being little and their gran making it. Sitting in the Ealing dining room on a Sunday afternoon, competing with Ava to see if they could fit a whole wedge in their mouths in one go, unable to speak and hardly able to chew. Their grandmother sighing that they were disgusting, while eating hers in two swift bites. Their mother lounging back, bored, the ice in a bright-red Campari chinking as she sipped.

'*Gracias*,' Ava said to the waiter, but he was gone, off to smoke a cigarette and check his phone.

They all stared at the unappetising little plates. No one wanting to try anything. Rory watched Flora wipe a bead of sweat from her forehead.

He looked around the ailing Café Estrella, with its peeling paint, broken awning and straggly orange trees, the old men on plastic chairs playing chess, the tables of dirty plates and the waiter on the phone by his scooter, and then compared it with the view of Nino's, with its black leather chairs, white walls, queue of customers. There was just enough sadness in seeing the café's fall from glory to make him forget his own misery for a minute.

'Maybe you should make another film,' said Ava into the silence. 'A follow-up on Flora.'

Rory immediately shook his head. Like a reflex reaction to any suggestion of Ava's. 'I don't have a camera,' he said, squashing down a small bubble of interest at the idea as he remembered the time he'd spent in the kitchen filming that first documentary, what he'd learnt watching Ricardo: the heat, the passion, the sweat and the adrenaline of success.

'I've got a camera,' said Tom. 'Go for it.'

'You do?' said Rory.

'Go on,' said Ava. 'You should do it. Definitely.'

He could see her working it out in her head, the whole thing already done and dusted as a fix-all solution.

'Don't you think it's a good idea, Flora?' Ava carried on, nudging Flora on the arm.

'Well . . .' Flora seemed both pleased for the distraction from the limp-looking food but also slightly worried at the idea of another film. 'I don't know. I haven't been on camera for ages. I'll look so fat.'

Ava rolled her eyes. 'You won't look fat, you'll look amazing.'

'It won't be a very happy story though, will it?' said Flora, adding with a mock-documentary voice, 'The couple have now split up, and as you can see Flora is failing miserably on her own, stuck with mounting debts and no customers under the age of seventy.' But the way she was running her hand through her hair and giving it a little flounce, the deprecating laugh she added at the end, it was clear to everyone she would adore being back in front of the lens.

'Well maybe this is the chance to make it something else?' said Ava, refusing to let it go. 'Maybe this will give you your confidence back?'

'Is she always this idealistic?' Flora said to Rory, leaning back, a little bamboozled.

Rory nodded.

Ava looked chastened. Like she did when she was a kid.

Rory felt bad. He realised part of the reason he was fighting the whole film idea was simple sibling rivalry. The desire for Ava not to be victorious. Not to be right. He wondered how often he'd made similarly based decisions. How often he'd wanted to keep her down. He had done so much to keep her happy when they were younger – soothe her as a baby while his mum walked to the end of the garden to escape the cries, make her laugh when they were left in the house on their own, let her sleep on his floor on folded up blankets when she had nightmares – it just seemed inconceivable that this needy little kid could possibly know better than him now.

And yet all Ava was doing was trying to help him. Trying to find a solution to restore balance.

Rory swallowed. He thought for a minute, looking from the slightly dejected Ava to Flora, sitting back, arms crossed under her chest, expression cynical, and said, 'It could very well give you your confidence back, Flora. You're one of those people who comes alive on camera.'

Ava's eyes narrowed just a touch, as though she'd clocked a victory. As though he was coming round to the idea.

Flora batted her lashes.

A little bubble of excitement fizzed in Rory at the idea of filming here again. The prospect of doing a job with no expectation. No one waiting for the end result. Aside from Ava, among these people Rory carried none of the weight of expectation that had been placed upon him in the last ten years. And how well did he even know Ava nowadays? They met up for the odd drink, birthdays and Christmas Day.

This would be something completely at Rory's whim.

'You know, I've still got the original,' said Flora.

'You haven't?' Ava gasped. 'Oh, can we watch it? Please?'

Rory made a face. 'Nah, I don't think we should—'

'Of course we should,' Tom cut in, and no one seemed to disagree with Tom, ever. He dropped something into conversation and people seemed to wilt in acquiescence. That was the upshot of fame, however distant.

As the others stood up, Rory remained, reluctant. He very rarely watched anything that he had made. It was in the past. History. He was on to the next thing. He knew that nothing he produced ever quite lived up to the epic vision that he had prior to undertaking it. And this being his first ever film, he expected a chasm between reality and perfection.

But everyone was already following Flora into the café. Rory pushed his chair back and sloped along behind.

It was dark and smelt slightly of old chip pan grease. The football was on the TV. Flora went round behind the bar while Ava perched on one of the high metal stools, paint flaking off the rust, and Tom and Rory stood.

'Isn't this exciting?' said Flora, bending down to scrabble through a huge stack of DVDs and VHS tapes on a shelf.

'I can't believe you still have videos!' Ava said.

'It's all that lot,' she pointed to the punters eking out their coffees and peering into the café to see what was going on, 'they want to watch their old films here half the time.'

Tom leant against the bar, hands in his pockets, and sighed. 'Ah, there's nothing like a rainy morning's viewing of *Casablanca*.'

Ava raised a brow.

'It's actually true,' he added. 'It's very relaxing.'

'It doesn't really seem your style,' she said.

'And yet you don't know me at all,' Tom replied, eyes narrowed, knowing grin.

Ava's cheeks flecked red and she turned her attention to Flora, who had stood up triumphant with a dusty copy of Rory's film in her hand.

As Flora was trying to work the DVD player, Max came charging in like a wet puppy, full of speedboat chatter, but then the sudden sight of Rory on the TV screen halted him mid-sentence.

'Urgh, is that you, Dad?'

They all stared at the screen in fascination. There was twenty-year-old Rory, all buff and tanned with his camera on his shoulder. He was talking to the mirror, the same one they were all facing now behind the bar. His blond hair thicker, his skin golden, his eyes glowing bright.

Something about seeing that energy, that confidence, that youth, made Rory unable to look away.

And then there was Flora, big laugh, shining hair, skin smooth as a cherry.

They were looking at ghosts.

He glanced at Flora across the counter and wondered if she was thinking the same thing as him. Is that person still there? Still somewhere living inside me?

He felt like he could say with certainty that it was still in Flora.

He swallowed. Which meant that *he* was still living somewhere inside him.

'Why are you doing that weird voice?' Max asked, face screwed up, hair dripping a puddle on to the floor. 'You sound really odd, Dad.'

'I know.' Rory had to look away because now they were getting into the actual film, the faux American accent the younger version of himself had put on for the voiceover and the thundering flamenco music he'd overlaid. 'I think we should stop it now.'

'No!' a chorus of voices undercut him.

Then Ricardo appeared on screen – all dashing Latin good looks, red neckerchief and casually half-unbuttoned chef's whites, rhapsodising about his future while he patted his wife's bottom – and Flora reached over and pressed STOP.

They all sat in silence.

It was Ava who broke the tension. 'Hey Tom,' she smirked, 'I bet you've got a stash of *Love-Struck Highs* at home, you should go and grab a couple, we could watch them now.'

Tom scoffed. 'Sounds to me, Miss Ava, like you might be the one with the *Love-Struck High* collection. What was it you were saying about a poster earlier, Rory?'

He glanced at Rory, winked conspiratorially.

Ava huffed, 'I did NOT have a poster!'

Tom beamed.

And Rory remembered what it felt like to laugh.

CHAPTER 13

Ava was still sleeping on the sofa in the living room. Max and Rory were sharing the spare bedroom. Ava was itching to tell Rory about the little room of their mother's stuff, but she'd figured it was better to wait till morning, let him get a good night's sleep.

She hadn't thought it possible for the days to get any hotter. She woke up damp from sweat, her hair stuck to her forehead, sun clawing its way in through the cracks in the blinds.

'Have you been asleep all this time?' Max asked, as she appeared in the hallway. He was slipping little feet into his flip flops. 'Dad's already been for a run and we're going out for breakfast.'

Ava looked behind her at the clock. 'It's not that late,' she said, although as Rory appeared, showered and changed from his jog, he shared a look with Max to say that it was.

Ava had been up in the night again, lying awake on the pulsing hot sofa, her hand itching to check her phone in the silent stillness. To feel the distraction of the little number of unread messages on the corner of her WhatsApp and email. To check her Instagram likes and her Facebook notifications.

In the end she'd caved, slipping it out of its hiding place in a living room drawer and turning it on, on the proviso of checking for emergencies. When she saw a text from Rory's wife, Claire – *Is he OK?* – she felt vindicated. So vindicated that, after replying – *Think so. We've given him a project. A x* – she treated herself to a little WhatsApp chat with Louise.

Ava is typing . . . *I'm meant to be digital detoxing.*

Louise is typing . . . *Unsuccessfully, clearly. How's the heart-throb?*

Ava is typing . . . *VERY smug and not that good-looking. How are the twins?*

Louise is typing . . . *Famous people have symmetrical faces, giving them universal appeal. You're lying. Twins size of lemons.*

Now as Ava stood in the hall, Rory and Max in front of her, she wondered where her phone was. She'd stayed up after the WhatsApping doing more Thomas King Googling. Looking at paparazzi pictures of him getting mad with photographers at airports, his hand trying to block their shots. There was a flurry of old articles about how 'strained' things were with Mia Martínez, the mother of his daughter, a one-hit wonder teen popstar, who became more famous for her wild-child antics as her subsequent releases failed to chart. Reporters made insinuations about whether she'd trapped Tom into parenthood in an attempt to stay in the limelight; others blamed him for the demise of her career. But it was generally implied that neither of them were mature enough for parenthood, and while there were staged pics of Tom all fresh-faced, holding the tiny baby in *Hello!* magazine, the majority of pictures were of him stumbling out of clubs, glassy-eyed, while Mia was papped out and about exhausted with the baby strapped to her front. It was only in later photographs that Tom appeared with the little girl, holding her hand, her face blurred out, him suddenly wearing glasses and shirts rather than ripped black T-shirts.

Ava had skimmed article after article and had no recollection of falling asleep. She certainly hadn't turned her phone off or hidden it back in the living room drawer. What if it rang now? She couldn't bear the idea of getting caught cheating in the detox. Max's little face would be pure disappointment. And she didn't want Rory to find it because he was just beginning to look more human again, and he would tell Tom that she'd failed in the detox, and that would make him even more annoyingly smug.

'Dad's going to teach me to be a cameraman,' Max was saying.

'That's nice,' Ava said, distracted. Wanting to find and hide her phone. 'I'll meet you out there, if you like, at breakfast,' she said.

'You sure?' Rory asked, shoving his feet into the same-brand pair of black flip flops that Ava recognised from when he was a teenager. Once Rory settled on something he didn't change.

'Yeah, fine,' she said, but as he started to usher Max out the door, Ava remembered the little room. 'No, wait, wait! I have to show you something.'

Rory stepped back into the hall. 'Right now?'

Ava nodded. 'Come with me.' She could feel herself holding in a smile at the idea of it. The rush of excitement she'd felt when she first prised the door open.

Rory and Max followed as she led them up the stairs into the main bedroom. It was labyrinth dark. She pulled the blind and the place shone. Rory looked immediately uncomfortable being in their grandmother's bedroom. He stood awkwardly on the threshold.

'In here,' Ava said, and jogged over to open the little door.

Rory and Max edged forwards.

'Ta-da,' she said proudly, pulling the scrap of light cord. 'Look, it's all of Mum's stuff.'

Rory watched from where he stood in the middle of the main room. Max went closer to peer in. Ava waited, expectant.

'It's very sparkly,' said Max as he touched a sequinned jacket sleeve.

Ava nodded, giving him a little wink as she slipped the green jacket off the hanger and put it on over her vest top. 'And look, Max,' she said, lifting up a dusty programme from a box of theatre memorabilia, 'this is her,' she pointed to the picture on the front. 'Isabel Fisher, one of the greatest mezzo-sopranos ever in the whole world.'

Max nodded like he had no idea what that meant, but as he glanced at the picture of the woman in swirling red skirts playing Carmen, he frowned and said, 'Isn't that you?'

Ava laughed. 'No, it's our mum. Mine and Rory's.'

Max took it off her. 'Blimey,' he said, 'you're identical.'

'Max, watch your language,' Rory cut in.

Ava bent down and picked another programme from the stack. There were hundreds of them. 'That's her as Cinderella,' she said, passing the glossy booklet over to Max. 'And here, in the *The Barber of Seville*. And look, this box must all be fan letters,' she said, gesturing to a pile of cards and envelopes in a tatty old shoebox. 'And this, this is a photo of her at The Plaza in New York. When we went to see her she always took us to The Plaza. Afternoon tea. It was amazing.'

That was when she heard Rory sigh. She glanced over to hear him say wearily, 'Ava, you're not going to get all starry-eyed about this, are you?'

Ava felt herself deflate. She stood up as straight as she could under the sloping roof, pushing the box of fan letters on to the nearest shelf, a couple of loose brooches falling to the floor. 'Oh Rory, why?' she said. 'Why do you have to always go and ruin everything?'

Max looked at the floor, his toe nudging a fallen leopard brooch.

'Because I know you, Ava,' Rory said, running a frustrated hand through his hair. 'I know what you're like. You'll get sucked in like you always do. Just close the door and walk away.'

'No,' she said, hands on her hips, still in the sequinned jacket.

Rory looked at her, eyebrows raised. 'You'll get hurt.'

'Well, good,' she said. 'Maybe that's a good thing.' She felt like she was five again, eyes blazing, chubby little hand bashing the table in a tantrum. 'Better than shutting the door and ignoring it.'

Rory shook his head, his voice staying completely calm as hers rose. As it always did when they fought. 'Don't come crying to me when you find something you don't like.'

'I want to find things, Rory. She was our mum.'

'Yes, and she left us, Ava. And it wasn't a bad thing. She made life harder. At some point you have to accept that.'

Ava looked away to the stack of glossy programmes, breathed in through her nose. Max was watching her.

She smiled at him, then looked back at his dad. 'The thing that you never seem to understand,' she said, 'is that there's more than one way. There's more than your way, Rory.'

Rory replied with a snort, as if that was ludicrous. 'Come on, Max,' he said, 'we've got work to do.'

Max, who seemed quite relieved to get the hell out of there, bounded over to the door saying, 'Assistant Director, if you don't mind, Dad.'

Rory did a mock salute. 'Yes, sir.' Then turned to Ava and said, 'We'll see you at the café.'

She nodded without looking up, pulling the glimmering jacket off and sliding it back on to the hanger.

CHAPTER 14

Flora's kitchen was dark. The walls were a deep blue, the paint chipped where delivery trolleys had hit the edges and feet had scuffed the skirting board. The beautiful big paella pans and giant stainless steel pots hung unused from a central pulley that had been fixed almost permanently up close to the yellowing ceiling, forgotten. A giant gold graffiti stencil of a bull's head dominated the wall between the kitchen and the bar, the window hatch in place of its nose, commissioned by Ricardo in the early days as a symbol of ambition. He'd give it a ceremonial smack first thing every shift.

Rory walked once around the space, noting the new addition of a microwave and the whiff of old chip pan oil, and came back out to lean against the bar.

'Didn't you use to have tapas out on the counter here?' he asked Flora, pointing to the space where he knew very well heaps of fresh tapas had sat on stands, all priced with different-coloured cocktail stick flags, ready to be picked by tempted customers.

Flora was standing awkwardly behind the bar, the counter top running along almost the complete length of the right-hand side of the room. She'd poured herself into a powder blue dress and done her hair and make-up beautifully. Her big blonde curls shone in the overhead lights, but she was clearly a little embarrassed about the place being under such scrutiny.

'You'll see all my tricks,' she'd said with a laugh when Rory had paused by the microwave.

Max was perched on a battered old bar stool. The camera was on the counter in front of him.

'We had to stop,' said Flora, in answer to Rory's question about the tapas. 'There was so much waste at the end of the day.'

Rory nodded. 'Who's cooking now?'

'Me, a bit. Igor,' she said, pointing to where the sullen waiter had just pulled up on a scooter.

'The waiter?' Rory asked, thinking maybe he'd got the wrong end of the stick.

Flora nodded, shrugged her shoulder, did a little laugh. 'We don't have a lot of business, Rory. Friday nights sometimes I get a guy from town to come in and help, but he wants full-time work and I can't give it to him. I don't have the customers.'

Flora broke eye contact and looked away towards the kitchen. Rory remembered Ricardo working his magic: chorizo flaming in brandy, lobsters screaming in the pan, clams popping open like flowers, crabs making a dozy dash for it in their chilled semi-consciousness.

'Do you want to film the kitchen?' Flora asked.

Rory had thought he did. But what would he film? There was no flamboyant finger-licking or spoon-slurping, wild gesticulations with a tea towel to get the point across. 'Maybe we should just start on you,' he said.

Flora struck a pose, arranging herself by the coffee machine like Marilyn Monroe. Rory caught Max's eye; even his ten-year-old was dubious.

'Maybe you should sit at that table,' Max said, pointing to a small marble table at the back with gold legs. On it was a cut-glass jug that had lost its handle and was filled with wild flowers, scrappy little things that had managed to chip their way through the fierce summer heat. Next to the jug was a pink snakeskin notebook, a fountain pen and a painting of a green parrot leaning against the wall.

'Oh yes, that's *my* table, my haven,' said Flora, 'where I write my books. Well, not *my* books any more, recipes for other people to say are theirs. But they still feel like mine. I buy all the books when they come out in the shops, I just have to pretend that it's my face on the cover.' Almost every one of Flora's statements was rounded off with a jolly little laugh, the sadnesses of her life seemingly more manageable when scraps of amusement.

Rory looked from the lovely little table vignette to the rest of the bar, then outside to the plastic tables and chairs and broken awning. 'Flora?' he asked, a little bemused. 'Why haven't you done the rest of the bar like this table?'

'Because, my darling, I love my table,' Flora said, sashaying out from behind the bar, her stilettos silent on the scuffed black rubber floor. She sat herself down, smoothing the front of her dress, positioning herself at the best angle, crossing her legs and folding her arms to push up her chest, before adding, 'And I hate this place.'

Rory wished he'd caught it all on film. Wished he'd captured the cool certainty and the raw hitch of emotion that she'd done well to almost conceal. He glanced longingly over to where the camera sat on the bar and saw with surprise the little red recording light. He looked up to Max, who winked at him. Bloody hell. The boy had nous.

'This . . .' Flora carried on, hand sweeping across the bar space, the dark industrial gothic chic, 'this was his vision, not mine. When I look at it all I see is my money. My naivety. My stupidity. Maxy, be a darling and lean forwards and flick that light switch will you, that one there on the wall.'

Max stretched as far across the bar as he could to where Flora was pointing and pressed the switch on. Fluorescent lights under the bar shone red, illuminating more smaller graffiti bulls' heads.

'Cool,' Max grinned.

'Dreadful,' Flora sighed. 'And do you want to know how much that cost me? No, I can't even say it. It's too depressing. What's so strange is that something – are you recording? Have we started yet?'

Rory nodded. He crossed the room and went to pick up the camera next to Max.

'No, I want to do it,' Max said with a firm whine.

Rory paused. 'How about I start and then you can take over?' he said with forced diplomacy.

'No, you said I could do it.'

Rory's hand was itching to get hold of the camera.

Flora was clearly keen to carry on with her sentence.

Max said, 'Otherwise I just sit here doing nothing. I want to do it.'

Rory swallowed. This was his thing.

But this was his son.

'OK,' he said, stepping back. 'OK, you do it.'

Max beamed as he hoisted the camera on to his shoulder and pointed it at Flora, who immediately carried on with what she'd been saying.

'What's so strange,' she said again, 'is seeing something that once held all your dreams, where you saw yourself getting old and still being happy, change into something so completely and utterly opposite to that.'

Rory was trying to listen, but he could see the camera wobbling on Max's shoulder. He was envisioning the shake on film. And what he half-heard, he was also trying really hard not to align with his own life. Rory had seen his future. It was there in his head like the AA Route Planner. He had always known he was going from A to B, in roughly this amount of time, barring any major incidents or illnesses.

'And for you, this place represents that?' Rory asked, tearing his focus away from Max.

Flora shrugged a yes.

'It's a real shame,' he said, 'because when I was last here, I wouldn't have said that this place was all Ricardo. It was you as well. Ask me then and I'd have said you could have done this on your own. Easily. It wasn't just his dream.'

'I know, but I'm tired, Rory. I'm tired,' she said. 'It's exhausting.'

'What is?' Max piped up, clearly a bit confused.

'Being so utterly furious, darling, all the time,' she said with a laugh and a smack of her hot pink notebook.

Max grinned. 'Maybe now you can get your own back, on camera. Say something mean about him.'

Rory wondered if this was in fact the best environment for his ten-year-old after all.

Flora guffawed. 'What a marvellous idea.' She thought for a second then leant forwards, smiling, and said, 'Well, the bandana is to hide an ever-increasing bald spot. He says it's his trademark, but it's a hundred per cent because of his hair. Of course I told him no one would notice, but they definitely would . . .' She chuckled to herself.

Rory shot a quick glance at his own hair in the mirror behind the bar. Claire was always telling him not to panic when he examined it for signs of thinning. Is this what separation would be like? Finding out that everything you've ever reassured each other about was a lie? Maybe the shirts he wore *were* too young for him? Maybe his stubble *wasn't* sexy with bits of grey in it? Shit, he thought, self-consciously covering his jaw with his hand.

'And another thing, he's utterly obsessed with Jamie Oliver. Can't handle him at all. Desperate to be as famous as him. Shouts at the television when he's on. Even started doing little affectations with his voice, you know, all pally and chatty? I caught him practising it in the mirror once and had to gently put a stop to it. This is quite liberating. Gosh. What else? Oh, well, there's always the obvious, he has a much smaller willy than one might think—'

'OK, that's enough.' Rory strode over and tried to prise the camera from Max.

'What?' Max protested, clutching on tight.

'Exactly – what?' Flora echoed. 'It's just a bit of fun. Max knows what willies are, don't you, Max? And if he doesn't, he should.' Flora arched a perfect brow and Max blushed and giggled. 'Leave the camera alone and don't be such a prude, Rory.'

Rory frowned. He'd almost grappled the camera away from his son and was reluctant to hand it back.

Flora watched him. 'We're not making a masterpiece, Rory.'

'No, but we want to make something,' he replied.

'And we will,' Flora said, in such a commanding tone that it made Rory stop and listen. 'But we'll laugh as we do it.'

Rory was very rarely told what to do. A little abashed by the ticking off, he found himself relaxing his hold on the camera and stepping away.

The waiter, Igor, marched past with no thought to the filming in progress and started banging and bashing with the coffee machine behind the bar.

'Igor, darling, we're filming,' said Flora. 'Do you have to make so much noise?'

Igor made a face. 'People need coffee.'

'*I* need coffee,' said Flora, her skin-tight dress impeding her movements as she tried to get up gracefully from her chair. 'Rory, do you want one?' she asked, smoothing herself down.

Rory nodded, 'I'll have one.'

'And grab a pastry. Sorry, darlings, I totally forgot to offer you breakfast. Max, take, take, take, whatever you like.'

Max did not have to be told twice. Putting the camera down, he started piling his plate with chocolate twists, then put a few back when he caught Rory's eye.

All the regulars had started to slope in. The squeak of Gabriela's pug on wheels was the first, then Rosa with her huge bag of knitting.

Igor finished frothing the milk, wiped down the nozzle and picked up the three cups of coffee from the machine. 'You can carry on now,' he said to Max, who nodded, half a chocolate twist in his mouth.

Flora, who was sipping the espresso she'd made, gestured towards Igor and said, 'Now *there's* someone who was very pleased to see the back of Ricardo. Igor and Ric did not see eye to eye on many things.'

Igor made a face and said something in Spanish, which Flora agreed with, then went outside with his tray of coffees and sticky pastries, muttering under his breath.

'Not the happiest of chaps,' Flora said, watching as Igor thwacked coffees down on various tables, 'but very loyal. You should see him. He's got these three little girls, all under five, I think. All black curls and podgy little legs. He adores them.'

Rory looked at Igor with some scepticism, watched him grumbling from table to table, arguing in Spanish with Rosa and the walrus-moustache man. 'Really? Igor does?'

'Oh yes. I think all this grumpy business . . .' she pointed towards Igor grimacing and shaking his head, 'is basically boredom. I tell him to go and get another job, but he won't leave. If he wasn't so happily married I'd say he was in love with me as well.'

Rory's lips twitched in amusement. Flora winked and gave her hair a pat. Max said, 'Why is everyone in love with you, Flora?'

'Because I'm bloody marvellous,' she said, then laughed. 'It's been a while since I've thought that.' She shook her hair like a horse. 'Gosh, I feel almost high. Giddy. Like I've been at Ric's wacky backcy.'

Max frowned and looked at his dad, confused. Rory was standing with one elbow propped up on the bar, and he shook his head a touch to suggest that Flora was a bit mad and that Max should just ignore her. Max sniggered to himself.

Gabriela was bending down to unclip the pug from his wheels, and when she looked up with the dog in her arms and saw Max holding the camera, asked, 'What's going on here?'

Flora did a little half-twirl and said, 'Filming, Gabriela. A documentary about me.'

'Why?' Gabriela looked suspicious.

'To try and make the café marvellous again,' Flora said.

Gabriela scoffed. 'Well, that's going to take more than a film.'

Flora looked suddenly mortified. Embarrassed by her own exuberance.

'It's hard work, Flora, hard work that'll make something great. You've got to put the work in,' Gabriela said, glancing around at the dingy décor. 'I've told her to get rid of it. Sell it, start again,' she added to Rory. 'Hasn't been the same since he left. People can sense unhappiness, sniff it a mile away.'

Flora stroked back her hair and inhaled a shaky breath. 'See what I have to put up with,' she said to Rory and Max, voice over bright.

On the wall the fly strip hummed as a wasp got caught in the fluorescent lines.

'Remember there'll be no more breakfast if I don't have the café, Gabriela,' Flora added, clearly hoping for something affirming in reply.

Gabriela shrugged. 'I'll be dead soon anyway,' she said, and turned round to go and sit with Rosa, who was already asking what they were talking about.

Rory watched them looking round the place, nodding. Saw them point at the cracks in the ceiling, the curl of damp wallpaper. Rosa wobbled the table with her hand to make a point of its faults. The wasp tried to free itself from the zapping wall trap. Rory couldn't look Flora in the eye.

No one said anything for a good minute. Max shifted uncomfortably on his stool. Rory ran his hand over his mouth, trying to think of the best way to steer the chat. Flora stood behind the bar, sipping her coffee, visibly deflated. As he watched her, Rory realised that this was Flora stripped of the show-pony bravado.

He shifted his weight, tried to act nonchalant as he glanced to Max to check the red light on the camera was on. Max nodded as soon as he caught his dad's eye, which made Rory smile inside.

Rory cleared his throat. 'Do you do much cooking, Flora?' he asked.

Flora examined her nails. 'No. No, not as much as I did.'

A fly landed on the pastries in the basket. Flora leant forwards and flicked it away.

If Rory had been filming he'd have filmed the fly. But then he would have missed Flora tie her hair back then remember she was being filmed and quickly take it down again with an exaggerated flounce. He would have missed that little moment of her, which Max had caught.

What was it Ava had said? *There's more than your way, Rory.*

'So why aren't you cooking?' he asked, trying to keep focused.

'I think you need a lot of confidence to be a chef,' Flora said, running her hand along the counter top. 'A good chef. And . . .' She paused. 'Well, I think maybe when you've believed in someone and trusted them and then that goes, you perhaps lose confidence in your own judgement. Every time I've stepped into a kitchen to do something – something proper – I've just been second-guessing myself. There's a little Ricardo sitting on my shoulder saying, "Not like that, you idiot" or "You think they'd want to eat *that*?"'

She said it all in great humour. Rory waited, listening. Max turned to check that he wasn't meant to be doing anything more, and Rory gave him a nod to just sit tight, camera steady. He was quite enjoying having this little sidekick; it was easy to work with someone who had half the same brain as him.

Flora took a sip of coffee, put the cup down, scratched her head, licked her lips, then as the silence hung she eventually said, 'We started getting knocks. People started saying exactly what I'd imagined Ric might say. You know how you were yesterday with Twitter?'

Rory had not thought about Twitter all day and the reminder was a kick in the gut. He nodded.

'That's how I was about bloody TripAdvisor. Golly, they ripped me to shreds some of them. And it's addictive. So I know how you felt.' She looked down at her blurred reflection on the counter top and then covered it with her hand before looking back up at Rory. 'What hurt the most was that some of them were old regulars. People who'd been coming here every year. I don't understand why they didn't give me the benefit of the doubt. Let me try and make it better in time. I don't know. Everyone's a critic now, aren't they? Maybe I shouldn't even have read it all, but then that lot opened up over there and we became like Team Flora and Team Nino. But there was no one on my team apart from this lot and Igor.' With a sweep of her arm she encompassed the knitters and chess players. 'I think my mistake was trying to keep his menu,' Flora sighed. 'It was silly. I couldn't cook like him, but that's what people were coming for. They wanted his soft-shell crab and the vodka octopus, and if it wasn't on the menu they felt they'd been hard done by, felt like it was a wasted trip. It was pretty much no win. Again, like you with the tweets. It's hard to watch your dream dissolve.'

Rory winced again.

He remembered the vodka octopus. It had been sensational. Under normal circumstances he would have been disappointed not to find it on her menu. He too might have ventured next door in protest.

He looked at Max holding the camera. Thought about the snippet he'd seen of himself filming the day before, wondering, as he had looked at Flora, whether that person still existed. He'd been so confident that strong, vibrant Flora was in there somewhere. Perhaps, he thought as he downed the rest of his espresso, it was up to him to help beckon her out of hiding, and maybe they'd stumble across the past version of him along the way. It was that simple hope that made Rory say, 'How about we find our confidence together, Flora?'

Flora tossed her hair back with a frown.

'Us,' Rory said, 'in there.' He nodded to the empty kitchen.

'Yeah! Do it!' said Max, jumping down off his stool.

Rory held back a comment about the camera shake.

'Go on, Flora,' Max said, pointing the camera up at her.

'Oh, that'll be a very bad angle, Maxy,' Flora said, trying to shield her chin and stepping back but finding herself blocked by the coffee machine. 'No. I don't know. I can't cook in this dress,' she said, looking down at her pale blue frock as if she had stumbled on the perfect excuse.

'Put an apron on,' said Rory.

'Dad wants to be on *MasterChef*,' said Max.

Rory made a mental note to edit that line out as soon as possible.

Flora was still uncertain. 'Really, I haven't cooked in ages.'

'Come on,' said Rory, a little softer, warming to the idea of getting into the kitchen. He cooked every night he was home. It was part therapy, to switch his brain off from the stresses of work, and part because he knew Claire loved everything he made. It had been their little joke that she'd never leave him because she couldn't live without his stroganoff. The idea of winning her back through kitchen prowess seemed a little far-fetched now the joke was a semi-reality, but there was a sliver there, enough to tug him towards the hob. His memories of Flora and Ricardo in this specific kitchen had been Rory's Spain. The two of them snogging in front of the flaming hobs, bum squeezing, sweat pouring, wine gulping. OK, they hadn't lasted as a couple, but in their heyday they had had energy, passion and excitement. Shouting, laughing, smoking, swearing. When Rory cooked now it was to Radio Four with a nice glass of Pinot Noir.

There must have been something in his expression to show Flora that this was as much for him as it was for her, because she suddenly stood up straight, shimmied the wrinkles out of her dress and said, 'OK, come on then. What have we got to lose?' She marched into the kitchen, all giant cleavage and faux-bravado. Rory followed, then Max with the camera.

But the cold, drab nothingness of the kitchen was an instant downer on Rory's burgeoning memories. He wanted dark and dingy, hot and close; to hear butter sizzling in the pans and chillies chopped nineteen to the dozen. He lifted Max up to sit on the corner of the work surface and noticed the mark his hands made in the dust.

Flora yanked open the fridge. 'There's not really that much food in here,' she said.

Rory glanced around. It was depressingly bare besides some milk, big tubs of olives and packets of tortilla and serrano ham.

'Oh well,' Flora said, happy for fate to have kyboshed the plan. 'Shall we go back out front?'

Max's little face fell.

Rory stared despondently out the dirty window. Of course they could go and buy ingredients then reconvene at another time, but there was something crucial about the spontaneity of this. Something precious in the fact that Flora hadn't had time to prepare. And Rory knew himself well enough to know that spur-of-the-moment wasn't his strong point, so an idea such as this should be grasped before there was time to analyse and dismiss it. If it didn't happen now it felt as though it never would; next time he would be behind the camera and Flora's Friday night chef drafted in.

Then through the grimy glass Rory caught sight of a sliver of foliage. 'Have you still got the vegetable garden, Flora?'

Flora made a face. 'Sort of,' she said a little guiltily.

They all trooped outside. The sun was scorching hot. Blistering. Blinding white on the eyes. Rory made Max stand in the shade because he didn't have any suntan lotion on. The hum of the cicadas felt like the noise of heat itself.

In front of them was a small vegetable patch and a decrepit greenhouse that had once been a verdant oasis, rich with nearly every vegetable imaginable, micro-managed by Ricardo's obsessive hand. There had been polytunnels and neatly written labels, intricately woven willow frames and immaculate beds with rows of perfectly manicured crops. Now, hanging on a couple of old bits of bamboo were some forlorn-looking tomatoes and a couple of fly-ridden green beans. Frazzled weeds crunched underfoot as they walked the network of paths, avoiding half-eaten peaches and rotting lemons that had fallen from the surrounding trees.

Rory glanced around, unable to believe that Flora had let this work of vegetable patch art go to such wrack and ruin, but then over the rickety fence his eyes landed on the bougainvillea-strewn railings of his grandmother's house in the distance, reminding him of the little room of his mother's stuff. His desire, as Ava and Max had leafed through dusty programmes, to gather it all up and throw it out the window. Treasure, like the garden, made toxic by the memory of the owner.

Max was sidestepping the outside wall, keeping out of the sun under the watchful gaze of his father.

'There's something!' he shouted, as Flora and Rory were about to forget it.

In the far corner next to a pile of rotting corn stalks was a leaf the size of a dinner plate. Max bent down behind it and twisted something off the stem while trying to keep the camera balanced on his shoulder.

'Be careful,' Rory shouted.

'Here!' Max held up a giant courgette, triumphant. 'You can cook with this, can't you?'

'God knows where that came from,' said Flora, kicking off her high heels to step over what was now scrubland to take it from him. 'Well done, Maxy.'

Heartened by the courgette find, Rory reached up and picked some peaches from the tree next to him, then spotted a gnarled lemon on a tiny bush at the back of the garden. Max rescued the few edible tomatoes and Flora picked a great bunch of stinging nettles and some dandelions.

'We're foragers,' said Flora when Max turned his nose up at her bunch of weeds. 'It's all the rage at the moment. There are restaurants charging thousands for a tuft of wild garlic and some road kill.'

It was only when they were back inside that, on a whim, Rory checked the freezer. 'Blimey,' he said, lifting out great bags of lobsters, langoustines, tiny prawns and a spindly legged spider crab. 'This is where all the food's hidden.'

'Well look at that,' said Flora, taking a bag of langoustines and inspecting it with genuine surprise. 'Who knew?'

Rory realised then how little she had been in this space in the last few years. How dire her situation was with the café. He knew then that if they hadn't come this summer they would never have seen this place again, nor glimpsed their forgotten selves on film. Everything suddenly felt a little more pressing. But was it possible to save a place that had two-year-old lobster in the freezer that the chef knew nothing about?

CHAPTER 15

Ava finally got to sample a croissant without Max running up to steal it from her plate. It would have been delectable – light, sticky, flaky, chocolatey – had she not been distracted by her annoyance with Rory.

She was sitting at the table closest to the beach, furthest from the café doors where Rory and co. were filming in the kitchen. Her back was turned on the breakfast crowd, all of them piling in for their thick milky coffees and chocolate whirls. Gabriela had tried to strike up a conversation when she arrived, looking Ava straight in the eyes, but Ava had picked up the shoebox of her mother's fan mail that she'd brought with her and pretended to be engrossed. Gabriela had made do with the walrus-moustache man, whose hard-of-hearing 'what was that?' questions drove her nuts. Ava's croissant-eating was punctuated with Gabriela's angry shouts for him to turn his hearing aid on.

For a moment she imagined her grandmother among them. Always the peacekeeper, Val would have had a sharp word to Gabriela and a clap to walrus-moustache man to get on with it. As Ava glanced up from her letters she wondered if perhaps the group was missing its glue; the one who brought them all together, repeated stories when one of them wasn't listening, pulled in the shy chess player, scoffed at the more damaging gossip, forced apologies and reconciliations. There couldn't have been that many people at her funeral singing her praises and no gaping hole left in her friendship group.

Ava suddenly felt a bit guilty for ignoring Gabriela.

But then the chair opposite her was pulled out and once again Tom sat down.

'Oh here he is,' she said.

Tom laughed, deep and self-satisfied. He pulled off his shades and squinted at the sun. His eyes a little red, his skin more pasty than normal.

'Heavy night?' she asked, surprisingly pleased to have him sitting there.

He shrugged.

She imaged scenes of debauchery in some bar in town where the girls danced in bikinis and the champagne fountains flowed.

'My grapes are suffering from the heat,' he said, and Ava had to pause, coffee cup halfway to her lips.

'Your grapes?' she said.

'Yes,' he said, confused as to why she didn't get it.

Ava realised she'd been doing too much Googling. Aligning personality to the famous cardboard cut-out sitting before her in his blue jeans and black T-shirt, his flip flops tapping on the cracked concrete. Stupidly she felt like she knew him. Knew almost too much about him. Too much Google. And of course it all seemed so definitely the truth.

'I thought you found this part too stressful,' she said.

He seemed surprised that she'd remembered. 'Yes, but all good plans go to waste. I do find it too stressful, but it's impossible not to get involved,' he said with abject sincerity. 'I love my grapes.'

Ava choked on her coffee as she laughed, having to pat the splashes away from her face with a napkin.

'I have no shame in saying that I love my grapes,' he said, staring at her with just a hint of amusement at the corners of his eyes. Then he reached over and picked up a couple of the letters on the table. 'What are these?' he asked.

Igor the waiter brought over an espresso and a plate of *pan con tomate* that Tom had ordered.

'Cheers, mate,' he said, pouring the gloopy tomato all over the hot, oily toast. 'I'm starving.' He took a huge bite. 'Go on then,' he said, mouth full, waving a letter. 'What are these?'

'Fan mail,' Ava said, reaching forwards to take the letter back so he didn't get it all sticky with tomato. Tom held it out of her reach. He flicked it open and had a read.

'For your mum?' he asked.

'Yes,' she said, surprised. 'How do you know that?'

'Chats with Val,' he replied, half-listening, reading the letter.

'Everyone just loved her,' Ava said proudly, sorting through the reams of envelopes. 'These are all essentially love letters.'

'Yeah?' Tom said, not quite convinced, as if that didn't sit well with the image he had.

'Yes,' Ava said firmly. 'I know she could be a pain, but she was also amazing. It goes with the territory, doesn't it? The artistic temperament.'

Tom looked happy enough to be persuaded.

'Look at this one.' Ava held up a letter. 'It's from a man who came to see her fifteen times as Carmen. Fifteen times! Even I didn't see her that many times as Carmen and we went a lot. I can see why he did though. She was incredible. You'd watch her thinking, wow, that's my mother. And my gran, well, her eyes would light up when she saw her. She was so talented. I mean, you can't ignore talent like that, nothing should get in its way.'

'No?' Tom asked, annoyingly non-committal.

'No,' said Ava. 'She's someone who *had* to follow her dream, otherwise it would have just eaten her up.'

Tom was watching her as she nodded away, wanting him to nod in agreement.

'She *was*,' Ava said, emphatic.

'I believe you.'

'Good,' said Ava, as though it was really important to have cleared that up, even though it was never a mess between the two of them.

Tom leant forwards, pushing one of the letters aside to reveal a photograph of a baby. 'Who's that?'

'Well, this woman, she named her kid Isabel after her, she sent a picture of the baby.'

Tom picked up the photograph and made a face. 'Not sure I'd be that happy with that,' he said.

Ava bashed him on the arm. 'You can't say mean things about babies.'

'Why not?'

'They're babies.'

Tom laughed. 'This one is a bit of a monster, come on! Give me another letter. Christ, it's so hot, why are we sitting out here?' he asked, wiping away the sweat on his forehead with the back of his hand.

Ava didn't want to admit that it was to be as far away as possible from her brother, so instead handed him an old flamenco fan of Val's that she'd been using when the heat got unbearable. 'You want this?' she asked, a bit dubious as to whether he would be happy to use a frilly plastic fan.

'Yes, definitely,' he said. 'And another letter, an interesting one, no more ugly babies,' he added, resting his feet on the opposite chair, fanning himself with the ruffled Spanish fan.

Ava flicked through the ones she'd already read. 'This is from a French guy called Christian, he wants to marry her. They all want to marry her.'

Tom read the letters, laughing from time to time. 'They're insane.'

'They're mesmerised,' she corrected. Then she rested the letter she was reading in her lap and said, 'You must have got stuff like this, didn't you?'

'A long time ago,' he said, fanning his fan while finishing off his toast. 'I think this thing is more efficient than air conditioning.'

He looked up and seemed quite pleased that he'd made her smile with his enthusiastic fanning, then folded the letter he'd been reading and put it back in its envelope. 'I was very bad at this bit. The fan mail. I didn't read any of them. There was a publicist who replied and I think there was probably a generic piece of paper with my signature on it. Or I signed them all. I have no idea. It was a very hazy time.'

Ava raised a brow. 'That bad?'

'I have snippets of memory. Women would send me their knickers through the post.' He laughed. 'I remember those letters,' he added, fishing about absent-mindedly through the fan mail box as he spoke. Ava resisted the temptation to bat his hand away, to tell him that this was precious cargo he was rifling through. 'It was a long time ago. Another era almost. It's all just a big blur really.'

Ava pulled the box away from him and started to work through the next block of letters. 'Good blur or bad blur?' she asked.

She tried to rise above her Googling. To not take as gospel the gossip column inches she'd read: the insider scoop from the angry ex left holding the baby; the photos of him stumbling out of clubs bleary eyed, next to rumours of rehab; the fights with top directors when trying to break Hollywood and storming off set.

Tom shrugged. 'It was like . . .' He paused. 'What was it like?' he asked himself. 'It was like going to bed and overnight everything changing. No one expected it to be as big as it was. I could suddenly buy my parents a house. And to be honest, I'm not sure they wanted a house,' he laughed. 'They had a house.'

'You forced it on them,' she joked.

'I did! This great big thing. They were rattling around in it. My dad complaining about the cost of heating it.' Tom sat back, hands behind his head, smiling. 'Overnight our lives changed and my parents had no idea how to handle it. They were just normal people. I thought it was great, they didn't.' He stretched up and yawned, put his sunglasses back on, then took them off again and looked out at the beach. 'So yeah,' he said, watching the speedboat take off with a waterskier in the distance, 'I just pretty much did what I wanted and the only person telling me what I could and couldn't do was a manager who, in retrospect, possibly didn't have my best interests at heart.' He looked back to Ava and added with a regretful wince, 'A lot of money was wasted.'

Ava imagined herself relaying everything he said word for word to Louise, trying to etch it on her memory because this was Thomas King talking. But at the same time it felt like a window into a world that she only understood from being on the outside. The glamour of fame that echoed the feelings of standing in her mother's dressing room as a teenager in some of the grandest theatres in New York, staring at the black and white photographs tacked to the mirror and the roses deep velvet red, and the stage manager in black with a headset tripping over her in her hurry, sweeping her to one side because this was the five-minute call. Watching the curtain rise from her seat in the stalls and feeling the monumental divide between where she was sitting and where her mother was on-stage.

Ava leant forwards, elbow on the table, chin resting in her hand, and said, 'So really it was just a big blur of hedonistic consumerism.'

Tom nodded as though he was pleased with her neat wrapping up of his life. 'Exactly,' he said, picking up his coffee. 'All hiding the fact that I wasn't really a very good actor.'

Ava did a mock gasp. 'You were a good actor,' she said.

Tom glanced up from his sip of espresso, brow raised, sly grin. 'You think so?'

She shrugged, knowing she'd been played. 'You were OK.'

'That's a very polite way of putting it,' he laughed.

'Do you regret any of it?' she asked, her fingers fanning through the letters, glancing from the rhapsodies about her mother to Tom, casually open about something that she had spent a life in awe of, an impenetrable world existing on a tier above her own.

'Some of it,' he said. 'I don't think I realised the impact it would have on my family.'

Ava had a vision of herself waiting for hours in a hot dressing room surrounded by a fog of perfume, empty champagne bottles and discarded make-up, her grandmother subtly trying to check her watch.

'You know I have this on my keys,' he said, holding up a dirty old plastic figure on a keychain.

'What is it?' she asked, staring at the odd little animal.

'It's Olly. One of the mascots from the Sydney Olympics.' Tom stared at her, looking for recognition, but got none.

Ava tilted her head to look at it from where it hung between his fingers. 'Is it a duck?'

Tom rolled his eyes. 'It's a kookaburra. Anyway. The summer I got it, I'd gone to Joan Peter's Drama School, basically because my best mate had. It was just messing about really. I was waiting for lunch every day so we could watch the Olympics. This kid had a portable TV and we'd cram round the screen to watch. I love the Olympics. And that year if you drank enough Coke you could send off for one of the mascots – there were three of them; Olly, Syd and Millie. So I did. We all did, drank loads of the stuff and sent off for these.' He held up the keyring. 'They made us a little gang. It was all very sweet,' he laughed, mocking the sentimentality of his story. 'Anyway, then the *Love-Struck* casting agents came at the end of the term and, well, that was it. So I don't regret it because if I'd turned it down . . . Well, then I'd be sitting here going, God, I was the idiot that turned down one of the biggest TV franchises ever made, wouldn't I? And I'd be all bitter, sitting at my desk somewhere, and I'd hate bloody kookaburra Olly because he'd just represent a time before my terrible decision. But I suppose I have it just to remind myself that there was a person before it all.' He paused, then frowned, rubbed his hand over his eyes. 'You know this story was going to have some really momentous meaning but now I can't actually find one. I'm really tired. Let me think. Maybe it's just a reminder that if I hadn't done it then I wouldn't have loads of the things that I have, but I would have had *other* things instead. Does that even make sense?' He sighed. Finished his espresso. 'Basically, there's no right path. There you go, there's some wisdom.' He laughed, hands outstretched like he'd hit the jackpot. 'And now, well, I know what success feels like. Now I'm free to do my own thing.'

Ava wondered if she was free. She would like to say that she was, but in reality she was tied by other people's opinions, to being valued by her friends and congratulated in her work; she was tightly enmeshed in the routine and certainty of her life back home, and, she realised as her gaze flicked over the letters, obedient to the memory of her mother.

She had a vision of herself standing centre stage, her own brief moments in the spotlight. Dressed up like Shirley Temple with her little-girl curls and rosy cheeks, ribboned white socks and green velvet party dress, next to her mother in matching emerald but looking more Jessica Rabbit, slinky and skin-tight with a V slashed most of the way up her thigh. Her mother's agent had leapt on their striking similarity, created the mother-daughter act as a great profile-raiser, and her mother had been sold the idea in an instant. Charity events, concerts, gala dinners, festivals at The Royal Albert Hall. Each time bigger audiences, bigger stages. Ava opening the show, singing shyly and out of tune, but so young it didn't matter, doing bobbing little dance moves that delighted the audience as her mother's voice wowed with crowd-pleasers like 'Somewhere Over the Rainbow' and 'I Feel Pretty'. Ava's chubby legs shaking with nerves, but the feel of her small hand in her mother's enough to keep her where she was. Her mother kneeling down at the end to envelop her in strong, toned arms, Ava's little face pressing into her soft, perfumed neck, red lipstick kisses on her cheek and the sound of her mother's squeal of delight in her ear as the crowd roared.

A crash from the kitchen brought her back to the present, a pan lid dropped like a cymbal. Everyone turned. 'Sorry! Sorry!' shouted Flora, arm raised. 'Our fault.'

When she turned back, Tom was holding up a strip of photos from the letter he'd opened. 'That your dad?' he asked.

Ava looked. Four black and white shots, all of her mother, big lips, nipped-in waist, short dark curls, sitting on a man's lap, massive smile, eyes alight, his face buried in her hair, his arms tight around her waist.

'No,' she said, frowning. Reaching to take the photos from him and stuff them back in the envelope. She didn't want to see them.

Tom watched her for a second. She looked at him looking at her. His face seemed suddenly less famous. Aligned with the glamour of her mother, he looked positively normal.

There was another noise from the kitchen, a flash and then the smoke alarm went off. 'It's OK, don't worry,' Rory shouted, climbing on to a chair to turn the alarm off while Flora wafted smoke out of the kitchen.

As Ava watched, she heard someone making clicking noises like they were trying to summon a horse. Looking around for the source she saw Gabriela desperately trying to grab her attention. Having keenly observed Ava's chat with Thomas King thus far, as soon as she caught Ava's eye, Gabriela started pointing excitedly at Tom's back and doing a succession of huge dramatic winks.

Ava rolled her eyes and looked away.

'What's going on?' Tom asked, glancing round to catch the tail end of Gabriela's winking, Rosa beside her grinning like she was at a wedding. 'Oh, I see,' he said, lounging back in his chair with a smile.

Ava felt herself blush against her will.

'I should warn you,' he said, legs up on the opposite chair, arms crossed over his chest, head tipped back to catch the sun, 'I don't really do relationships.'

'Oh my God,' Ava felt her mouth drop open, incredulous. 'You're so unbelievably arrogant. You're not even my type,' she said, shaking her head and trying not to laugh as she put the lid back on the box of letters.

Beside her Tom smiled, satisfied, as if he was everyone's type.

CHAPTER 16

Rory and Flora cooked all afternoon. The haze of smoke that danced in the air was evidence of Flora's lack of practice and Rory's novice status. Igor had come in to complain about the burning smell and rescued the frozen spider crab from the out-of-date seafood stash about to be binned. He'd bought it off a fisherman the other week and forgotten to take it home. The crab had been immediately commandeered by Flora.

Max filmed it all from where he sat on the counter, eating olives straight from the giant tub and sampling the charred garlic courgette. But when his shaggy-haired friend Emilio poked his head through the door, coughing from the smog, and asked if he wanted to go waterskiing, his ambition to be a top director was suddenly put on hold as they raced out together in the direction of the jetty.

Rory and Flora called it a day when Flora, red as a beetroot, sampled the stinging nettle stock she'd been reducing all day and proclaimed it revolting, tasting like dirty dish water. Rory, who had been struggling to steam the huge frozen spider crab, battling to get all the legs in the pot, had been unable to disagree. It was more than a little disheartening to realise that the sum total of the day's work was some stringy over-cooked spider crab, burnt courgette fritters and stock that tasted of dirty water.

It was quite a relief therefore to come home and find Ava sitting on the narrow veranda out the back of their grandmother's kitchen on a rusted yellow chair, her feet up on the railing, a bottle of what looked like Licor 43 on the table next to her. The sun was just skimming the edge of the hillside and drifting on to the courtyard garden in hazy evening beams. The air was laced with the scent of warm figs and oranges, so heady he could almost reach out and touch it.

Ava opened one eye and looked behind him. 'Where's Max?' she asked.

'Dinner and a movie with his new best friend. What's that you're drinking?' he asked.

Ava bent to the floor to pick up the bottle. 'It appears to be something called Licor 43.'

'Claire and I used to drink that.'

Ava held up the dusty bottle for him to see.

'How old is it?' Rory made a face.

'Best before 1999.'

'Excellent,' he said, 'pre-millennium.'

Ava smiled.

Rory got himself a glass and some ice, then poured a slug of the fluorescent orange liquid.

'Have you texted Claire?' she asked.

'Just to say we arrived.'

'Don't you think you should—' she started, but he cut her off, holding his hand up.

'Honestly, Ava, just leave it.' He knew he was putting anything more off because he didn't know what to say. Claire would be looking for some sort of apology but he didn't quite know yet what he was sorry for.

They both sat back and looked at the view. Pots of geraniums lined the walls of the house opposite like big, colourful buttons.

'How was the filming?' she asked.

'Alright. We cooked.'

Ava rolled her head to look at him. 'I always forget you like to cook.'

'Yeah,' said Rory. 'It was a bit of a balls-up actually. Pretty soul destroying.'

They sat again in silence. Looking and drinking their bright orange drinks.

The sun dipped below the hillside leaving a hazy dusk behind. Car doors slammed and outdoor lights flickered. All around them was the gentle roll of the sea and the last buzz of the cicadas.

'Well, look at us,' Ava said after a while. 'Never drink together and then twice in a matter of months.'

'When was the last time?' Rory asked, puzzled.

'The funeral,' Ava said, slightly exasperated.

'Oh yes.' He nodded. 'We should do it more often.'

'Yeah.' Ava finished her drink. 'Rory, I have to ask you something.' She turned to look at him and the expression in her eyes caught him completely off-guard. A flashback to young Ava crying out for reassurance. 'Mum wasn't having an affair, was she?'

Rory downed his luminous orange drink.

He could feel her waiting. Sometimes Rory wanted to grab her by the shoulders and say, 'Why do you do this?' But he knew why. He knew that it was because only he remembered the tough bits. The bits that being three years younger Ava never saw or were kept from her, protected as she was. Lifting his mother up from the kitchen floor as she wept in great hiccupping sobs about her awful life. How trapped she was. How unhappy she was. How she'd been consumed by motherhood. Robbed by motherhood. How she was more than this. That if this was to be her life she wished she was dead. Rory getting tissues. Rory wiping her nose. Rory holding her hand. Their dad quietly swooping in and taking her up to bed. Then an audition or a party invite and she was off out the door, make-up immaculate, heels, dress, hat . . . Ecstatic. Gone.

Ava said, 'Rory?'

His instinct was to say nothing. To gloss over it as they always had. Ava's way of dealing with their mother was to romanticise her. Look up at her in awe where Rory looked down with anger and pity. But he wondered as he looked at Ava now, big expectant eyes, hair curly like a kid from the sea and salt water, if he'd been saying nothing for too long.

'Yes,' he said, 'I think so.'

'Well why didn't you tell me?' she said, starting to stand up. 'Why do you think yes? If you don't know for sure, why would you think yes?' She squeezed past the side of the table.

'Where are you going?' he asked.

'To try and bloody find out,' she said, stalking inside.

Rory sat where he was for a moment, alone on the veranda with just the pots of geraniums for company, looking out at the monster shadow cast by the palm tree in the garden.

He remembered a time when his mother had locked them in the car to go to an audition. They'd sat in the car park for hours, the air gold with autumn, chart hits on the radio, a blanket over the seats for a den. Quite fun at the time. But he'd seen her with him. Seen him tilt her chin up with his fingers, his cigar so close to her hair that he thought it would burn. And he had hated that he'd seen. Hated her desperation.

Rory stood up with his drink. He walked through to the hall, up the stairs and into his grandmother's bedroom. Ava was standing in the doorway of the little ante-room. He came to stand next to her and stood there for a moment in silence by her side. Inhaling the scent of mothballs and the dark familiarity of Shalimar. After their mother had left he remembered Ava dowsing herself in the stuff until their dad had convinced her otherwise. The hint of it now was like nicking at a scab, a moth flickering at a light; he could inhale but it would never be quite enough.

'I'm going to start with that box,' said Ava, pointing to another shoebox of cards and envelopes, her tone businesslike.

Rory nodded. 'I'll take the one next to it,' he said, feeling suddenly like he had to do this for Ava. That he had let her down by keeping her out.

He leant against the wall and started leafing through the box he'd pulled from underneath the clothes rail, a sea of glitter and frosting. The letters were all in different handwriting, all different colours. He read a couple. Rolled his eyes at the effusiveness of fans. Then he came across a signed photograph of his mother, unsent, the sight of it like a sharp blast of air. He tucked it straight back in with the fan letters and put the box back where it had come from.

'Have you looked at these?' he asked Ava, pushing aside another shoebox at the back, under the coats, so he could put the one in his hand back into place.

'I haven't looked at anything yet,' she said, snappily.

Rory dragged it into the light and flipped the lid. It was more battered than the other box, the seams of the lid torn and the cardboard frayed. Opened more often, handled a lot.

Rory skimmed the contents. These letters were different to the others. All airmail. White envelopes cuffed with blue and red chevrons. All from New York and addressed to Ms Isabel Fisher. *Ms* rather than *Mrs*.

He opened one, tucking the box under his arm. It wasn't fan mail. He turned the letter over for a signature.

The scent of the room seemed stronger, the movement of the fur coats disrupting the mothballs and lingering perfume.

He turned the letter back over to check the date.

It had been sent when Rory was three years old.

'What is it?' Ava asked. She was kneeling on the floor, rooting around at the back of the shelf to see what was there. She'd found more shoeboxes but they just contained shoes.

He had the overwhelming instinct to lie.

Instead he handed her the box.

She picked up the letter that he'd only half-tucked back in.

'Syd?' she said, looking up at him. 'As in Syd from New York? The producer guy with the shiny suits and the old Cadillac?'

Rory nodded. 'And the cigars.'

'But he was gross,' she said, confused, as she started to read.

My darlingest Isabel,

I suffer without you. My divorce I think might kill me, if I don't kill her first. Read that as a joke, unless of course she dies, in which case destroy this letter as soon as possible. Sorry, I'm trying to amuse myself. She's claiming insanity, she needs me. Threatening to do herself in. And she's going for the money. My lawyer says she's within her rights. Darling, it seems that if I were to divorce and we were together properly we would be in absolute poverty and I can't bear the thought of reducing you to this. You deserve more. One day, I promise, I will give you everything you were born for. For the moment, we will have to be more circumspect than ever.

Ever yours, Syd

'He's an idiot,' Ava said, voice thick with distaste. 'He's clearly just stringing her along. When was it written?' She turned the envelope over in her hand and looked at the postmark. 'Oh my God, it's the year I was born.' She looked up at Rory. 'Shit . . . is he my father?'

In all of this, Rory had never considered the possibility.

Ava pressed the heel of her hand to her forehead and almost laughed.

'No,' he said, immediately. 'No way.' He sat down on the floor next to her.

'Oh God, Rory,' Ava said, half-nervous giggling, half-despairing, fingers pushing into her eyes. 'This is not what I thought would be in this room.'

'It's alright,' Rory said. 'We'll read the rest, we'll work it out.' It felt suddenly unbelievably important to keep their normality. To keep her normality. In adulthood Ava infuriated him – her lack of direction, her flightiness, her refusal to settle down – because to Rory it felt just like his mother all over again. And this time he wanted someone else to take the mantle of responsibility. He had always loved Ava and wanted rid of her at the same time. But the idea that perhaps she was Syd's, that perhaps the mantle would pass in a direction he wasn't prepared for, made it suddenly important to prove the status quo. However annoying he found her, she was still this little kid that he had made laugh and feel safe.

They sat on the floor, rifling through the letters, their knees pressed together uncomfortably in the tiny space.

Ava held up an envelope. 'This one's from, like, eight years later. How long did this bloody affair go on?'

My darlingest Isabel,

I'm counting the days till we can be together properly. Moments with you when I don't have to glance to one side. There is some justice! Hold tight. Don't listen to Leonard. He doesn't understand. I can make you a star! I'll take you with me to New York. I can put you in the spotlight. I can put you where you were born to be. With me, you will shine, I promise.

Ever yours, Syd

'Leonard?' Ava looked up at Rory. 'As in Dad?' she said. 'Dad knew?'

Rory shrugged. 'I didn't know that he knew, but I suppose it doesn't really surprise me. He'd have put it down to one of her whims.'

Rory rifled through the letters like a Rolodex, stopping when he recognised the big loopy handwriting, confident in fountain pen, of his father.

Ava watched as he opened it, the paper thick and mottled brown with age and damp. Half the writing had been blurred, the ink running from a long-ago spill, but the last paragraph was intact.

'Here you go,' Rory said as he read it out loud.

Isabel, I'm of the opinion that a person invested with the ability to find interest and adventure in the everyday things of life has a much more enjoyable time than a person who is always seeking to be amused. You are chasing something that does not exist.

In the end I'm sure you will do as you please, Isabel, you always do, but just remember, there is a family here and it is yours.

Faithfully,
Leonard, your husband

Ava looked at Rory. Rory looked back at her.

The room seemed to shrink in his mind. This letter hit harder than he had imagined.

Suddenly they were dolls in the memory of his house, the tiny mother shouting while the tiny father's voice rumbled deep through the royal blue carpet. Tiny Rory upstairs listening, knowing she wasn't getting what she wanted. Knowing she didn't want his father to be as measured as he was. Crossing his fingers as he sat at the top of the stairs, *Come on Dad*, willing him to make some massive gesture because then everything might be alright.

Ava was watching him. 'What's wrong?' she asked.

Rory shook his head. He thought about his own belief in setting a path through life and sticking to it. 'I'm beginning to see how infuriating rationality can be.'

Ava laughed. 'You never say things like that. I've never heard you not take his side.'

Rory exhaled, long and slow, then ran his hand over his face. He suddenly wanted to text Claire.

He looked at Ava and pointed to his father's letter. 'One guy's offering her everything she ever wanted. The other one's telling her to find it in everything she doesn't want. It's not really a tough choice, is it?'

'She didn't not want us, Rory.'

Rory scoffed, like he didn't want to get into an argument about it.

'She just had a talent that was bigger than us,' Ava went on, determined.

'No, she had an ego and a vanity that was bigger than us. Look at this,' he tapped Syd's letter. 'She left us for a bloke and what he promised. If it was pure talent she wouldn't have needed him, would she?'

Ava didn't reply. She went back to the letters. 'We're meant to be finding out if this idiot's my dad,' she said. 'Remember.'

Rory went back to his box. They opened envelopes and they read. The room got hotter, the overhead light fizzing on occasion. The sleeve of a fur coat brushed against Rory's face as he moved and he pushed it away in disgust. The letters droned on. More of Syd's fawning. Rory's mind wandered.

'What did you do with the money Dad gave you?' he asked. 'I was wondering that the other day. I got my Nikes but I couldn't remember what you got.'

Ava shook her head. 'I have no idea. Probably in my piggy bank or something.'

'Ava, there was nothing but buttons in your piggy bank.'

'How do you know?'

'Because I'd check it to see if there was anything I could steal.'

'Shame on you.'

Neither of them said anything.

Rory scratched his head.

Ava took the last letter from her box. 'Oh, it's all OK, look at this,' she said, waving a scrap of paper from an old telephone memo pad. There was a space on the memo to write who had called and at what time, but that had been ignored in favour of the hastily scrawled note. It was dated, like the first letter, from around the time of Ava's conception. Before Syd's promises to take their mother to New York, to make her a star. 'It's from him. He's not my father.'

Darlingest, things here awful. Absolutely no chance of divorce at present. Maybe Leonard's right, another baby might be the best thing for you right now. Give you something to focus on till we can finally be together. Syd

'That's good,' said Ava. 'I suppose,' she added, a little more tentative. 'So I was basically a solution to a broken marriage and a stop-gap in an affair. Lovely.'

Rory found he didn't have anything to say. He just looked at her and nodded. They didn't do things like hug any longer so he gave her a quick tap on the arm.

When the room became too unbearably hot to sit in any longer, Rory said, 'Shall we go and have another drink?'

Ava nodded.

On the way through to the veranda he dropped back a touch, took his ancient Nokia out of his pocket and typed a message to Claire: *Hello.*

Ten minutes later, as they were drinking the last of the Licor 43, his phone vibrated with a message from Claire. He opened it, nervous, fingers shaking slightly. *Hello,* it said.

And Rory put his phone back in his pocket with a smile.

CHAPTER 17

The morning was perfect. Sky poster-paint blue. Sea calm as ice. Sand raked in perfect grooves like a comb through slick, gelled hair.

Ava had slept badly, her dreams filled with images of Syd and her mother in an open-topped Cadillac. To block it out she'd got up when she heard Rory go for his run and took Max to Café Estrella.

The view on the walk over was like staring at a painting come to life: breakfast was in full swing, everyone gossiping over their coffees and pastries, the birds jumping in and out of the fallen fig tree, Igor with a tray of toast and jam held high above his head to squeeze between the tables, and along the path from the car park a tiny ramshackle market – just a couple of stalls selling vegetables, fish, socks, pants and polyester housecoats. One old guy with a flat cap and a bushy black beard sat behind a small table selling mushrooms, big ones and tiny ones, measuring the weight on his scales before bagging them up. A woman opposite him was selling glistening fluorescent sweets, and next to her was a baker's van, the infamous Everardo standing alongside selling bread.

'My friend Emilio says it's going to get windy,' Max informed Ava as they perused the stalls.

She squinted towards the glassy sea. 'Really? Looks pretty calm to me.'

'Emilio says his dad says that it'll be windy this afternoon. That's why he's retying all the boats.'

Ava looked out to where the path narrowed into a peninsula of towering pine trees and then down to the pontoon where, as Max had predicted, the boats rented out by the watersports shop were being fastened in preparation.

They ordered some croissants and took the only vacant table, the market bringing everyone in early.

'Emilio reckons I'll be ready to mono-ski soon. That's with one ski not two, Aunty Ava.'

Ava made an impressed face.

Igor brought their pastries and drinks.

'I'm really good on two skis,' Max carried on, delighted that he had such an interested audience, slurping chocolate milk so thick the spoon almost stood up on its own. 'I wanted to go out today but they reckon the water will be too choppy for the speedboat. I hate the wind, don't you, Aunty Ava?'

Ava shook her head at him. 'It's not even windy yet, Max.'

Max shrugged like that was of no consequence.

Ava laughed, sitting back and holding her coffee cup in both hands.

Everyone was there: Gabriela and her pug with a big bag of vegetables from the market in her basket, Rosa with her unfathomable knitting, the walrus-moustache man sitting back from the chess players, making comments to the mushroom seller when he didn't agree with one of the moves.

Ava watched Flora take Everardo an espresso then stand next to him, chatting while he drank. She studied him over the rim of her cup, his tall frame like a praying mantis. His skin was worn and pock-marked and he had the kind of eyes that might slide off his face, droopy but kind. She couldn't work out whether he was incredibly ugly or dramatically stunning. He seemed to be able to make Flora laugh with very little effort; all dry one-liners that had her chortling away. Ava watched, intrigued.

Then she looked at Max. It seemed like his kind of question. 'Max,' she asked, 'do you think Everardo is really ugly or really good-looking?'

Max swallowed his bite of pastry and did a full unsubtle twizzle in his seat. '*Really* ugly!' he said immediately.

Ava heard a tut from the table next to them. Gabriela was listening. 'You are very naughty.'

Ava winced.

Max slithered down into his chair.

Rosa stopped her knitting. 'What are they saying?' she asked.

'They're discussing how handsome Everardo might be,' Gabriela explained. 'And deciding not in his favour.'

'That was Max!' Ava said, momentarily thinking perhaps she shouldn't pass the blame to a ten-year-old.

Rosa lowered her knitting and turned to peer over her reading glasses to where Everardo was chatting to Flora.

Gabriela sat back, arms crossed. 'What do you think?' she asked Rosa.

Rosa scrunched up her face as if undecided, but veered towards Max's opinion.

Gabriela shook her head as if they were all being unfair. 'I think that you can settle something like this by imagining them in a movie. Imagine him,' she said, pointing at Everardo, 'in something at the pictures. How many women would fall in love with him?'

Ava laughed. 'Would name him as their guilty crush?'

'Ex-actly!' Gabriela pointed a finger at her. 'You've got it.'

All four of them turned to stare at Everardo, Max squinting his eyes to get a better impression, Rosa leaning forwards to look over her glasses.

Everardo, sensing he was being watched, glanced up, and they all sat back in an instant, like some choreographed comedy sketch. He frowned self-consciously and said something to Flora, who turned around to check, by which point they were all concentrating really hard on their individual tasks. Rosa's knitting needles click-clacking away. Gabriela patting her dog. Ava furiously stirring her coffee, feeling the satisfaction of being in cahoots, being part of the gang.

Flora shook her head and turned back. Everardo still looked wary as he folded himself into his van.

Gabriela glanced across to catch Ava's eye and gave her a thumbs up. Ava laughed, 'Yes,' she said, 'I see it.' While Rosa sat back a little stunned as she nodded appreciatively.

Flora strode over. She looked better. She'd had her roots done. Her hair was glossy and flounced and she was wearing a white dress covered in lemons. 'What are you lot up to?' she asked, eyes narrowed with suspicion.

'Nothing,' said Ava innocently. 'So, Everardo?' she said, pointing to where the white baker's van was driving off up the hill. 'Very handsome.'

'Do you think?' Flora asked, looking back to where the van was just disappearing round the bend. 'I never know really.'

'Oh yes,' said Ava. She could see Gabriela and Rosa leaning forwards to eavesdrop in the background. 'In a sort of unconventional Hollywood way.'

Flora didn't say anything, just looked and thought. 'Interesting,' she said in the end and wandered off towards the bar, the tanker of opinion slowly U-turning in her head, spurred on by someone else's assessment.

Once Flora was gone, Rosa did a little clap. Gabriela's face concertinaed up in a satisfied grin, and Ava understood the camaraderie of gossip.

Max turned, confused, and said to the three of them, 'I still don't get it. He's *really* ugly.'

Ava leant forwards and ruffled his hair, 'You're so cute. I think it's probably a girl thing.'

'Get off,' Max batted her hand away with an imperceptible smile, smoothing his hair back into place.

As Ava watched him preening himself, she realised that now would be the time she usually got her phone out – if she had ever found her phone since the night of Googling – to mark the end of an event. Rounding it off like a half-hour sitcom episode. And Max would no doubt have disappeared into his laptop doing whatever it was ten-year-olds did on their computers. And that was no bad thing. She and Max had fun together, even if that involved sitting side by side, both lost to their screens. But as she felt for a minute the absence of her phone, the desire for a pause, she realised that on the other side of that desire came a space to be filled. Like long car journeys or delays at airports. Time expanded before her like a bubble. Things were being said, innocuous things that might not have been said with the distraction of Instagram. The discussion about

Everardo would have been a covert snap on her phone
and a WhatsApp to Louise saying, *Ugly or hot?* But
instead it got her an in to the gang, a shared laugh and
a covert little matchmaking plan. She realised that at
home all her friends were the same age as her, so when
their life stages changed they did so *en masse*, with
or without her. Here she was just one of many, age
irrelevant. It was as liberating as not having her phone.

As she sat pondering this little interlude of wisdom,
wondering what she might discuss next with Max,
realising that his impending teenagehood would soon
greatly reduce the opportunity to chat, it appeared that
Max had been undergoing the same technology-free
epiphany.

So when Ava asked, 'Hey, Max, have you got a
girlfriend?', he filled his time-expanding bubble with
his own probing question: 'Why aren't you married,
Aunty Ava? Dad says it's because you've got FOMO.'

CHAPTER 18

'Jesus Christ, Max.' Rory appeared fresh from his run, showered and changed but still a little red in the face and now even more so. 'You can't ask questions like that,' he said, raising his hands either side of him in disbelief. But in so doing he knocked into Flora who was carrying a tray of espressos and a plate of *pan con tomate*. The coffee, the toast and the little jug of pulped tomato flipped forwards on to the table and Ava and Max jumped back as the liquid hit.

Rory grabbed a bunch of waxy, unabsorbent napkins from the dispenser and started to mop it all up as best he could. 'Sorry,' he said to Flora. 'Sorry,' he said again, trying to control the mess but only making it worse.

Ava had grabbed a wodge of napkins too and was trying to dab at the mixture.

'I'm really sorry,' said Rory, as he tried his best to clear up the spilt tomato. 'Not for this,' he added, pointing to the soggy napkins. 'For that,' he said, pointing to where Max was looking on with intrigued confusion. He'd picked up the camera Rory had brought with him and started filming with it on his shoulder.

'You can't blame him!' Ava said, incredulous. 'You're the one that said it.'

'Yeah, but not for you to hear,' Rory replied, tone beseeching, hands dripping with tomato- and coffee-covered tissues.

Ava stared at him, wide-eyed.

He looked back at her, apologetic, then shrugged one shoulder and took the risk of a smile.

'You are unbelievable,' she said, sitting back with a half-laugh. 'You get away with murder.'

Flora bustled over with a roll of blue paper towels and, wiping up all the chaos on the table, said, 'Are we still filming today?'

Rory was standing to one side, quietly smiling to himself. 'Yes. Absolutely. Let's get started.'

This should have been Ava's cue to have another coffee or go for a swim, but today something made her want to join them. The appeal of company? The emptiness left by her mother's letters? A desire to keep being part of something?

She followed Max in the direction of the kitchen, dragging a high stool with her to sit in the doorway. An attempt had been made to wipe the window clean and the sun was streaking the air through the greasy smears.

'So what are you cooking?' Ava asked, quite excited to be in the hub, backstage, where customers weren't usually allowed. The giant hobs and big stainless steel oven doors seeming vast and important. Like getting a glimpse into the staffroom at school, wondering what went on back there, what secrets were whispered.

But to her disappointment, Rory and Flora looked equally unsure, turning the question back on each other.

'I don't know,' Flora said. 'What do you think, Rory?'

'I don't know either. Fish again?'

Ava had been expecting to be wowed.

The kitchen was stuffy. It smelt unused. A broken extractor fan ticked annoyingly in the corner.

Next to her, Max sighed. 'You need a thing,' he said from behind the camera.

'A thing?' said Rory, perplexed, wiping the sweat from his face with a piece of kitchen towel.

'What's your thing?' Max asked.

'Honestly, darling,' said Flora, 'I have no idea what thing you are referring to.'

'Your brand,' said Max, poking his head out from behind the lens. 'What you're gonna market yourself as.'

Rory shook his head. 'What do they teach you at school?'

'It's branding, Dad, they don't teach it to ten-year-olds at school. You just have to look around you. At Apple. Or Nike.'

'Or the Kardashians,' said Ava. 'Or the Spice Girls,' she added, getting into it.

Max gave her a very dismissive look.

'Well, what's their brand?' Flora asked, pointing towards Nino's restaurant over the way.

'I don't know. They're cool,' said Max.

'Cool can't be a brand,' said Ava, like she was suddenly an expert. 'Hipster Spain,' she added after some thought.

'Good one,' said Max.

'I thought so,' Ava agreed.

Flora was still uncertain. 'Well, what was Ricardo's brand, what's my brand going to be? I don't have a brand!'

'We'll find you a brand, Flora, don't worry,' Max said, precociously consoling.

Rory was standing back, arms crossed, looking impressed at his son, like he was basically an extension of himself, as if his right arm was the one doing the talking. Then he said, 'I think Ricardo was all about gastronomy. Modern Spain. I think he'd want to be known for Spanish fine dining, wouldn't he?'

'So what am I?' Flora was starting to look quite despondent. 'An overweight British woman with a speciality in comfort food?'

'No!' said Ava, leaning forward and giving Flora's shoulder a squeeze. 'You're a beautiful Brit–Spanish fusion.'

'I hate the word fusion,' Rory said, shaking his head. 'There's too much fusion in my opinion.'

'Alright, MasterChef,' said Ava, giving him a warning look. 'We're trying to look at the positives here.'

Then suddenly they heard a hand smack the bar top and all turned to see raisin-tanned Gabriela waiting there, a startled pug sitting on the stool next to her. 'All anyone wants,' she drawled, 'is simple, good food. That's it,' she said, making a final gesture with her hands. 'You're all sitting in there talking, time-wasting, when the answer is right in front of you. Get the bloody paella dish down. Get a pan on the hob. Fry up some peppers. Look at the lot of you! Talk, talk, talk, nothing gets done. That pan is not just for show, you know! Use it!' She shook her head, exasperated. 'You should be outside buying up the bloody market.'

Ava was slightly concerned that Gabriela might have a heart attack, her wrinkled face flushing with exertion. 'Come on!' Gabriela raised her hands. 'Get a tortilla going.'

Flora was looking a little shell-shocked, as was Max.

Ava turned to nod in agreement. 'Oh, Flora,' she said, 'remember your tortilla? It was to die for.'

Flora shook her head. 'Ricardo axed it from the menu.'

'So bring it back!' Gabriela was not letting up. She was sighing heavenward as the pug quivered into the back of the stool. 'Give me strength,' she said, when none of them seemed to do anything. 'You are a bunch of idiots!' Then picking up the pug and depositing him on the cushioned chair at Flora's desk, she elbowed her way into the kitchen, past Ava who got a sharp dig in the ribs. 'If you want something done properly . . . I don't know,' she shook her head. 'Rosa,' she called through the hatch to her friend. 'Rosa, get in here.'

Rosa looked up at the sound of her name and immediately put her knitting away to scuttle towards the kitchen and join Gabriela.

'Right,' Gabriela said, pushing her sleeves up, bracelets clattering as she pointed to each person. 'You,' she said, pointing to Rory, 'I saw you boiling that poor crab. What do you think you were doing? Cremating it? It's already dead!' she shouted like he was a complete imbecile. The tips of Rory's cheeks flushed. 'You have to be quick, you need to move.' She went over and slammed her bony, ring-covered fingers on Rory's hips. 'Get these moving,' she said. 'You need *el duende*.'

Max made a face to Ava, having no idea what Gabriela was talking about.

Gabriela bent down, her face almost touching his, and whispered, '*El duende*. It's the spirit, the emotion,' she clicked her fingers, 'it's the passion, the magic. You can't cook without any magic. It's the thing that makes the little hairs,' she took his arm and pulled his sleeve back, pointing to the fine blond hairs, 'stand on end. *Comprende*?'

Max nodded, absolutely terrified.

Gabriela looked back to Rory. 'Let me see the hips.'

Rory, who clearly had no intention of gyrating his hips in a kitchen full of people, stepped back and nodded. 'Will do,' he said.

'Now,' said Gabriela. 'Do it now. We want to see you can be trusted with the crab. Don't be shy. You want to cook, first you've got to move your body like this. Look. I'm eighty-two . . .'

They all watched as Gabriela started flicking her hips like a flamenco dancer, clicking her fingers above her head. Ava and Max giggled. Rory stood stiffly.

'All of you, move them,' Gabriela shouted, pointing to them each in turn with a wooden spoon that she'd picked up from the side.

Ava wiggled her hips as best she could without getting off her chair, Max got right into the swing of things, circling around and around with the camera wobbling. Flora did some moves like a belly dancer, then giggled at herself, a little breathless.

'Now you,' said Gabriela, bashing Rory on the thigh with the spoon like a reluctant horse.

The contact seemed to surprise Rory into a full gyration. He shocked even himself with the movement. But then, intrigued by the feeling, he did another, and another, then laughed, chuffed with himself as everyone cheered.

'That is more like it,' said Gabriela. 'You are on the crab. We'll make croquettes. Now you,' she turned her wooden spoon on Ava.

'I'm just watching,' said Ava from her stool.

'No one is just watching. Here,' she reached into her shopping and pulled out a bag of potatoes, 'you want tortilla? Get peeling. You,' she looked at Max.

'I'm filming,' he said, voice high and nervous.

'My left side is my best side,' said Gabriela, pulling her lips into a deep-grooved pout. Then her eye was caught by something out the side window. 'Is that the fish man?' She pushed past Rory and opened the window, letting in the noise of an engine ticking over and the dismantling of the market stalls. 'Marcus!' she shouted. 'Marcus, what fish have you got left?'

Ava could just see a man through the window, tired and stressed, sucking a final drag on the stub of a cigarette, shake his head. 'I got nothing spare.'

'Oh come on, Marcus, you must have something?'

'Nothing, Gabriela. Sold out.'

'You want me to tell your mother you gave me no fish?'

He flicked his cigarette away and sighed. 'I got an octopus, that's it. But it's for the hotel up the road.'

'Is it big?' Gabriela asked.

He nodded.

'Cut me off a few tentacles, tell them it was in a fight.'

Marcus couldn't hide a smile. Ava watched him get down from the driver's seat, his movements slow and tired from overwork, and go round the back of his van, shaking his head as if he couldn't believe he was doing this. Then with a knife from his pocket he lopped off two giant tentacles and brought them over to the open window.

'You tell my mother I gave you the octopus,' he said, his tone looking for confirmation.

Gabriela snatched the tentacles. 'I'll tell her you gave me two tentacles. Under duress,' she said, and shut the window.

Moving the camera to one side, Max made a face at Ava. 'Urgh, octopus. Yuck.'

'Max,' Rory cut him off. 'Don't be rude.'

Ava caught Max's eye and winked, mouthing 'Yuck' back at him.

'Ava!' Rory snapped at her.

'Sorry, Rory,' Ava said, going back to her pile of potatoes, faux-chastened, making Max laugh and Rory sigh.

Gabriela deposited the tentacles on a chopping board next to Flora. 'You,' she said to Flora, 'I don't know what you've been doing for the last year or so, but now you can do some bloody work. Get that pan down, get a paella going. Rosa will help you.'

Flora raised her brows. 'I know how to make a paella, Gabriela.'

'You know how to make nothing,' said Gabriela, crossing her hands with finality. 'Zilch. All his fancy stuff he did, all the piling on top of each other, all the bloody truffles and burning hay, that's not cooking. You think you know more than Rosa? A woman who's been making paella for more than seventy years? Since she was standing on a stool in her mother's kitchen. You think you know more than her? You think you know more than me? Who do you think worked here before you lot came along? It was us. We worked here. We cooked here. None of you ask for our advice because you all know better. You all know everything. But this place has been here longer than *any* of you. You go. It survives.'

Flora looked away.

Gabriela nodded, battle won. 'As I said,' she continued, all powerful, 'you know nothing. None of you.'

CHAPTER 19

They cooked and they cooked some more, the kitchen reaching the same inferno temperatures as the sizzling pavement outside, Gabriela shouting orders, taking a seat when she got too tired, standing only to inspect the paella, a small teaspoon slurped through cigarette-lined lips.

Garlic hissed, chicken fried, crabs fizzed and stock popped in bubbles on the stove, while under the grill tortilla gently browned and green peppers spat in the pan.

Max had propped the camera up on a giant tin of olives and was playing pinball with Emilio, who'd arrived with his sister and her gang of friends, the two boys desperately trying to impress the gangly butterscotch-tanned girls chewing their lemonade straws and feigning disinterest, watching music videos on their phones.

Ava had spent what felt like hours peeling potatoes and vegetables and was taking a break for a glass of water, leaning against the kitchen door, watching the kids circling each other, while Gabriela lined up her next task.

She straightened up when she saw Tom saunter in, just as Gabriela hollered, 'Ava, come here! There's washing up to do. Ava!'

Tom paused when he heard the shouting and came to stand next to her, peering through the door, intrigued to see what was going on.

Ava whispered, 'You have to save me,' through ventriloquist teeth.

'I have to what?' He was confused.

'Get me out of here,' she muttered, before shouting, 'Coming!' to Gabriela.

Tom cottoned on as Gabriela bashed the kitchen surface with her wooden spoon. 'Quickly, quickly, quickly!' she shouted at Ava.

'But Ava, I thought we had a lesson?' Tom said, looking at his watch, feigning puzzlement as he frowned at her to question why she'd double-booked.

'Oh my God, of course we do!' Ava sighed with mock forgetfulness.

Gabriela's face screwed up. 'What lesson?'

'Paddleboarding.' Tom grinned.

Ava's face fell.

Little Max looked over from the pinball machine. 'Oh man, jealous.'

Ava was tempted to tell him to go instead of her – the last thing she wanted to do was make a complete idiot of herself on a giant surfboard in front of Thomas King – but then she glanced at the mountain of filthy washing up.

'Coming?' Tom asked, beckoning her with a nod of his head as he started to stroll out of the café.

Ava winced but then caught Gabriela watching and turned it into a weird grimacing smile. Gabriela's eyes narrowed as she realised this was lies, but seeing it wasn't wholly to Ava's advantage her face softened and she trotted back to her stool with a gleeful 'You have fun!'

Outside the weather was glorious. No sign of the howling gale that Max had predicted.

'You get your stuff, I'll meet you over there.' Tom pointed to the shallows near the pontoon.

Ava shaded her eyes from the sun and peered over to the racks of paddleboards. 'We don't have to actually do this. I just needed to get out of there – so thanks for the excuse.'

'Oh, we're doing it.' Tom laughed.

'But I don't really want to do it.'

'You'll love it.'

'I don't think I will. I'm not really a watersports person.'

Tom thought for a moment. Behind him the beach was in full swing. Ava decided she would sneak to a sun lounger out of sight and read her book for an hour or two.

'OK,' he said in the end.

She felt the inner glow of victory.

'I'll just go back in and get my coffee.' He started to walk past her.

'No, you can't do that. You can't go in there. We're meant to be paddleboarding.'

'But we're not paddleboarding.' He shrugged like it was one or the other.

Ava's victory was short-lived. She groaned like a teenager. 'OK, OK. I'll go and get changed.'

Tom grinned with winner's delight.

Ten minutes later, choppy little waves had started to pick up on the water, the crests glistening like diamonds, as Ava shuffled reluctantly through the sand to where Tom was already waiting, top off, bronzed torso on show, next to two giant paddleboards lying on the sand.

She half-listened as he went through the instructions, her concentration mainly focused on all the people watching on the beach, and how she was going to get on this thing and paddle and stay upright, all while dressed only in a swimming costume, without it being completely mortifying.

The little waves lapped giggling against her feet.

'OK, ready?' Tom asked.

She nodded. She had no idea what she was meant to be doing. She picked up the board and immediately put it down again. 'It's really heavy.'

'It's not heavy,' he scoffed.

She picked it up again, glanced back to the café and saw Max and all his little friends had come outside, some of the boys kicking a football, the girls still on their phones. Max was pointing towards Ava and her lesson and one of the boys looked over and wolf-whistled. The girls sniggered.

'Concentrate,' Tom said.

'I *am* concentrating!'

He raised a brow to imply she wasn't at all, picked up his own board and paddle and walked into the water. Ava struggled after him, making faces behind his back. He turned and caught her and she grinned childishly down at the sea.

'You're so mature,' he said, sardonic.

'Look, OK, I'm doing something I don't want to do *in the slightest* in front of a whole beach of people who have nothing else to do but watch me make a complete idiot of myself. Please, just let me do what I have to do to get through it.'

Tom stared at her for a second or two, then, holding his board steady with one hand like a pro, came back to give her a hand. 'Let me help you.'

'No. I'm fine,' Ava said, just as the wind caught the edge of her board and it smacked her in the face.

Tom winced.

She heard one of the teenagers crack up. It wasn't necessarily at her but it felt like it. It felt like the whole beach was enrapt, books and sudokus discarded.

She stood very still. Breathed in through her nose. The little waves pushed and pulled at her like excited children. 'OK,' she said. 'Yes. Some help would be greatly appreciated, thank you.'

Tom's mouth twitched as he tried not to smile. 'Right.' He held the board steady so she could clamber on, flapping around, it felt to Ava, like a whale. She wobbled herself up to kneeling as she heard Max whoop and clap and shout, 'Go, Aunty Ava!'

'That's not helping,' Ava said, nodding back towards the shore and the whooping.

Tom handed her the paddle. 'It's OK, just stay kneeling like that for the moment and we'll get ourselves round the headland out of sight.'

Ava nodded, feeling better now she was actually on the board. 'OK,' she said. 'Thank you.'

'You're welcome,' Tom replied, as if through unnecessary herculean effort they'd finally reached an understanding.

Now that Ava was tentatively paddling, Max got bored, the show over, and turned his attention to the football as a couple of English kids from the beach asked if they could join in the game.

Ava felt herself start to relax.

Tom was shouting instructions.

She listened this time and found herself actually moving quicker. Realised it was more successful if she put herself in his hands rather than try and do it stubbornly on her own. She breathed out, shook her hair out of her face, wobbled, gripped the paddle.

'Relax!' he shouted.

She forced herself to relax and it was easier again.

They reached the headland. 'Ready to stand?' he asked.

She shook her head.

'You'll be fine.'

'No, I want to stay kneeling.'

He brought his board close to hers. 'Ava, I promise, you'll be fine.' His big blue eyes were fixed on her.

She wanted to shake her head. But she also knew it would be better to trust him. That she wanted to trust him.

He nodded, as if coaxing her into agreement. She nodded back, mute, tense.

He touched her arm. 'You have to relax.'

Touching her arm was not helping. Her whole body popped at the contact.

'So you place the paddle horizontal here, below your hands, and jump to your feet.'

Ava laughed. 'That easy?' she said, glancing at him, eyes catching, looking away quick, suddenly shy.

'That easy.'

So she took a deep breath and she jumped. And she wobbled, and her mouth made funny noises that she had no control over, and she tensed and she wobbled and she clenched her stomach muscles and thanked the lord for all her Pilates, and then finally she was steady and she laughed. 'I did it!' she shouted. 'I did it! I'm standing!'

Tom glided up beside her. 'See, I told you you'd be fine.'

Ava nodded. 'Yes,' she said, feeling a sense of pride massively out of proportion with her achievement, and at the same time suddenly more aware of Thomas King –

flattered by his kindness, wanting to stay under his scrutiny, craving more of his one-to-one attention as he paddled ahead, golden tanned, muscles rippling. She shook herself for being ridiculous, for succumbing to a teenage crush, which in turn made her lose her footing, then her balance, and topple straight into the sea.

She came up spluttering.

'What happened?' Tom was looking back, confused.

'Nothing,' she shouted. 'Nothing, I just . . .' She paused, couldn't think of an excuse quick enough. 'Nothing,' she repeated, climbing back on with no trouble at all because her attention was now on something else; internally chastising herself for being such a cliché. For fancying the movie star.

'OK, come on then.' Tom beckoned for her to get moving.

They paddled the headland one in front of the other. Tom deliberately keeping the pace slow, pausing to check on her and shout more instructions. Ava's entire focus on getting it right to keep her mind from straying on to other thoughts.

And without realising, suddenly she was gliding along beautifully and she didn't have to stop herself from thinking about anything because she was completely consumed by the magic of the water, of the coastline, the fish jumping, the bright horizon and the giant glowing orb of the sun.

She felt completely calm. Her mind silent.

And her whole body was smiling. As though for those few minutes she was free.

CHAPTER 20

Ava strolled into the café, high on life. Giggling and chatting, reliving paddleboarding moments that she'd loved, Tom nodding in agreement.

'And I'd thought it would be really boring,' she said, chucking her towel over a chair. 'But it isn't, is it? It's magical. I know it sounds stupid but it actually is—' She stopped short when she reached the door of the kitchen. 'Blimey Rory, is that a bandana?' she asked, with more than a hint of surprise.

'It is indeed, Ava, it is indeed,' her brother said, hands moving from pan to pan, flipping peppers, sliding croquettes into the oven, burning his hand, running it under water for a second, then back to his pot of bubbling stock. Hips moving like there was a place in the *Strictly* finals up for grabs.

Ava stood in the doorway, arms crossed, smiling in amazement at the scene in front of her. Flora was on fire, tea towel tucked into her waistband, sauce down her dress, hair pulled high in a messy knot on top of her head, sweat on her brow and a smile on her lips.

'You've got *el duende*,' Ava laughed, as Tom reached over to sample a chunk of marinating octopus.

From her seat in the corner, Gabriela made a grumbling noise as if to say this was not yet *el duende*, but she didn't say it out loud, kind enough to spare the enthusiastic cooks.

'Tell you what, Ava,' Rory said, without looking up, 'instead of standing there commenting, you could make yourself useful and go out and see what you can find in the garden.'

'Yes, Chef!' she said, with a sniggering salute.

Flora handed her a cardboard box. Tom sauntered along behind.

Outside, the promised wind was starting to pick up, gusts taunting the feeble vegetables, unsettling the leaves of the fruit trees.

'This is ridiculous,' said Ava, holding her hair back from her forehead as the weather wreaked havoc with her curls. 'It was calm a minute ago.'

'It's the heat,' Tom shouted over another big gust, a peach falling from the tree beside him. 'Messes with the weather. Think of my poor vines.'

'You and your bloody vines,' Ava laughed. 'Shouldn't you be up there battening them down?'

Tom bent down and picked the peach off the ground. 'Not a lot I can do, there are trees planted as windbreaks, so . . .' He shrugged, taking a bite of the peach. 'They'll be OK.'

Ava walked past him with her cardboard box to the lemon tree at the back. 'It's quite sweet really,' she said, 'they're like your children.'

'Less demanding,' he said drily, chucking a couple of peaches into the box as she went past.

The wind rattled the ancient wooden fence. The fat waxy leaves of the lemon tree knocked together like nervous clapping.

'You have a daughter, don't you?' Ava asked, as casually as she could, but the moment she said it she regretted it. It felt like prying rather than conversation, simply because she'd learnt it from

Google. She was annoyed with herself, felt like Gabriela and co. trawling for gossip rather than continuing the relaxed chat. So she turned, holding her hair back from her face and said, 'Forget I asked. You don't have to talk about it.'

Tom paused as he took another bite of the peach, chewing slowly as he watched her, brows furrowed.

Ava knew she'd overplayed it. Why couldn't she have just left it? Pretended that it was as it was, simple conversation, they'd been getting on so well. Sweat trickled between her shoulder blades. Taunting gusts of wind pushed at her face and body, tugging at her clothes. She felt caught on the back foot, halfway to becoming Tom's friend but still hampered by the glamour of fame. Muddled by the moments out on the water that now seemed a million miles from reality.

'I do have a daughter,' Tom said. 'Lola. Do you want to see a picture?'

The simplicity of the gesture cut through all her internal panic. She paused. 'OK. Yes.'

Tom reached into his back pocket and took out his wallet. He passed over a photo booth picture of a teenage girl, black hair pulled into a ponytail, huge wide smile, eyes slicked with heavy black kohl.

'Very pretty,' Ava said, clutching the photo tight as it flapped in the breeze.

'Smart too,' he said, looking at the picture over her shoulder. 'And very demanding,' he added, in reference to the earlier alignment with the grapes.

The wind seemed to wrap them together in blustery spirals. Ava was suddenly super aware of how close he was. She could smell the soap and the aftershave and the heat. 'Do you see her a lot?' she asked, trying really hard to stay focused on the picture.

'More now I live here. I'm not her mother's favourite person and neither is she mine,' he said, taking another bite of peach, seemingly immune to their proximity and the weather. 'But she's sixteen now and at college in Barcelona so she's more her own person – decides who she wants to see and no court's going to stop her.'

Ava nodded. Feeling a bit of a fraud for knowing half that info already. She turned to hand the photo back and found herself eye to eye with his chest. She stared a fraction too long as the wind caught his T-shirt, skimming it over the muscles of his chest, glanced at the sharpness of his jaw, took a step back, wondering if actually a quick one-night stand might be the answer, but then she looked up and recognised the look that she'd seen when he'd checked out the women on the beach, when he'd offered her a bed at his house for the night, a well-perfected louche prowess, an automatic response to any woman standing this close.

She almost laughed out loud but kept it in. 'I'm going to get more lemons.'

Tom shrugged, finished his peach and chucked the stone towards the compost heap, but the wind caught it and it curved in mid-air, landing with a metallic thud.

'What was that?' he asked, looking over at the space between the overgrown compost heap and the tangle of brambles in the corner of the plot.

'A wheelbarrow?' Ava said, no idea what made metallic noises in gardens.

'Doesn't look like there's space for a wheelbarrow,' Tom said, striding over to have a look, weeds squashing beneath his flip flops, blustery breeze getting stronger.

Ava continued picking lemons, but when he said, 'It's not a wheelbarrow,' curiosity got the better of her.

'What is it?' she asked, going over to join him, stuffing lemons in the pockets of her shorts.

'I don't know,' he said, his arms scratching on the brambles as he hauled out a giant metal bowl thick with spiders' webs and sticky with sap and old leaves.

'There's another bit,' Ava pointed to a square-looking machine and some spokes in the thicket.

They both reached in to get it. The machine was heavier than it looked and stuck. The sides of their bodies pressed together as they pulled, the brambles drawing blood, the wind battering them into the fence.

Ava laughed at the effort, heaved again, pushed her hair away with the back of her wrist, and out of the corner of her eye caught a glimpse of him watching her, thick black lashes and gaze less lascivious.

She paused. Thought for a second that he looked like his character in *Love-Struck High*. Young. Normal.

Then the wind bellowed and her hair swept in front of her face again and the crusted earth and brambles gave up the machine and they both landed on their bums in the middle of the old courgette plant.

'Well what the hell is it?' Tom said, examining the silver tower, the moment between them over. He spun the big spoked wheel attached to the side, the edges scalloped with rust, the base of the tower speckled with mud, a fat black spider scurrying away over the levers.

'It's the churro machine!' they heard a voice exclaim, and turned to see everyone outside watching, the wind flapping their clothes and aprons. To their surprise it was Rosa who had shouted. Quiet, knitting Rosa.

'This was my father's,' she said, treading carefully over the weeds in her black leather lace-up shoes. She put her hand on her heart when she looked at it, knelt down and ran her finger along the edge of the spider-webbed bowl. 'The best churro maker in town,' she said, a sparkling smile beneath increasingly damp eyes.

Ava thought she might well up herself from the obvious emotion on the old woman's face.

'He won awards, you know?' Rosa continued. 'I have the trophies at home.'

'Yeah?' Ava smiled at her pride.

'Oh yes, he was the very best.'

Ava looked up and caught Tom's eye, watching her again, and he winked, mouth half-smiling, and she thought maybe the moment wasn't over. Something between them had shifted. And unusually for Ava, it didn't make her immediately want to back away.

'Can we bring it in?' Rosa asked, turning to seek permission from Flora.

'Of course we can bloody bring it in,' snapped Gabriela. 'It's gonna be the star of the bloody show.'

So together they hauled the machine inside, Rosa pointing to a spot underneath the television at the far end of the bar where it fit perfectly, like a lost relic swathed in ribbons of spiders' webs. And they all sat, drinking red wine out of little glasses, listening to Rosa as she carefully wiped the dirt from the metal bowl and spoke about the history of Café Estrella: waiting tables after school, her mother in the kitchen, the whole town lining up for her father's churros on the weekend, the queues snaking out on to the beach. And as they sat they ate all the amazing food that

Flora and Rory had cooked. The paella bubbling with bright yellow rice and plump pink prawns, the chunks of oily purple octopus, the soft warm crab croquettes and the langoustine stew. And it made them think of possibilities. That maybe the café could rise again.

CHAPTER 21

For Ava and Tom, the next few days were spent cleaning and fixing the churro machine. Dashing from the safety of the covered bar area out into the battling wind to chuck soapy buckets of blackened water down the drain. Talking about not much. Laughing. Sort of flirting. Trying to work out how the stupid machine fitted together. Tom driving into the town to track down a new handle for the tap that the mixture came out of, and a new stand for the bowl of boiling oil that fried the churros. Every now and then Max would join them, bored of filming, moaning about the wind, and the flirting stopped. Just the odd covert look. It was all a nice distraction from her mother's letters. Ava felt light. In the moment. Everything else shoved to the back.

She wondered how they were getting on without her at work. If she could only find her phone she would have texted Peregrine to check all was OK. She had a momentary vision of her desk, Hugo sitting there on the phone, doodling on her pad, a little jealous that they were no doubt getting on fine without her.

She had wanted to be deemed irreplaceable, but catching sight of Flora sashaying towards them, hair piled high, bright pink apron tied tight, phoenixing out of Ricardo's ashes, she realised that no one was. The job would just be done differently. It would change to fit whoever took it. She wondered, giving the big churro bowl a last polish, whether she had convinced herself she was indispensable in order to never have to leave.

'Darlings,' Flora said, giving the wheel of the churro machine a little spin, 'this looks sensational. Rosa is raring to go. She's been here since dawn whipping up the batter.'

They looked into the kitchen to see Rosa with a dotty headscarf on, sleeves rolled up, stirring two huge vats – one of batter, the other dark chocolate dipping sauce. There was a giant lipstick-glistening smile on her face and she looked about twenty years younger.

Next to her Rory and Gabriela were prepping lunchtime tapas.

Flora stood with her hands on her hips, casting her eyes over the usual breakfast crowd. 'Thing is we're not really getting the word out,' she said, concerned.

'You need a sign or an A-board saying Tapas and Churros,' Ava said, pointing to the front of the restaurant.

'I do, but in this weather it'll blow away,' Flora said, looking out to where the wind had dropped a touch overnight but still whipped and bellowed enough to steal sun umbrellas from the sand.

'We could do it,' Max piped up. 'We could shout for business.'

Ava made a face; she didn't fancy walking up and down the beach calling for churros punters.

Tom, however, like her brother, seemed to have a knack for sensing when she was out of her comfort zone and a similar enjoyment of her discomfort. 'I think that sounds like a great idea,' he said. 'Nice one, Max.'

Ava shook her head. 'There's no way I'm shouting on the beach.'

'That's very unsupportive, Ava,' Tom said, tone serious, eyes laughing.

'Yeah, Aunty Ava, VERY unsupportive,' Max chipped in.

'Oh God.' She put her head back to stare at the ceiling. 'Come on then,' she sighed, resigned.

Flora clapped with delight and beckoned for Rosa to come out and get the churros show started.

Two minutes later, all Rory could hear was Max's voice yelling, 'Best churros in Spain – freshly made, see it now. Get yours while it's hot. Fool to miss it!'

Rory turned to see him through the kitchen hatch, on the beach, walking up and down in the sand, wind ruffling his hair, ushering people inside. Ava stood with her hand over her eyes, refusing to join in until Max pushed her towards a group of suntanners shielded by a windbreak, while Tom looked on grinning before casually chatting up passers-by, laughing with them, leading them in the direction of the bar where Rosa was stirring great wheels of churros in hot, sizzling oil. They'd watch her fish them out with her wire net and drench them in sugar, then nod as they tasted, dipped the warm churros into glossy sweet chocolate, and Tom would smile as they sighed, his look plain, 'I told you so,' and then he'd leave them charmed and beaming so they could fill up with more. Rory watched him turn to Ava as if to say, that's how it's done, then saw Ava's competitiveness fire up in an instant, saw her push her hair back with her sunglasses, roll her shoulders and stalk off down the beach to do better. Her stubbornness made him smile with recognition. The ease with which she could be wound up.

As kids, their arguments would go on for days. He'd put up a wall of silence as she ranted and raved behind him and their dad went into the garden for some peace. He wondered if he was doing the same thing now with his wife.

Watching Ava he realised that Claire would describe him exactly as he had his sister. They were as stubborn as each other. He wanted both Claire and Ava to see the world as he did. The past as he did. Because he knew he was right. But then, even if he discovered he was wrong, he knew he wouldn't back down. Just maybe tweak his argument a little bit.

He ran his tongue along his bottom lip as he thought. As he pieced together these discoveries about himself by watching his sister. Considered his final argument with Claire. Re-ran everything she had said, and wondered, if he'd just listened to her point, whether he might have agreed with her and they could have moved on.

He thought about his dad's cool, considered response to his mother and wondered, if he asked him now whether it would have been better if they had tried harder to find out what she was chasing rather than just telling her she would never find it, what his answer would be. It would be no, he knew it without having to ask. A stubborn no. The past unwavering.

Max was still shouting. Rory briefly wondered if he should go out and tell him to be quiet. He didn't want him upsetting people. Out the side window of the kitchen he could see the guys from Nino's watching, shooting daggers their way. But Rory held himself back because as many people as were walking past with brows raised, were poking their heads in, were edging into the darkness to have a nose at the churro machine, to watch Rosa expertly piping her fluffy delicacies, to sample a strand drenched in the chocolate that Flora poured. And Rory thought, why not? Why not make a bit of noise for once?

Somehow Max's yelling was like the complete antidote to everything he felt about his job and his life, to all the Twitter vitriol and his stupid #SwanLovesGoose kidnapping error. Like Pac-Man gobbling up the tweets. Max shouting at the top of his voice into the wide open air.

'Are you planning to do any work?' The snap of Gabriela's voice brought him back down to earth.

'Sorry,' he said, turning from the scene outside and going back to prepping his sardines.

So he cooked. And cooked and cooked. His mind quietly at peace. He could hear Max shouting, Tom charming, Ava nattering, Flora laughing. He burnt things, he underseasoned, he overseasoned, he got told off by Gabriela, he started again, he got stressed when orders started pouring in – the churros customers were intrigued enough to sample the tapas – and relaxed when it started to settle down.

Relaxed enough to turn to Gabriela in a moment of quiet and say, 'Why, before, when we started filming, did you make Flora think it would be better to sell this place?'

Gabriela looked shocked at the very idea. 'I never said that.'

'Yes you did. You said it would take more than the film to make this place anything, that she was better off selling.'

'I do not think I did, young man.'

Rory frowned, pulled his bandana off and stood with his hands on his hips. 'I can rewind the tape.'

Gabriela's lips pursed. Then she went back to the scallops she was opening, prising the shells apart expertly with the tip of her knife. 'Do you know what it's like to watch someone fade away in unhappiness?'

Rory was struck by a blinding image of his mother sitting at the dressing table in her bedroom. The curtains closed. *'This isn't the life for me, sweet Rory. This isn't the life I was born for.'*

Looking straight at Gabriela, he swallowed and said, 'Yes. Yes I do.'

'Well then, you know you try everything you can to make them happy again, yes?'

Rory licked his lips, nodded.

'We've seen what this place can do to people. It's not easy. We've watched Flora. We've seen who she has become. For you she's got her act on. But I've picked her up, sobbing, off the floor.' Gabriela put the shell down on the chopping board, stood with both hands braced and turned to look at Rory, 'You know what that's like?'

Rory paused, glanced briefly at the floor then nodded again.

Gabriela studied him. Seemed to see straight into his soul. 'Yes,' she said, 'I suppose you do.' She looked down at her hands, twisted her rings, seemed to be taking a moment because she had forgotten about Rory's mother – her dear friend Val's daughter – and when she spoke again there was a new respect in her voice. 'I will admit that it has been different though, since you all came. I think maybe she's starting to realise she can do it without him.' She sighed, as if she wasn't sure either way, picked up the next scallop from the bucket and went back to work.

Rory thought she had finished, but then she said, 'I admit, I was wrong.' He felt his mouth pull into a smile. Then she turned to glare at him, waving her knife as she added, 'I won't say that on camera.'

Rory shook his head.

'No,' she said, emphatic. Then opening the next scallop shell, she added, 'Sometimes you need other people to help you see things. Maybe that's the case,' as if pondering to herself. 'Look at Rosa. She's been my friend for sixty years, I never thought she'd tear up over some churros. I've never seen her so happy.'

Rory watched Gabriela shelling the scallops for a moment. Then glanced over his shoulder at Rosa cleaning down the churro machine ready for tomorrow's breakfast, and next to her Flora, glowing with confidence, holding court with the customers.

He thought of his wife. He thought about everything she did. Everything she had done. All the time at home when he had been away filming, that in his mind was blank – it wasn't blank at all, but her getting on with things. Getting on with life, with Max's life. From this vantage point, relaxed and calm in the café kitchen rather than caught up in the domestic melee, he could see that she had picked up the flak for him over the years, held the fort, been the mainstay of their family. Unsung. Unthanked. He could see it. Suddenly it seemed so obvious. And suddenly his need to be right lost all its power.

Pointing to the back door, he said to Gabriela, 'I'm just going to take a break.'

She waved her knife again. 'Not for long, young man.'

'Be careful with that thing,' Rory said, backing away as he untied his apron and, leaving it on the surface, stepped out into the humid, breathless heat of the vegetable patch, the warm wind taking a rest.

He sat down on the rickety bench, hands clasped in front of him, elbows on his knees, and looked out at the dying tomatoes.

He took his old Nokia from his pocket.

I'm sorry, he wrote.

The response came back immediately. *That's a good start.*

CHAPTER 22

Igor the waiter watched on, eyes curious with suspicion as the queues for churros grew, as the smell of garlic frying and chicken roasting wafted out from the kitchen, as customers edged in and tables filled. And tapas now sat temptingly on big white plates, tiered on the old silver stands at the end of the bar. Igor's days of cleaning glasses and watching TV were over as hands were raised in his direction. People wanted coffee with their churros, beer with their tapas, ice cold sherry or a fruit-packed jug of sangria.

'Sangria?' he frowned, as he sloped behind the bar. 'No one's drunk sangria here in ten years.'

'Sangria?' Flora exclaimed. 'What an excellent idea, I'll have a sangria. Igor, make some for us back here in the kitchen will you?'

'A good sangria has to sit,' said Igor.

'Oh bugger that,' Flora scoffed. 'Just get it made.'

Igor grumbled, pulling an ancient bottle of brandy down from the shelf, expertly concocting what looked to Ava, who was sitting on one of the bar stools sampling the tapas, like a lethally strong jug of sangria. His movements became lighter, quicker, the more he made. The weight of boredom beginning to lift.

'I'll have one of them,' she said. Tom, who was next to her, eating little anchovies and bread warm from the oven, held up his hand for Igor to include him in the order.

Max had been invited to a pool party at a house up on the hill by one of Emilio's sister's friends. He'd gone home to get changed and appeared back now all dressed up in his jeans and a shirt, a million freckles on his excited face, sun-bleached hair slicked back with what Ava presumed from the scent as he came closer was her phenomenally expensive styling foam.

'Nice hair,' she said. Max blushed. She'd asked him to pick up her towel and swimsuit for her, and he threw the hastily stuffed bag her way to distract from any more embarrassing grooming comments. 'Oh this is nicely packed, Max, thanks,' she added, brow raised as she looked down at the crushed towel and squidged-in swimsuit.

Max just grinned and, looking past her into the kitchen, shouted, 'Dad, I've gotta go,' hopping from one foot to the other. 'Come on, we're going to be late.' The only thing stopping him looking like a teenager was the chocolate round his mouth from all the churros he'd eaten that day.

'OK, I'm coming,' Rory shouted as he came out from the kitchen, then turned immediately around and returned with a roll of kitchen towel which he chucked at Max. 'Use this,' he said, gesturing towards Max's mouth.

They all watched as Max made a hash of the kitchen roll, trying to tear a sheet off but ripping it in half, wiping his face but missing the crucial bits of chocolate, distracted by the fact that he was already late as well as by a couple of the girls he'd been hanging out with strolling past arm in arm, wearing cropped tops and skinny jeans, pointing his way before starting the walk up the hill. 'Gone?' he asked his dad, anxious to get going.

Rory shook his head and ripped off another piece of paper, subtly wiping off the chocolate so none of Max's friends would see and adjusting his half-upturned collar. 'There. Very handsome,' he said.

Max nodded, not really listening.

Rory tried not to smile.

Ava watched as she popped little meatball tapas into her mouth. She'd never really seen Rory as a dad. She'd seen Claire as a mum and Rory unpacking the car, or going back to the car to pick up the things that had been forgotten, or coming in for a bad-cop tell-off when Max wouldn't listen to Claire. But she'd never really seen him as a lone parent. And she was surprised to find in him an unexpected sweetness.

'Looking good, Max!' she called, as he smoothed back his hair.

Max gave her a glare, a silent warning not to embarrass him in front of the girls.

Ava grinned.

A large group of locals came in, all chatter and big laughs, pushing tables together and sitting down under the awning, their day-at-the-beach paraphernalia propped up around them. A woman in a gold bikini and white shorts strutted up to the counter to take a look at the tapas.

'Excuse me, is there going to be more?' the woman asked, pointing towards the almost empty plates, then added, 'Hey Tom,' with a smile and a wave when she recognised him at the bar.

Tom nodded a polite hello.

Ava tried not to notice.

Flora wiped her hands on her apron as she leant through the hatch to have a look. 'Absolutely, darling, coming up,' she called, and when the gold bikini woman went back to sit with her friends, Flora added, 'Rory, we're going to need you back here.'

'Can't. I have to walk Max.'

'Come on!' whined Max.

'We'll walk him,' Ava said, sliding off her seat. She'd said 'we' without really thinking about it, because somehow over the course of the last few days she and Tom had become a 'we', everything they had done they had done together.

She glanced back at him, suddenly a little embarrassed by her assumption. Embarrassed that he'd be looking at her like there was no chance he was walking up the hill when there was fresh sangria being poured and a woman in a gold bikini waiting.

But he was already wiping his hands of tapas oil, already standing up ready to walk out with her.

'D'you want to go swimming after?' Ava asked, grabbing her beach bag from the floor.

Tom thought about it for a second, then shrugged. 'Why not?'

'Let's go!' Max didn't seem to care who escorted him as long as they got moving ASAP. He was off before Ava and Tom had barely left the restaurant, the two girls strolling in front of him turning round and giggling every now and then, Max puffing his chest out, trying to put as much distance between him and his aunt as possible.

Ava and Tom hung back so he could do his stuff. They watched with amused fascination as one of the girls dropped back to ask Max a question then ran back to her friend, Max's swagger increasing with every burst of excited laughter.

At the top of the hill his shaggy-haired friend Emilio appeared, arguing with his sister who trotted off when she saw the girls. A car pulled up and the English boys who'd played football with them got out, high-fiving Max and Emilio. They all loped off together towards one of the big white villas that overlooked the bay.

'Bye Max!' Ava shouted.

He turned. 'Oh yeah, bye,' he said, all nonchalant cool.

Ava and Tom watched him go into the house then turned to walk back, silently smiling.

Ahead of them was a view of the whole beach, from the pedalos waiting on the straw yellow sand, out to where the sea met the sky, the sun hovering low over the water ready to drop, and round to the tourists walking the blustery headland, the houses, the café and the bright pink daubs of bougainvillea.

The only noise was the sound of their flip flops and the breeze rustling like animals through the leaves.

A phone beeped.

'Is that yours?' Tom asked.

Ava paused. 'No,' she said, too quickly. Realising immediately that it must be somewhere in her cavernous beach bag. Either thrown there after her night of Googling or bundled in by Max along with the towel.

It beeped again.

'It is yours!' Tom said, his mouth open in mock surprise.

'It's not,' said Ava, starting to walk a little quicker.

'It is,' he said, jogging to catch up with her. 'You're the worst detoxer ever.'

'I'm not, I am detoxing,' she said, emphatic.

They were both walking really fast, side by side, him trying to get her to stop.

'You're also the worst liar.' He was laughing.

Ava was slightly out of breath. 'I'm not, it wasn't my phone,' she said, stumbling on the incline of the road.

Tom put his hand out to steady her at the same time as whipping her bag off her shoulder.

'Give it back!' She dived towards him to yank it back but she was too late. Tom's hand fished around in her bag and pulled out the iPhone, triumphant.

'Give it back,' Ava said, half-laughing, half-serious.

'No way,' he said.

She tried to wrestle him for it. Jumping up at him in the road, his arm outstretched, the phone out of her reach. Even with the wind it was swelteringly hot. The air swirled thick and glittering from the sun. She suddenly registered that they were touching. That his arm was tight around her as she grabbed for her phone, that she could feel his breath from laughing and his heart beat through his chest.

But then his fingers holding the phone nudged the Home button and the screen lit up. She saw the exact moment his eyes registered what was on the screen and in that second it was all gone.

She felt his grip loosen around her. 'Here,' he said, handing her the phone and her bag.

'Thanks.' She took it from him, not quite sure what had happened.

Tom pointed up the hill and said, 'My house is just up here. You'll be alright going back on your own, won't you?'

Ava nodded. There would be no swimming.

He jogged away without looking back.

She looked down at her screen.

A WhatsApp preview from Louise: *The kid's not his! Massive super injunction. Lawyer friend told me so don't tell anyone. Best bit of gossip, EVER?!*

CHAPTER 23

Rory was madly frying up *pimiento du padron*, the little green peppers hissing and crinkling as they blackened in the pan. From the kitchen window he caught sight of Ava walking alone down the hill. 'Where's Tom?' he asked, as she appeared back at the bar.

'He had to go.'

Rory frowned. 'Why, what's he doing?'

'I don't know,' she said.

He came out with the pan of sizzling peppers and slid them on to a plate at the far end of the counter, scattering little crystals of sea salt over them like a pro.

'Is he coming back?' He walked past Ava back towards the kitchen.

Ava sighed and got her phone out of her pocket.

'I thought you were detoxing?' he said, as she tapped the screen a couple of times and brought up a WhatsApp text, holding it up for him to read.

'I am,' she said, and explained what had happened. When she was finished she stared at him, her hair hanging windswept and curly half across her face, her huge eyes trained defensively on him as she said, 'Go on then.'

'What?' Rory asked, inwardly cringing at the message.

'Tell me how awful I am.'

Rory frowned, his fingers thrumming on the counter top. He *had* been about to say how awful she was.

That it was a stupid thing to be messaging about. And that with regard to the detoxing, she'd promised not just him but Max that she'd lay off her phone. But now she was expecting a telling-off he realised how predictable he was. How quickly they reverted to type when together. Or maybe he just told everyone how awful they were.

He thought of all the times he'd told Claire how she could have handled a situation differently when she came home bitching about some workplace injustice. 'I don't want a solution, Rory! I just want you to listen to me,' she'd groan in frustrated annoyance. 'I just want to be able to say it and for you to nod in sympathy.'

He thought of his plans to kidnap the #SwanLovesGoose and how easy it would have been not to action it, but equally how easy it was for a silly plan to run away with itself. A five-minute meeting and an idea that would probably have disappeared just as quickly once they'd seriously examined the logistics if it hadn't been for the Twitter leak.

He looked at Ava looking at him, eyes blinking. Instead of saying anything he nodded towards the frothy jug on the counter and said, 'Igor's made some sangria. Have some. We'll join you in a bit.'

Then he went back to the kitchen. Flora and Gabriela were frying up more meatballs, steaming lobster, whipping up fresh garlicky aioli and flash-frying tiny white clams. There was a call for more tortilla. 'That's you, Rory,' Flora shouted, face pink, hair a bit sweaty, glass of sangria on the go next to her chopping board.

But Rory had paused.

'Everything OK?' Flora asked, when he didn't jump to it.

'Yes, yes. Absolutely,' he said, giving himself a quick shake. He'd been distracted. Wondering how often in his life he might have been wrong. It was still virgin territory for him, to question his watertight resolve, the possibility that he might have won arguments, bulldozed through chats, made decisions not necessarily because he was right but because he was so stubbornly headstrong.

He was feeling more and more like his father every day.

As he whisked up the eggs for the tortilla, he was caught by his own reflection in the window overlooking the garden. He remembered a similar moment as a teenager, catching sight of himself in a giant hallway mirror, the time he stood at the top of the stairs, Ava trying to get through to their mother in New York, and him saying, voice completely neutral, *'Unless she calls to talk to me herself, I'm never calling her again.'*

His dad at the bottom of the stairs, standing next to Ava, looking up and saying, *'That's up to you, son.'*

And his mother didn't call. She was terrible at keeping in touch. So he didn't speak to her again.

In the hot, smoky kitchen, Rory rubbed his hand over his eyes. Stood holding his fingers over his temples.

A soft touch to his shoulder reminded him where he was. 'Have a break,' Flora said. 'Go and sit with Ava.'

Rory would usually have pulled himself together, said absolutely not and got on with his work, but this time he nodded, handing Flora his whisk, sloping out the kitchen door to take a seat next to Ava at the bar.

'That was quick,' Ava said, sucking on a slice of orange from her sangria.

'I got dismissed. Mind not on the job,' he said, pouring himself a glass.

She nodded.

Rory realised how nice it was for someone just to agree with you and not try to fix the problem. He bobbed the ice and fruit around in his drink with a plastic cocktail stirrer shaped like a palm tree.

Out front, the café was quietening down. The beach almost deserted. The wind causing havoc for the man collecting up the sun umbrellas.

Rory had a slug of the sangria and just managed to stop himself coughing. 'Blimey, that's strong.'

Ava laughed.

He took another gulp, then pushed his glass to one side and leant forwards, elbows on the bar, fingers steepled under his chin, and stared at the lines of optics and liqueurs in front of him. 'Do you want to know something?'

'Always.'

'I did sometimes want to come with you, you know? With you and Gran when you went to New York. When you went to watch Mum.'

'You did?' Ava said with surprise. He could see her image reflected back at him in the wall of mirror behind the bar.

'Yeah.' Rory nodded, sitting up straight, bobbing the fruit in his drink again.

'Well why didn't you?'

'Stubbornness, I suppose. I'd made up my mind.' Rory licked his lips, rolled the next idea through his head before saying, 'I don't think I wanted Dad to think less of me.'

'But he told us to go. He paid for it.'

Rory shook his head. 'Yeah, but I knew he thought she'd made the wrong decision by leaving and I felt like I should show that I supported him in that. That he would judge me somehow if I went too. That it would make me seem weak.'

Ava listened.

Rory scratched his head, felt like a polar bear at the zoo, suffocating in his cage. 'And I actually think that I'm right,' he carried on. 'I think he would have done.'

Ava couldn't deny it.

'But what did I end up with?' he asked, glancing across at her. 'Dad thinking I was a strong young man and not getting to see my mum.' He sighed with annoyance. 'In retrospect it means *nothing* what he thought.'

There was a pause.

'I wish you'd come,' said Ava.

'Yeah,' Rory nodded. 'Me too.'

They both toyed with their drinks in silence, Rory twirling the plastic palm tree stirrer between his fingers.

'It's very unlike you though, Rory,' Ava said, fishing out a slice of peach to eat from her glass. 'You suddenly taking Mum's side.'

'I'm not taking her side,' he said. 'I just feel like I maybe took the wrong side. That there shouldn't have been a side at all.'

The awning flapped in the wind. The light dimmed as the sun began to sink. Chairs scraped. Igor came round to make a drinks order. Sploshing more sangria into their glasses with a wink as he left.

Flora appeared with the fresh, warm tortilla sliced into chunks and added it to the plates on the bar, then scooped two portions up on to a separate little plate, added a blob of aioli, and set it in front of Ava and Rory. 'Here,' she said, sliding the plate on to the counter. 'Get it while it's hot.'

Rory hadn't realised he was quite so famished until he took a bite.

Ava picked up her diamond-shaped wedge, looked at Rory and then shoved the whole thing in her mouth at once, hardly able to cram it all in.

Rory was momentarily stunned by her table manners, then the memory sparked of them doing the same as kids and he shook his head in disbelief. 'You are kidding?' he said.

She shook her head, having trouble chewing.

Unable to resist a challenge, no matter how uncouth, Rory picked his tortilla chunk up and did the same, stuffing it into his mouth, worrying for a moment that he might have to spit the whole lot out on the floor.

Seconds ticked by as both of them sat side by side trying to chew, trying to get their teeth to do something when their mouths were unable to move. Ava laughed and tiny bits of tortilla shot out. Rory worried if he laughed it might come out of his nose. He caught sight of the woman in the gold bikini from earlier giving an unimpressed sneer, and he had to hide his face in his hand as he started to laugh and choke at the same time. It was all strangely liberating. He knew exactly why his grandmother had looked at them with such disdain and why his mother had angled her chair away when they'd played the game twenty years ago. He would struggle to watch Max do this without telling him off for messing with his food. Because he had forgotten how much fun it was to be a participant in simple silliness. Again he realised that maybe he should let a few more things go.

'I win,' said Ava in the end, opening her mouth wide so he could see there was nothing left while Rory was still struggling to chew. She took a self-congratulatory gulp of sangria.

Rory finally finished. 'That was very immature,' he said, still unable to quite give in.

Ava rolled her eyes.

They sat side by side in silence as the sun disappeared into the trees like a flickering bonfire.

Then Ava held her curls away from her face, sighed, and said, from out of nowhere, 'I don't see how you think having FOMO would stop someone getting married.'

Rory nearly spat his drink out.

'Do you really think I've got FOMO?' she asked.

'Ava, seriously, I can't even remember what FOMO means,' he said. 'Fear of something.'

'Missing out,' she said, picking another bit of peach from her glass.

'Oh yeah. Well, yeah, I do think you have that. But I don't think that's why you're not married.'

'Why do you think I'm not married?'

'You're too picky.'

Flora appeared behind the bar, service finished. She scoffed as she poured herself a huge glass of sangria. 'No one is too picky, Rory,' she said. 'It's good to be picky. Golly, take it from me, there's nothing worse than marrying the wrong person.'

Rory huffed. 'OK, fine, fine, I'll give you that,' he said.

'Maybe you're just not the marrying kind,' Flora said to Ava, fanning her flushed cheeks with a menu. 'I'm going to be absolutely squiffy by the end of today. What Igor's put in this, I have no idea!'

'No, forget marriage then.' Ava waved the comment away. 'Just a good long-term relationship. A great one.'

Rory propped himself up on the bar, starting to feel the effects of Igor's lethally strong mixology. 'I think maybe it's that you can't settle. Look at Jonathon, he was perfectly nice.'

'Nice. See.' Ava raised her hands in the air, slipping slightly on her stool. 'He was nice. It was just nice. It's either nice or it's sex.'

Rory shuddered. 'Do you have to talk about sex? You're my sister.'

'Yeah, I'm your sister, not your mother.' Ava made a face.

Rory shrugged. 'Well actually, if you're looking for a reason, that's probably it.'

Flora started unloading the bar dishwasher. 'What is? Sex?' she asked through the plume of steam.

Rory sighed. 'No, our mother,' he said. 'Fear of being left,' he added, as if he had landed on the definitive answer.

Ava screwed up her face. 'No.'

Flora was reaching up to put the wine glasses back on the shelf. 'Don't write it off,' she said, voice strained from stretching. 'It's horrendous. Being left.' She went to get more glasses and paused by the dishwasher. 'I can only tell you from my point of view, but it's a killer because you spend your whole time thinking: why wasn't I good enough? And there's no one there to answer you.'

Rory stilled his glass and turned to watch Ava. She was looking down, playing with the straw of her drink.

Flora carried on. 'So you just go round and round in your head coming up with new, more self-damning answers. *If only I'd done such and such we'd still be*

OK . . . I wake up in the middle of the night sometimes with the answer and then immediately forget it.' She laughed as she collected up the remaining glasses.

Igor came round to give her a hand, but she told him he'd done enough and to go home. Clearly delighted, he grabbed his keys and gave them the cheeriest goodbye Rory had heard since he'd been there. He watched him scoot off on his moped with a satisfied smile that changed the whole shape and look of his face. Rory could suddenly see him as a doting, happy father of three.

Gabriela had strapped the wheels to her little pug, who'd been curled up in the corner of the kitchen most of the day eating scraps, and Rosa was collecting up her knitting. They left the kitchen, Gabriela tying a scarf around her hair, saying, 'A very good day. Same time tomorrow, Rosa?'

'Oh yes, Gabriela.' Rosa nodded.

'Goodbye all,' they waved, and off they went, pug wheeled along behind them.

Flora flopped forwards over the bar, hand over her eyes. 'The woman's a tyrant.'

Rory topped up all their glasses. 'She got you your customers back.'

'And your brand,' said Ava, turning in her chair to watch them go.

Flora peeked through her fingers. 'And it is quite fun, I suppose.'

'It's really fun,' Rory said.

'Yes,' said Flora, standing up a little more proudly, shoulders back, chest out. 'Yes it is,' she repeated, as if it had only just dawned on her. 'Maybe I'm not washed up after all,' she said, looking out at her café, then she glanced at Ava and said, 'See, I'm the perfect example of getting married for the wrong reasons.' She came round to their side of the counter and pulled one of the stools out so they were sitting in a triangle. 'Having thought about it *non-stop* for two years, I know that I got flattered into marriage. Ricardo knew just how vain I was and made me feel incredible at a time when I was beginning to feel old.' She touched her face on instinct, smoothed the lines by her eyes. 'And insecure. There were suddenly lots of spring chicken cooks on the TV and I was no longer flavour of the month. Sales of my books were catastrophic. I liked Ric's youth. His energy. And I think, perhaps, I used him to tackle something I should have done myself. I should have been able to do *this* on my own, but I hid behind him. I've never been very brave,' she added with a little chuckle.

'I think you're brave,' said Ava.

'Well I think you're brave too, darling,' Flora drawled, patting her on the arm. 'IMHO!' she added. 'That's one of those things like FOMO, isn't it? *In my humble opinion*. See, I'm still young and cool.'

They were all giggling.

'Cheers!' Flora held up her glass and toasted the air before taking a long gulp. 'And you of course, darling Rory. You're very brave.'

'I'm not brave,' he said, 'Not in the least. I only got married because Claire was pregnant.'

Ava scoffed, 'Oh come on, Rory, that's always been such a trite answer. It wasn't just because of that.'

'It was. She told me she was pregnant. I said we had to get married. That was it.'

Ava blew out a breath as if that wasn't it at all.

'What?' Rory asked.

'That wasn't it,' Ava said.

'How do you know?'

'Because you'd been together a year before then. And after she found out about the baby she spent half her time sitting at my kitchen table trying to work out what to do. What *she* wanted to do. It wasn't all based on your command, Rory,' Ava said, going to pick up the sangria jug but finding it empty so standing up to go and get something else to drink.

'I didn't know that,' said Rory, the news making his voice quieter. Wrong again.

'Well,' Ava shrugged, rummaging around in the fridge. 'Sherry?' she said, holding up a bottle of Manzanilla dry sherry.

Flora nodded. 'Glasses are up there,' she pointed to where the small wine glasses hung from hooks.

'I thought she just agreed with me,' Rory said, still flummoxed that there had been any procrastination on his wife's part.

'So it wouldn't have mattered?' Ava asked. 'Anyone could have been pregnant, Rory, any girlfriend you had. You would have just married them, no question?' She looked up while pouring sherry into three glasses. 'Perhaps you would,' she said, shaking her head like she despaired of him.

Flora was watching. 'Rory,' she said, 'what if Claire hadn't been pregnant? Do you think the two of you would still have got married, eventually?'

Rory had asked Claire to marry him because she was pregnant. That was the fact. Plain and simple. Twenty-one, accidentally pregnant. He didn't give time over to wondering if they would have got married if she hadn't been, or what he'd have done if it had been a different girlfriend who had been pregnant. It wasn't in his make-up to think about other potential paths.

He left things like that to alternative therapists and Ava.

He had never given much credence to the fact that they'd been in a fairly decent relationship before Claire got pregnant. Forgotten it to be honest; forgotten that actually she had been here that holiday he'd made the film about the café. That they had flown out together straight from uni. He had failed to remember those quieter moments; the times when he wasn't behind the camera being awed by the larger-than-life Ricardo, but sitting in this bar drinking cold beer with her, trying to make her laugh.

He realised, as he took a sherry from Ava, his fingers damp from the condensation bubbling on the glass, that for ten years he hadn't thought about Claire specifically. She'd been part of a situation. He'd never separated her out.

He imagined Claire's voice: 'Of course I've thought about it, Rory. How could you not have thought about it? I chose *you* because I liked *you,* baby or no baby. I mean, yes, maybe we wouldn't have got married so quickly, I'd have liked a dress that didn't make me look like a giant whale, but I chose *you.*' He imagined her standing with her hands on her hips, exasperated. 'I liked your drive and you were funny. You made me laugh. *But I wouldn't choose you now.*' Rory halted his imagination. Claire had turned bad in his head.

Ava slurped her sherry, then, eyes twinkling, said, 'I mean come on Rory, think about it, ten years is a long time to stay with someone you only married because she was up the duff, you silly idiot.'

Flora guffawed.

Rory raised his brows, turned slowly to see Ava giggling, a little nervous. 'I don't know what you think is so funny,' he said drily. 'As far as I can see you still have commitment issues, FOMO, and a man who won't speak to you because you're addicted to gossip and crass WhatsApp messages.'

Ava snorted into her drink, clearly a little half-cut.

Flora guffawed again and almost fell off her seat.

After a pause, refusing to counter Rory, Ava leant forwards across the bar, big smile on her face, and said to Flora, 'I think you should get together with Everardo.'

Flora flushed tomato red. 'Well luckily,' she said, standing up a little wobbly and going to stack the tapas plates at the end of the bar, 'we're not talking about me, are we?'

Ava grinned, all pleased with herself.

Rory went over to help clear the tapas. 'It's pretty much all gone,' he said, as he removed the plates from their stands. 'Only a few bits of octopus left. Ava, you want it?' He wafted the plate in front of her.

She screwed up her face.

'Oh Ava, it's nice, you should try it,' said Flora.

'No way.' Ava shook her head. 'It has suckers.'

Flora looked at her, disappointed. 'Shame on you, Ava. You should be open to new tastes.'

'And new opinions,' said Rory.

'What new opinions?' Ava asked.

He held his arms wide in disbelief. 'All my suggestions as to why you've never been in a serious relationship.'

'Oh please.' She made a face at him.

'Very grown up,' he said.

They carried on clearing up. Flora was on her way to the kitchen with the plates when she said to Ava, 'You should apologise to Tom, darling. You'll feel better if you do.'

Ava looked down at the floor. 'I know,' she said. 'I know I should.' She started to walk round from behind the bar. 'Maybe I'll go now while I've still got some Dutch courage.'

'He won't be at home,' Flora said, leaning on the counter top.

'No?' Ava frowned.

Flora shook her head.

'Where will he be?' Ava asked, confused.

'I'll tell you what,' Flora said with a cheeky smile. 'You eat the octopus, I'll tell you where Tom is.'

Rory looked over, impressed.

Ava straightened up. 'Flora! You set me up!'

Flora pointed to the octopus.

Outside, the lights from the little fishing boats were bouncing on the choppy water as the evening breeze picked up. The noise of restaurant-goers still at Nino's mixed with the sound of waves tumbling on the sand. The dark sky painted with smears of grey cloud.

Rory watched intrigued as Ava tentatively pronged a bit of octopus on a cocktail stick. He had never seen her publicly put herself out for someone she was in a relationship with. And she wasn't even in a relationship with Tom. He'd never seen her show any level of deep emotion for someone that wasn't their mother or Max. She usually kept things light and funny and glossed over everything with a witty one-liner. He was surprised she was even contemplating it.

Ava turned the octopus over on the stick, examining the suckers. 'This is so unfair.' She looked around, disgusted.

Flora was fiddling with her hair, clearly willing Ava to eat the octopus. 'It really is very good. Very fresh.'

Rory wanted to say, '*Just eat it, for goodness, sake.*' But he didn't. Simply because he himself had just been called out for showing a similar lack of emotional openness for his own wife; he could barely admit that he loved her out loud. And he knew as Ava deliberated, prodding the suckers, her hold on the cocktail stick shaky, her eyes pained, that she wouldn't eat it. That she would walk away. As he would. Because they were too stubborn and it was too open. The motivations too silly, too weak, too vulnerable.

But then, to his disbelief, Ava picked up the octopus and rammed it into her mouth. 'Oh God, it's disgusting, it's disgusting,' she said, her face screwing up, her mouth hardly able to chew, her eyes tight shut.

Rory watched, stunned.

'This is so gross.' Ava was flailing her arms about. 'You can feel the suckers. Yuck, yuck, oh my God, it's all squishy. Eugh. I'm going to be sick.' She chewed and chewed and then swallowed, downed the rest of her sherry in great gulps and said, 'OK,' shaking herself once, 'OK, where is he?'

Rory was baffled. Suddenly uncomfortably ashamed of himself. Would he have eaten it for Claire? He paused. Maybe he would.

Flora stood back, crossed her arms over her chest and smiled, satisfied. 'At the marina,' she said. 'You'll work out which boat.'

CHAPTER 24

Ava hadn't cycled since she was a kid, and even that had just been up and down the pavement listening to the satisfying click of the Spokey Dokeys clipped to her wheels. So she eyed her grandmother's rusting black bone-shaker bicycle with some trepidation. She remembered it from holidays. Val with her shopping in the red beer crate fastened with electrical ties to the rack on the back, a loaf of bread and a bunch of flowers poking out like a commercial for moving abroad. But after years left decaying under tarpaulin at the side of the house, it was barely fit for use.

There was nothing more sobering, Ava discovered, than having to detach mammoth black spiders from a rotting leather seat, grapple with a loose chain, hands covered in sticky oil, and pump perished tyres till they were as fat as sausages, praying the rubber would make it across town to the marina.

She hauled the ancient bike out into the square, conscious of Rory and Flora watching, lounging back in their seats with their sherries, enjoying the sight as she clambered ungainly on to the three-gear bike. Buffeted by the breeze, she wobbled, she twisted, she accidentally rang the bell, she squeezed the brake too hard and pulled up short, her foot slipped on the pedal, her bag swung round in front of her, and when she took one hand off to push it back she swerved and hit a brick wall.

Flora put her head in her hands.

Rory called, 'Maybe this isn't such a good idea. Maybe wait till morning?'

But Ava wasn't giving up now. 'No, I'll be fine.' She took a calming breath. The wind whipped at her hair. The air smelt thick with sweet figs and sea water. She took her bag off and put it in the red crate on the back. Then she tried again. She remembered her dad teaching her, his hand on the back of her seat as he cycled alongside, Rory up ahead. She had no memory of her mother in the scene.

This time she still wobbled, but with more pressure on the pedals she started to move. The front tyre clipped the edge of the path but she righted herself and turned with shaky confidence to wave at Rory and Flora, ringing her bell for fun.

She cycled along the hillside through the gusts of wind and the soupy fog of heat in the direction of the marina, silently praying that, having survived the bus, this wouldn't be the vehicle that finished her off. She'd been to the marina once before with her parents, Rory and her grandmother when she was much younger, seven or so. She remembered they'd had ice cream and looked at the boats. Her mother had walked slightly ahead with her choc-ice, a pale cream coat tied at the waist. She'd suggested a game in which they picked the boat they would have bought if they'd had the money. Rory chose instantly, a canary yellow speedboat with blue go-faster stripes. After much inspection, her mother had settled on a sleek white yacht with tinted windows, the name written in scrolled italics. Ava had watched one of the staff polishing the cabin windows while the owner sipped champagne in a hot tub and had been so awed by the effect it had on her mother that she'd instantly agreed. Her father, she remembered, had taken his time surveying the options, then finally picked a tatty little fishing boat that was mooring to drop its catch off at the flash restaurant. 'That'd be mine,' he'd said, licking his lemonade lolly. 'Oh me too,' Ava had said, immediately swapping, charmed by the cute, brightly coloured old boat. Her mother had sighed. 'Oh you're so humble, Leonard,' she'd said to their father. 'Well you know what, that –' she'd pointed to the super yacht, '– that is what I want. Not that,' she added, pointing to the barnacle-covered fishing boat and stalking off back to the car.

Ava could still remember the feeling of wishing she'd stuck to her mother's choice as she'd stared at the fish flapping and gasping in their buckets. As her grandmother bellowed for their mother to come back and her father said, 'She's just being difficult, let her go.' In Ava's mind it had been disappointment in her change of allegiance that had made her mother walk away. After that she had sided with her forever.

Now, as the marina rose in front of her as she cycled closer, it seemed more likely her mother had just been scouting for trouble. Looking for a way out. A way to justify a hop across the Atlantic to be with her lover and become the star he'd promised he would make her. It was the last holiday they'd had all together.

Ava clattered up to the water's edge, braking by a giant *No Swimming* sign, and scoured the area for a similarly flashy boat to the one her mother had chosen. She was nervous, aware of the awkward apology on the horizon, aware how much she wanted Tom to accept it.

The water was teeming with mega yachts: big gin palaces illuminated with colour-changing lights, cocktail parties in full swing as the boats bobbed and bashed in the sheltered but still choppy water. She wondered which was Tom's as she wheeled her bike along the network of jetties, peering into the sea of white boats, laughter drifting up from soft leather seats, mast ropes clinking in the wind.

'Well well, what do we have here?' said a voice behind her.

'Oh God.' Ava jumped in shock.

Tom walked past her without stopping, carrying a bucket of water, a rope, an anchor and some other boat paraphernalia, his clothes old and well-worn, his cap pulled low on his head yet still somehow exuding the glow of a movie star.

Thrown by his casual disinterest, Ava found herself saying, 'I was just taking a cycle.'

'Oh yeah?' said Tom with a half-laugh, unconvinced. He didn't turn round.

Ava jogged to catch up, the bike rattling alongside. 'Do you need a hand?' she asked.

He stopped and handed her the bucket. The water slopped over their feet. 'Sorry,' he said, completely unapologetic.

'That's fine,' Ava said.

Tom had already walked off.

She followed, hauling the heavy bucket and the bike, the boats beside her clacking like teeth in a crocodile's mouth. 'Which one's yours?' she asked. 'I was trying to guess.'

'Which one did you pick?'

She looked at his back, his washed-out black shorts and equally faded grey T-shirt, his flip flops and cap, and knew immediately his boat wasn't any of her choices.

So instead of pointing to one of the colour-changing mega yachts, she did a really quick scour of the shabbier boats on the dock. 'I went for that one at the end,' she said, relieved to have spotted the small paint-chipped turquoise motorboat with a faded canopy and a red cool box sitting on the bow.

Tom looked to where she pointed. 'Interesting choice,' he said in a tone nicer than she'd been expecting. 'I kind of wish it was mine.'

'Yeah?' she asked, tentative. Like she'd broken through a tiny crack.

'Yeah,' he nodded with a fraction of a smile. 'Damn it. I like that version of me.'

Ava chanced a laugh. 'I actually thought it was that one,' she said, pointing to where the uniformed crew were polishing the mega yacht.

'OK, that makes me feel better.' Tom nodded. 'But still, mine feels a bit schmucky now. I might not be *that* guy,' he said, pointing to the mega yacht, 'but I'm still not *that* guy,' he said, nodding to the little turquoise dinghy.

She laughed more freely. 'I don't even know what you're talking about now. Go on, where's your boat?'

He nodded in front of them. 'Down the end.'

'There are quite a few down the end.'

'The very last one on the right.'

She looked. She could hear the hint of pride in his voice, even though he'd feigned embarrassment.

'Oh wow,' she said, unable not to. She took a few steps forwards, the bucket of water bumping against her legs, the bike pedal scraping her ankle. 'That's stunning.' Glossy wood shone bright like treacle in the moonlight. A thin red stripe ran the length of the amber hull. 'It's like a pirate ship.' Ava looked back at Tom. 'But more glistening and yacht-like.'

'She's alright, isn't she?' he said, walking to the end of the jetty where he dumped all the stuff he was carrying on the ground.

'She's OK, yes,' Ava said, following along behind, one brow raised as if it was the understatement of the year. She put the bucket down next to him and rested her bike against one of the mooring posts.

'Jump on,' he said, pulling the boat level with the jetty.

Ava was about to jump when she paused and said, 'I actually came to say sorry, you know, about the message.'

He half-smiled. 'I know.'

She nodded and stepped on to the bobbing stern. Tom followed, pointing for her to sit on one of the blue cushioned benches that ran either side of the hull in front of the little cabin as he ducked his head and went inside.

Ava perched herself on the edge of the seat, looking around, wondering how she was going to bring up her apology again, and whether Tom would let her. That couldn't be it. It was too awkward to gloss over.

He came out of the cabin with a bottle of brandy and two glasses.

Ava watched him as he sat down on the seat opposite hers. Further away than they might sit as friends. He'd taken off his cap and pushed his hair back with his hands, the salt making it stay off his face. He looked more rugged, weather-beaten, like he'd been out on the water since he'd seen her phone.

'I really am sorry, you know,' she said, launching in as he was about to offer her a drink. He poured anyway. 'It was just stupid WhatsApp stuff, you know what people are like in messages? More uncaring,

I suppose. Trying to be funny. You weren't meant to
see it.'

'So I gathered,' he said, handing her a glass, the
fumes strong, the liquid gold. He swirled his own
brandy round in his glass, elbows resting on his knees,
looking at the floor.

'Oh God, can you just be angry with me?' Ava said,
sliding her drink on to the table.

'I am angry with you.'

'So can I explain and we can move on?'

Tom turned his head to look at her, a strand of
shaggy hair falling over his eye. 'Thing is, Ava, it was
about my daughter, and for you maybe it was funny
but for me, it just made me feel shit.'

'I know, I know, and if someone said that about
Max and Rory, I'd be furious, but if it makes any
difference, the whole chat started before I knew you.
It was all based on you as a famous person who, and
I know this sounds really bad, but who isn't really
real.' She winced at her own explanation. 'Look,
I mean, I didn't have a poster of you on my wall,
whatever Rory says, but I did sleep on your face when
it was on my best friend's pillowcase, for God's sake.
You weren't real when we started messaging about
you. You were a pillowcase,' she said, exasperated.

Tom looked back down at his drink and she thought
maybe she saw the hint of a smile.

She tried to tuck her hair behind her ears but the
curls wouldn't stay. She did it again, holding it back
with her hand. Above her the sail rope tinged against
the mast like a bell ringing. 'OK, not actually a
pillowcase but . . . you know? I would never talk about
you like that now. Well I would because it's gossip and
I like gossip, but I wouldn't let the conversation be

said the way it was said, so you'd just have to get cross with me for gossiping and knowing that your daughter might not be yours but that you still look after her, which is actually really lovely.' Ava bit her lip, mainly to stop herself from talking.

Tom didn't say anything, just looked down at his drink.

'If you have a mother like mine,' Ava went on, 'who to be honest I'm now realising probably wished that we hadn't been hers, to find a person who loves someone regardless is really touching. And I haven't rehearsed this part of it because I've only just thought it. But I think if Louise, she's my friend, knew you a bit, she'd have written something like, *Oh and he still loves her, it's so sweet,* with loads of kitten and heart emojis.' Ava drank her brandy in one big gulp. 'I'm not going to say anything else.'

Tom stood up, fiddled with something on the boat, which Ava presumed was to buy himself some time, then sat down again. She watched his calf muscles, the lines flexing and relaxing.

'It wasn't something I liked reading,' he said.

'No.' She shook her head, her throat still burning from the brandy. 'I'm sorry.'

'I was most annoyed because I was starting to like you,' he said.

Ava swallowed. 'Please still like me.'

He laughed. 'I do still like you.'

She felt a bubble of pleasure rise. She exhaled, shoulders relaxing, not quite aware how tense she'd been until the relief of knowing that he didn't hate her.

'I'm just annoyed with you for being the same as everyone else, I suppose. And usually I wouldn't care.

But for some annoying reason, I care.' He glanced up, eyes almost smiling. 'I blame you for that, by the way.'

'I'm *not* the same as everyone else,' she said, frantically shaking her head, hair going everywhere. 'I promise. Tom, I know what it's like to be in the public eye. I know what's it's like and I hated it. I used to be dressed up like this mini version of my mum and taken round to everything. Every opening, every gala dinner. I'd stand on those bloody red carpets that were always dirty and smelt of damp, with all these stupid cameras everywhere. I hate having my picture taken. I hate it. I hate people looking at me. I hate having to perform. And I don't know if it's because of the pressure or if it was there in me in the first place, but I hate it. And I could never admit it because I didn't dare disappoint her.' She chewed on the inside of her mouth as she thought about what she'd just said. The fact that she'd never said it out loud to another soul, and here she was saying it to a guy she quite fancied, who in the past would have been the last person she'd say it to.

Tom looked across at her. Seemed to see the difficulty she'd had admitting what she'd said. He nodded. 'The thing is, I think it's quite lucky it all stayed out of the press – up till now anyway,' he said, resigned. 'And it wouldn't even be big news any more. What's that bit called in the *Daily Mail*?'

'The sidebar of shame?' Ava offered.

'Yeah,' he laughed. 'We'd be right at the bottom of that. I think the problem is that I spent so many years protecting that right to be her father that it's a shock to see it written down as otherwise. To me she is mine and I don't want the world to know she isn't.'

'I can see that.' She nodded.

He went to top up her brandy.

'Any chance I could have a cup of tea?' Ava asked, beginning to feel a little ill from the effects of sangria, sherry and now brandy.

Tom raised a brow like she was asking a lot for someone who was meant to be grovelling. But he stood up and went downstairs to make her a cup of tea.

Ava leant back against her seat. Tipped her head and looked up at the clouds moving fast through the darkness, like sliding doors across the smattering of stars.

She realised that unlike most of the guys she'd ever dated, she didn't have to remind herself why she liked Tom, remind herself of the list of good points and bad, because she didn't even have to think about it. She was well aware that nothing had actually happened between them, but she liked his presence. She wasn't worried about him as a reflection of her choices because he existed so completely on his own. And maybe the safety of being on holiday meant she didn't have to worry about the best time for it to end before it had even begun. It just was.

The notion made her feel both excited and a little bit sick. A sick that had nothing to do with all the alcohol. Rory's flippant *'fear of being left'* comment was lit up neon in the night sky.

Tom came back out with her tea. 'Sugar?' he asked.

'No thanks.' She took the mug, smile overbright.

Tom narrowed his eyes like he could see her smile was fake. Looked a little puzzled about what had happened while he'd been down in the galley.

Ava wanted to change the subject and said the first thing that came into her head, no thought of decorum or sugar-coating. 'Did you always know she wasn't yours?'

Tom seemed surprised by the bluntness of the question.

Ava didn't shy away. She wondered if she was attempting some kind of strange self-sabotage.

But he wasn't biting, seemed almost relieved to be able to answer, to get it out in the open. 'No,' he said. 'No, I thought she was mine. And conversely, for most of the time I thought she *was* mine I didn't want anything to do with her.' He blew out a breath, sat back against the blue leather seat with his hands on the back of his head.

Ava thought about the Google images she'd scrolled through. From glassy-eyed band-T-shirt Tom holding the baby to bespectacled grown-up walking hand in hand with his kid. 'What changed?'

He smiled. 'My ego, I think.'

The smile made Ava's stomach tighten. It made her want to edge her way along the seat so she was right there next to him. But she didn't. She stayed where she was, sipping her tea.

Tom stood up, went over to the jetty side of the boat to haul in all the boat stuff he'd left on the worn wooden boards. 'I came back from LA having royally messed everything up and pretty well aware that acting was not my vocation, and then suddenly there was this great, funny little girl who made none of the other stuff matter and I really loved being her dad. I wasn't her mother's favourite person because I'd been pretty useless up to that point.' He went to lean the anchor against the side of the cabin and coil up some of the ropes he'd brought on board.

Ava felt guilty for staring at the muscles in his arms as he was telling his heartfelt tale.

'But it was great for a while,' he said, winding the rope from hand to elbow in a neat loop. 'Then Mia met someone else and suddenly denied paternity.' He shook his head. 'Then it was fucking awful. Sorry,' he waved an apology for his language.

Ava put her cup on the table and watched him. She almost didn't want to know this stuff. It was as though he was handing her something that came with the requirement of something in return. A closeness. A friendship. A tethering.

'Did she set you up?' she asked. 'You know, about being the father?'

'Her lawyer claimed it was a genuine mistake, but I, er . . .' He searched for the polite words. 'I find it hard to believe. I was pretty easy pickings at the time – I had a lot of money and zero guidance. She liked being famous and at the time I was. And I had a manager who was more than happy to get a bit of cheap publicity anywhere possible.'

She felt sorry for him. She didn't want to feel sorry for him. She wanted him to remain the cardboard cut-out of himself. It was all much easier if he was just a token famous person and this was just a filmic fling.

'Was it really hard?'

Tom looked up from the rope. 'Yes,' he said, with simple conviction. 'Because she was my kid and I didn't want her not to be. We had this great little relationship. I loved her. I still love her. Then suddenly I've got lawyers on the phone saying none of it's true. It was, I don't know, the worst time of my life,' he offered, before going to lift the bucket of water on board and put it down on the glossy wooden floor.

Then he came to sit next to her in silence. Close.

'Hence why you've axed all stress,' she said.

'Hence why I've axed all stress.' He grinned.

'How did it end?' she asked. 'The case.'

He turned and looked at her. 'Money,' he said. 'And I moved to Spain. I bought the vineyard because I needed something to do, and a little flat in Barcelona so during the week I could walk Lola to school every day.'

'So you moved away from everyone you knew?' Ava asked.

'Yeah,' he nodded. Shrugged like it was no big deal.

Ava laughed. 'You're such a saint.'

He put his hand on his heart. 'Aren't I just.'

He watched her for a second, eyes smiling, satisfied, confident.

Ava tried but couldn't hold the gaze. She looked away. Out past the sleek yachts to the pitch dark water. To cut the tension she asked, 'Can we go for a sail?'

Tom glanced out to sea, a little dubious. 'Now?' he asked.

'Now,' she said.

He laughed. 'OK, why not?' Then jumped up and went over to untie the jetty rope.

CHAPTER 25

Outside the confines of the marina the water was rough. Rougher than Ava had expected. White horses cresting black waves and crashing into the darkness. The clouds had closed over the moon. The distant lights from the restaurants danced like silver snakes in the water.

'Is it safe?' Ava asked.

'Of course it's safe,' said Tom, jumping all over the place to readjust the sail. 'You're with me.'

Ava held on a little tighter to her seat.

When they were finally cruising, Tom sat, hands on the wheel, the wind streaming past them, the boat thwacking up and down on the waves. 'Do you want to come and sit up here?' he asked through the smattering showers of spray.

Ava shook her head.

'Come on,' he called.

She edged her way gingerly to join him.

'Nice, huh?' he said, turning to look at her, the wind blowing their hair and skin like an overzealous shampoo ad.

'Sort of,' she said, clutching on to her seat.

'You want a go?' he asked, pointing to the wheel.

'No thank you,' she said, trying to sound stoic.

He laughed.

The waves danced and licked around them, crashing with almighty bursts of energy, like planes taking off overhead. The boat yawed, the sail billowed like a giant white ghost. Ava thought of whales and sharks sliding through the black water beneath them.

'Shall we go back now?' she said.

Tom looked down at her and laughed again. 'I thought you wanted to sail?'

'I did, but now I don't,' she said, more seriously than she'd meant to, more openly afraid.

Tom paused. 'Are you really scared?'

'Yes,' she said.

He studied her face for a second, then said, 'Hold the wheel,' and went to do whatever it was he did with the sail, the great white ghost screeching and flapping till it was safely away and Tom was back in place next to her. He turned a key and the engine roared to life. They turned in a wide circle and motored slowly back through the tumbling white water, the waves like punches on the side of the hull. He had to shout now they were facing into the wind. 'I didn't think you'd be scared.'

'Why not? This is scary. It's dark. The waves are ginormous.'

'Yeah, but you don't seem the type to scare easily. You slept on your own at the house.'

'I was terrified at the house,' she shouted.

'You still slept there,' he shouted back.

Ava thought about it for a moment. 'That's true,' she said, wondering if, as Flora had said, she was a little braver than she'd thought. It wasn't an adjective she'd have used to describe herself. Brave people didn't hide and she was beginning to fear that she had hidden a little from life; stayed put and edged back when things got serious. But maybe brave was something she was learning how to be.

Then the boat sliced into a massive wave and she screamed.

'Try to enjoy it,' Tom yelled, carving them diagonally through the choppy water.

Ava did some deep breathing in an attempt to relax her muscles, but every time they hit a wave she tensed again, holding on for dear life. 'I think I'm going to be sick,' she said, feeling her face whitening like the sail. She could taste the sangria, the brandy, the octopus . . .

'OK, think about something else,' Tom said. 'Talk to me. Tell me about your job.'

'That's not going to help. I'm going to be sick. I ate octopus for you.'

'I don't know what that means.' He laughed, then saw the serious expression on her face and made himself stop. 'OK, just try and talk about something else. Tell me about your mum. When did she leave?'

'When I was nine. She died of a heart attack when I was eighteen.' Ava held her hand over her mouth. 'This is no good.'

'Carry on. Did you see her at all after she left?' he asked, concentrating on the black abyss in front of them, the sea and the sky merged as one, grinning occasionally when they hit a particularly giant wave, clearly enjoying the choppy night ride but trying hard not to show it.

At this point in the line of questioning, Ava would normally change the subject, but right now she didn't have the wherewithal so she kept it brief. 'Yes. A bit. Oh God, can someone stop these waves?' She inhaled as much as she could but tasted only salt water spray. A great mouthful of sea water. She felt her whole body tense.

'Talk, Ava!' Tom shouted at her.

'We saw her more to begin with. Then not so much.'

'Why not?' He clicked his fingers for more quick-fire answers.

'She moved to New York.' Ava leant forwards with her eyes shut, breathing like she was in labour. She sat up again, tried to swallow down the bile in the back of her throat. All she could taste was octopus.

'And you went to New York? You and Rory?' Tom was watching her.

'Don't look at me. Concentrate on the waves. Rory never came. I'd go with Val. On the plane. Please keep looking at where we're going.'

'That sounds like fun,' he said. She felt as though she'd morphed into his child, his tone cajoling, buoying.

'Yes,' Ava said. 'It was. I loved it. I thought she was amazing. We'd go to all her shows and she'd take us to tea. At The Plaza. Always at The Plaza. People would stop her for autographs. Oh shit . . .' She stood up and vomited octopus and alcohol all down the side of Tom's boat, just as they turned the corner and cruised into the safety of the marina. 'I'm really sorry,' she said, wiping her mouth with a tissue from her pocket.

'It's fine,' he said. 'The water will wash it off. I'm sorry I took you out there.'

Ava sat down on the wood of the stern, lying backwards to stare up at the wisps of grey cloud, her body like it was made of jelly. 'I'm sorry I suggested it,' she said, her voice shaky.

Tom steered them to the mooring. The party-goers on the gin palace whooped as they went past. A couple on a neighbouring yacht waved.

'Bit choppy out there, Thomas,' the man said.

'Yes.' Tom nodded.

'Braver than me.' The man laughed and ducked into his cabin.

Ava rolled her head to look at Tom. 'Just enjoy it?' she said, tone sceptical.

Tom grinned. 'I don't suppose you feel up to grabbing that rope, do you?' he said, pointing towards the jetty.

Ava heaved herself up. 'Not really,' she said, swaying her way to the front of the boat to loop the rope around the mooring post, then sitting down on the leather seats.

Tom came to join her, handing her a bottle of water.

'That was horrendous,' she said, glugging down the water. 'I'm sorry you had to listen to all that about my mother.'

He shrugged. 'It's fine. It's quite interesting hearing it from the other point of view.'

'What does that mean?'

'Well, Val would talk about it quite a lot. About you and Isabel. That was her name, wasn't it? Your mum?'

Ava nodded. Intrigued. Concerned that she'd been talked about. Wanting to know every detail that had been said. Wondering about the nuggets she didn't know. 'What did she say?'

'I don't know,' Tom said, unscrewing the cap of his own water and gulping it down. 'Loads of stuff. I can't remember specifics.'

'Well just have a think,' said Ava, trying to sound nonchalant.

'Alright,' he laughed, holding his hands up as if under fire. He sat back, resting his ankle over his knee as he thought. 'We mainly used to talk about it in relation to me. Not about me personally but about stuff with Lola.' He turned his head to check that she wanted him to go on and Ava nodded, a little too eager. 'Well, it was because I was ready to walk away cos I was so furious with the whole thing. Whereas Val's belief was that a person should have as many people in their lives who love them as possible, and she would cite her daughter as an example, you know, Val making sure that your mum didn't cut herself off from her family. She thought it was really important that she see you and your brother, and clearly it was. And in the same way, she knew Lola's life would be better with all of us in it – getting along,' he paused. 'She actually forced me to see Mia's side, which I don't think I would have done otherwise. It's Val who got us on vague speaking terms.'

Ava looked at him a bit puzzled. 'What do you mean, cut herself off?'

'What do you mean, what do I mean?'

'You said she made sure my mum didn't "cut herself off from her family".'

Tom sat up straight, confused. 'She left, didn't she?'

'Yeah, but we still saw her. I still saw her.'

'Yeah, but I think Val would phone her telling her she had to get her act together,' Tom said, and as he said it Ava saw the moment it dawned on him that he was talking to the daughter in question rather than to some interested bystander. That perhaps this wasn't something to be relayed.

'She *wanted* to see us,' Ava said, a little more quietly than she'd expected. 'She just wasn't very good at keeping in touch.'

'Yes,' Tom nodded. 'Of course she did,' he added, trying to cover his tracks.

'Yes,' Ava agreed. Less convinced than she had been in the past.

She turned to look out over the marina. In the distance music still thumped from the party boat.

A sudden break in the clouds basked them in moonlight. Tom closed his eyes and stretched his arms out along the back of the seat. Ava sat where she was, still, conscious of his arm behind her. The closeness of his hand to her shoulder. The brush of his fingertips. The electricity. The amplification. The sense that her shoulder was suddenly the focus of her whole being. She could hear her heartbeat thrumming like wings in her head, drowning out any thoughts of her mother.

Tom rolled his head her way and opened his eyes. 'I'd probably kiss you now if you hadn't just been sick.'

'That's nice.' Ava tried not to smile.

Tom looked away, across at the party on the boat, a grin on his lips. 'There's a spare toothbrush in the bathroom cabinet.'

'Interesting,' she said.

'I thought so.'

They sat for a few seconds. Champagne popped on the mega yacht.

Then Ava stood up and walked down into the cabin to go and investigate the bathroom.

She blanched at her wind-battered appearance in the mirror, skin pale with the residue of the sailing trip fear and sickness. She splashed cold water on her face to get rid of mascara smears then looked in the bathroom cabinet for a new toothbrush, surprised by how little stuff was in there; she'd expected evidence of vanity, imagined a plethora of men's grooming products, once again resorting back to her Google version of him.

As she stood, cleaning her teeth, looking at herself, she wondered how she'd gone from being hit by a bus to about to snog Thomas King. Her pre-bus self would never have even imagined such a thing.

The thought struck her of how proud her mother would have been of her, mixing with Hollywood royalty. She imagined how it would have felt to walk into The Plaza, Tom's arm around her, the look of pleasure on her mum's face as people stopped to stare.

Ava rested the toothbrush on the side of the sink, unable to shake the image. What was she thinking? Was that what she was doing this for? Because his fame would have made her mother sit up and take note. Hang off his every word, eyes widening when people asked him for an autograph. And in turn she would put her hand on Ava's arm the moment they were alone and congratulate her. Maybe stroke her face and tell her how lovely she was, how happy she hoped she was, then giggle conspiratorially about this gorgeous new boyfriend.

God.

Ava covered her face with her hands. What was she thinking? What was her imagination doing? She was as bad as he'd thought her to be when he'd read the WhatsApp. She *was* the same as all the rest.

Her heart was booming through the tiny bathroom. She held on to the sink and stared into the mirror.

Or are you just making excuses, she asked herself, like Flora and Rory said, for fear of being left?

No. She shook her head.

It wasn't fear of being left. It was a desperate need to impress. As it had always been. A desperate need to be noticed. And Tom fit the bill so perfectly it made her feel a bit sick. Again.

She rinsed her mouth and tried to think of reasons to leave. Excuses she could give to jump on the bone-shaker bike and rattle away.

In the end, when she couldn't come up with a decent excuse – no phone to claim had rung with an emergency – she just walked fast up the cabin steps, out on to the deck and said, 'I'm sorry, I have to go.' And jumping up on to the jetty, before Tom really had a chance to register what was happening, she pedalled off as fast as she could.

CHAPTER 26

Rory couldn't sleep. Too much sangria, he decided as he lay in bed, heat filling the air, bursting the room at the seams. The sheet over his legs as heavy as lead. Max snoring softly in the bed next to him.

He heard Ava come in, clatter around a bit, then when he was certain enough time had passed for her to be asleep, he got up, pulled his jeans on and creaked his way up the dark staircase. He could hear Ava's breathing from the living room, the occasional murmur and a turn on the squashy sofa. Outside it was quiet aside from the occasional gust of wind. The hallway clock ticked monotonously into the blackness.

At the doorway of his grandmother's bedroom he stood for a moment, looking around at the outline of the bed, the wardrobe looming in the shadows, the flicker of a streetlamp through the sides of the blind.

He could hear his own breathing as he crossed the bare floorboards. Felt like a child, nervously trespassing, as his arm reached out to open the door of the little ante-room, to search around for the light switch, to smell the perfume as though she was in there waiting for him.

Then he pulled the cord and the room blazed bright and he felt like an adult again. Almost. His hand touched the collar of one of the jackets. Lifted a cuff. Peered into boxes of handbags and purses. Stilled on the stack of programmes, Isabel Fisher as Carmen in her bright red dress on the front. He perched on the edge of a small set of shelves and looked through every one. Every picture. Every smile. Every dressing-room snap of her face turned, caught, lipstick in hand. Every posed laugh. Every spotlight shot.

He stared through anger. Through frustration. Through pity. Through disappointment. Photos of her holding bouquets, radiant on stage, merged in his head with images of himself as a kid, when he'd spent so long trying to work out how to keep her. Coming home with pictures he'd drawn of the family, as if he could glue her to them with poster paint. Making dinner, learning recipes, while his friends played football. He'd tidy his room, take Ava out when she cried, wash up, dry up, close the curtains when she sighed at the familiar faces of the neighbours, open them again when she cried about the stifling suburban predictability, listen as she screamed in fury about his father, get her a towel as she retched, hysterical, after failing an audition. He would pour her afternoon martini and fetch the matches when she smoked secret cigarettes on the back doorstep. He'd read her bloody reviews out loud when she lay in the darkness. Even, he thought, pausing as the box of letters caught his eye, go to the post office to buy the stamps. The stamps that sent the letters that took her away.

Rory stood staring at the tattered box in front of him. The blue and red chevrons on the airmail envelopes.

'I bought the stamps,' he said to himself softly. Then he kicked the box with his bare foot, the wedged-in letters unmoving. 'Urgh,' he shouted under his breath so as not to wake the whole household. But it wasn't enough. So he smashed his fist into the wall and instantly regretted it.

The pain was unimaginable.

The thin wooden strut snapped on impact, collapsing the shelf that held the boxes of handbags, purses, belts, brooches, so they tumbled down like a jumble sale on to the floor.

'Shit,' he said, voice a loud whisper, sliding down the side of the shelves to the floor, clutching burning knuckles to his chest.

Then, staring at the mess, he stood up and started to ram everything back into the boxes, hating himself for pausing his own frustrations to clear up. Hating that he was so measured he couldn't even feel the thrill of a good wall punch. All the while terrified he'd broken all the bones in his metacarpus.

The pile of programmes had slipped and his mother watched him like the Mona Lisa from her picture on the floor. He left the room and went to get ice from the freezer. Then opened the back door to the veranda and sat with it wrapped in a damp cloth around his hand, the geraniums in pots on the opposite wall craning to see what was going on.

Rory stared out into the dusky night. White clouds in the moonlight stilling as the wind died. He thought about all his errands, all his attempts to please his mother. And they merged almost seamlessly into his life with Claire. The haste with which they'd had to marry never properly acknowledged. Just stride on forwards. Why had he never paused to think: I want this. I choose this. Of course it was something that should have been said. That should have been spoken about. Why had he not realised? Because, with the stubborn rationality of his father, it had simply been something that had to be done.

He thought about his dad, all calm and measured. Did he ever punch walls silently in the night? No. Even now he was stable, traditional. Still calling it the wireless. Shaking his head when Ava said she cried during acupuncture. Still happy to dismiss the entire canon of film and television with a downward turn of his mouth. But kind, Rory thought. His father's saving grace. Always kind to them as children. Kind to them as teenagers. Practical. Patient. But watching from the side lines. The cool observer. All of them butterflies he'd collected.

Rory thought about his own marriage. How much of it he had spent absent with work. Coming and going through their life, dipping in and out. There but not there. A marriage that he filled with things: Audis and loft extensions, bi-fold doors and hot-off-the-press iPhones.

It felt suddenly like all of it was a trick. Too similar to a way of life with his mother that had been proven not to work. A trick to make sure that she stayed. To keep buying, to keep making sure they had more to cover up what they lacked. He was finding it hard to pinpoint the time they spent together, the honesty, the fun. All he could see was Claire loading the dishwasher, Max lost to his laptop, him trying to grab five minutes on his phone. Where was the passion? The now? The I-can't-live-without-this? Where had it gone? Was it ever there? Was he just his father, watching as wings flapped furiously in a jar?

Rory bashed the table, then immediately remembered his injured hand as the pain shot up his arm.

He took a deep breath and exhaled. The scent of jasmine and fig sickeningly sweet in the darkness. The tiles cold under his bare feet. He thought of all the pensioners in the café. Gabriela bashing him with her wooden spoon. Rosa piping churros. The man with the white moustache bantering with the cheating chess players. They didn't have swanky new iPhones and they were much happier than him.

As he sat and thought about it all, the loneliness of dark windows all around him, he wished his father had realised that the responsibility of propping up his mother was too much for him as a kid. Wished that his father had pushed him to go to New York so his memories weren't severed on a whim. Wished that somewhere along the line one of them had ranted and raved and been listened to and understood and wishes had been acted on.

And he wondered if he was just repeating it all. Repeating it now with Claire because he had never confronted it. How do you break a pattern if you've always refused to acknowledge it exists?

He got his phone out and scrolled back and forth through Claire's replies since he'd been there:

Hello. That's a good start.

He held the crappy old Nokia to his chest, his eyes shut.

He breathed in, he breathed out.

Then he opened a new text and wrote, *I have always loved you.*

Then he immediately deleted it because it felt too corny.

Then he typed it again.

Then he sent it.

Then he waited.

But there was no reply. It was four thirty in the morning.

CHAPTER 27

'Aunty Ava, Aunty Ava!'

She woke to a hammering on the living room door. All bleary eyed and no idea where she was, coming up from an abyss of sleep and head sore from sangria, Ava fumbled about with the sheet as Max's little voice shouted through the door, 'Aunty Ava, Aunty Ava, Dad's gone.'

'Oh shit.' She jumped out of bed, stumbling to pull on a pair of shorts, tripping over the glass coffee table, stubbing her toe. 'Hang on, I'm coming,' she shouted, running her hand over her face and through her hair to force herself awake. 'OK,' she said brightly, opening the door to a panicked-looking Max, his eyes already damp with the threat of tears. 'What's this about your dad? Tell me what's happened,' she said, arm round his thin little neck, ushering him inside, sitting him down on the end of the sofa.

Max sniffed, wiping snot away with his sleeve.

Ava pulled out one of the lavender tissues from the box on the coffee table and handed it to him. 'Blow your nose,' she said.

Max blew his nose. 'Dad's missing,' he said, through a torrent of snot.

'He's not in your room?'

'No, and I've called Mum and he sent her a text at four in the morning and now he's not replying and I've been down to the café—'

'You've been down to the café? Without anyone Max, why didn't you wake me up?'

Max looked a little sheepish, then said, 'Because everyone was there.' Ava glanced at the clock, it was nine o'clock already. 'But no one's seen him,' Max carried on. 'He hasn't been for a run because his trainers are still here. He's gone.'

'OK,' said Ava. 'OK, we need a plan. Let me get dressed and we'll go and get something to eat and talk to everyone about where he might be and what we do in this situation. Yes?' she said, looking at Max, who nodded back solemnly.

She thought about the beginning of the holiday, when she could barely be responsible in the face of her brother's authority, and felt quite proud of herself.

'How was your party?' she called from the bathroom as she got dressed.

'Good.' There was a pause. 'A girl called Talia kissed me.'

'Go, Max!' Ava shouted, picturing herself fleeing from Tom's boat and cringing with embarrassment at the prospect of seeing him.

'Yeah, except I really like Selena,' Max said.

Ava laughed. 'You little stud.' She ruffled his hair as she came out into the corridor and grabbed her keys. It made her think that Tom was probably already on to the next one too. An idea that brought less relief than she'd hoped.

The café was a hive of activity when they arrived. The wind had dropped completely and the air hummed thick with heat. Gabriela and Rosa were holding court. A new energy around them like a halo. Less stooped, less old. Rosa's churros queue already snaked out on to the pavement. The walrus-moustache man, who Ava had now learnt was called Gael, was helping dollop thick, glistening chocolate into little pots for dipping, Rosa tipping piping hot churros on to plates quicker than he could keep up.

Flora appeared, whisking past Ava with a tray of pastries. 'You've lost Rory?'

'Seem to have done,' Ava said.

She did a quick scan of the beach and her gaze landed on Tom, sitting out the front, sipping espresso and watching the women go by. Ava rolled her eyes at the cliché of it and looked away. Concentrated on Max's little hand in her own. But when she sneaked another glance she realised it was she who was the cliché. Tom had been reading a book, which he had now laid on the table and was coming over in their direction.

'I hear you can't find Rory,' he said.

Ava shook her head. Nothing mentioned about the previous evening.

'Have you tried calling?' Tom asked.

She hadn't. She hadn't even brought her phone down with her. She'd turned it off after the WhatsApp debacle and put it in a drawer in the kitchen, officially detoxing.

'I'll go and get it' she said, and dashed back to the house.

Standing in the living room with her phone in her hand, she felt strange having the outside world so readily accessible. There were fifty-eight emails from work, Hugo panicking and then emailing back to say that he'd sorted it and not to worry. She felt less pleased than she thought she would that he was finding it hard. On Instagram there were thirty-two likes of her croissant picture and a question about whether one of her friends would like it as a holiday destination. On Facebook there were reams of shared news articles, Monday blues gifs, and interestingly a picture of her ex Jonathon with what looked like a new girlfriend. Mind distracted from Rory for a second, she clicked on the photo. Very pretty. Exactly the kind of person Jonathon should be with. A sweet, kind, smiley person who – she clicked on her profile – worked at a zoo and got into the spirit of things with his rugby friends. And it wasn't that Ava was jealous, because this was a lovely thing to have happened, almost a relief, it was that he had moved on. While she was seemingly in exactly the same place, mentally if not geographically. Still running.

She looked back at the photo. Jonathon taking the selfie of the two of them as they grinned up at the screen, Twickenham stadium behind them. And that was when she saw that her brother had liked it.

Rory Fisher was online.

Ava ran back to the café, breathless by the time she arrived. She held up her phone to Tom. 'He's somewhere with a computer,' she said, hand on her chest as she got her breath back.

Ten minutes later they were pulling up in Tom's Jeep outside a grotty looking internet café in the backstreets of the main town.

'Gig-A-Bites,' Ava said, looking up at the half-lit flashing sign. The words 'INTERNET 24 HOURS' were written on an A4 sheet of paper and sellotaped to the window next to a guy having a fag on the step. She peered in the door. There was her brother. Wearing what looked like his white pyjama T-shirt and jeans, his hair greasy, his neck slumped forwards as he sat, nose close to the screen.

Ava looked down at Max who had come to the window to stand next to her, his eyes all concern. 'He's had a breakdown,' he said.

But Ava shook her head. 'No, I don't think he has.' She pushed the door open. Rory didn't move. The two guys behind the counter looked up. 'I think maybe he's just had a relapse,' she said, trying to sound as confident as she could.

Ava walked up to her brother slowly, like one might an injured animal. Worried that Rory might roar. She pulled over the broken swivel chair from the computer next to his.

'Rory,' Ava said softly.

'Oh Jesus, you gave me the fright of my life.' He spun round, startled.

Ava felt a little foolish for being so tentative. 'What are you doing here?' she asked.

Rory turned to the screen where his Twitter feed was cascading in front of him. 'Look, it's all gone,' he said. 'All of it. Not a #VileRory in sight. They've moved on. That was it. Done.'

Ava looked at the screen. All the #SwanLovesGoose stuff was back to being cute shots of the pair snuggled up in their Tesco trolley.

'And the little bugger's gone and laid an egg.' Rory sighed, then rubbed his face as if trying to keep himself awake.

'Well, it's good that it's gone,' Ava said, glancing back at Max and Tom, watching. 'Isn't it?'

'It's still killed my career,' Rory said, rubbing tired eyes. 'That was all it took. And strangely it's almost a relief. Who'd have thought that?' He laughed. 'You know, I remember Claire reading an article in the *Telegraph* about families upping sticks and heading off on grown-up gap years together. I thought it was complete and utter bullshit. No one's going to quit a perfectly good job for a long holiday, are they? It was just for people who'd been booted out and couldn't get another job. But now, as someone who has, indeed, been booted out, I fear maybe there is more to life. I don't know. I feel like I've completely and utterly ballsed it all up. Everything. I'm so tired,' he added, hands pressed into his eyes. 'And I can't see a way out.'

The guys behind the counter were leaning forwards, one of them talking rapidly in Spanish. Ava wondered if he was translating. She imagined they were doing some whizzy search of Rory's internet history already, piecing together a little story for themselves.

Ava took a breath, tried to think of how best to handle this. 'Well maybe you don't have to see a way out. Maybe you have to look at each different bit and sort them out separately. I don't know, Rory. Maybe the Twitter thing was a good thing, maybe it gave you a shove to realise what you value most. You need to focus on the important bits, and that's you and Max and Claire.'

Behind her she could see Tom trying to coax Max away to play pinball, but he wasn't having it. He was staying put, listening.

Ava rolled her lips together, thinking. Looking from scrawny Max with his worried little freckle-covered face back to completely knackered-looking Rory. Then she said, 'You know, Rory, the other day I realised that I'd never seen you as a lone parent before. Until now. Until this holiday. And I know you think you're just like Dad, but you're not. You're lovely. You're a lovely dad. He was lovely and everything, but in a different way. He was more right-brained,' she said, taking a risk because she had no idea which side meant which.

Rory immediately corrected her, even in his moment of crisis. 'Left-brained,' he said. 'Dad was left-brained. Logical. Rational.'

Ava rolled her eyes. 'Yes, exactly. And as you have just demonstrated, you are that as well. But you're also a really right-brained parent, I think, because I'm not a hundred per cent sure what being right-brained means, but I'm going with that it means you're a natural at it, you're kind and you do what is emotionally right. You think about him in your actions. I've seen it, Rory. Take the film as an example. That was going to be your thing, your challenge, and you gave it to Max. You let him do it because he wanted to and we all know that it's going to be all wobbly and everyone's heads will have been cut off – sorry, Max – but I think that will make it even lovelier.'

Rory snorted a laugh. Max giggled.

'I've watched you, Rory, and you're so lovely with him. Honestly. You haven't blown this. There's still time.'

She saw his shoulders drop as he exhaled. He looked down at the floor, his forehead resting on the heel of his hand.

Ava didn't know what else to say.

Then Max put his little hand forwards and, clutching Rory's shoulder, said, 'I think you're the best dad in the world.'

And that was it. Rory crumbled. 'You do?' he said, trying to hold it together as he looked up at his son. 'I know I haven't been as good as I should be. So honestly, I won't mind if you don't really think that. I won't mind either way.'

Max frowned, a bit puzzled by the comeback. Ava thwacked Rory on the leg. 'He just said you were the best dad in the whole world, for God's sake. Give him a hug, you idiot.'

Rory took hold of Max by the shoulders and squeezed him into a giant hug, surreptitiously trying to wipe away any moisture from his eyes behind Max's back.

The guys at the counter got bored and went back to their screens.

Then Rory opened his eyes and saw Tom. 'Oh God. Hi, Tom. Sorry you've had to witness my idiocy again.'

'Seriously, it's fine. Totally fine.' Tom took a step back, embarrassed that he was intruding in this family moment.

'Come on,' Rory said, standing up slowly like a robot learning to walk, but still managing to resume his natural command. Max gripping his hand. 'Let's get as far away from here as possible.'

Ava stood up. Tom went over and held the door open.

'Did you see Jonathon's got a new girlfriend,' Rory said to Ava as they stepped outside. 'That's good isn't it? A relief.'

'Yes,' she said, pulling on her sunglasses, unable to believe he could still be quite so Rory, even on the verge of meltdown.

Outside the gloom of the internet café, the sky was a sheet of blue, not a cloud in sight. The green of the orange-tree leaves and the pink of the bougainvillea framed against it like a painting.

Max and Rory walked ahead, Rory's legs creaky and stiff, his hand clutching Max's like he might never let go.

Tom lagged back next to Ava, his knuckles grazing hers as they walked through the square, past the bubbling of a fountain tiled white and blue and kids playing football on the sandy path.

'That was good,' Tom said. 'You did that well.'

She turned to look at him, surprised by the compliment, and just caught his eye before he went back to looking straight ahead, almost as if he'd said nothing. 'Thanks,' she said to his profile, quietly proud.

CHAPTER 28

To lighten the mood, Flora was throwing what she had endearingly termed a 'painting party'.

Gabriela, Rosa and all the other grannies were armed with rollers, headscarves and yellow rubber gloves. Ava had always wondered who it was that bought the flowery polyester housecoats for sale at Spanish markets, and now she knew; in front of her was a sea of lurid drip-dry floral. Gael, who was always so impeccable in his suit, was currently up a ladder in jeans and a checked shirt, pencil behind his ear, drilling a hole for a new shelf with Igor.

They'd had another great day of service. People popping in from the beach, intrigued by the wafting scents of garlic frying, their eyes caught by the plates of prawns with long, curling whiskers and sizzling fritters of tiny shrimps. The man with the fish van was now delivering a full order of only the best catch of the day, on pain of his mother's approval. The guys from Nino's had been seen watching suspiciously from their doorway.

And Flora was flourishing with each bill paid and each meal eaten. Hair a little more bouncy, skin a little brighter, even a new bra to make the boobs as bedazzling as they once were. The dishes served were hers, and Café Estrella was no longer the enemy.

'But it can't look like this,' she'd said, waving a hand at the dark blue cave-like walls, the huge bull's head graffiti, the ugly bare interior.

Max was there with the camera, teaching his new BFF, Emilio, how it worked. They were swapping it between the two of them and Ava watched Rory as Emilio filmed the floor rather than Flora, his expression one of fondness rather than flinching annoyance. When he glanced over and caught her looking he did an embarrassed half-shrug, as if trying to excuse his softness. Ava pretended she hadn't seen anything.

Flora was standing in front of everyone holding up a mood board she had made. There were images of little white Spanish villas, orange trees lining the river in Seville, colourful courtyards dotted with terracotta pots, a decaying wrought-iron staircase, the Moorish tiles of the Alhambra, a flamenco dancer in a pink spotty dress. 'This is the effect I'm going for,' said Flora, who'd clearly put a lot of work into her board, all the little pictures carefully trimmed and neatly Pritt-sticked.

'Yes, yes, very nice,' said Gabriela, dismissive, eager to put her roller to use. 'Are we starting?'

'Yes, Gabriela,' Flora sighed, resigned now to this new force in her life. Propping up her beautiful mood board on the bar, she allocated jobs.

Ava was given the outside wall to paint, currently on her own. 'I'm going to need some help, Flora,' she said when everyone got down to work. 'It's a huge wall!'

'Don't worry, darling,' Flora said, unfolding giant, billowing dust-sheets, 'more help's on its way.'

At that point, Everardo pulled up in his van and Ava found herself intrigued at the prospect of spending an evening painting a wall with the beautifully ugly baker, his imposing stoop quite mesmerising as he stalked over to where Flora was taping the dust-sheets to the floor.

But to Ava's disappointment Flora said, 'You're with me, darling,' and ushered Everardo into the kitchen, where Flora had given herself the task of painting over the giant bull's head stencil that her ex had commissioned. 'Don't worry, Ava honey, you just get started,' she added, wafting Ava outside into the dusk, only the string of half-blown outdoor bulbs for company.

Ava stood staring at the dirty, weather-beaten wall. A vast expanse punctuated with two huge double doors. She dipped her brush into the white matt emulsion, watched the thick paint drip into the pot, and made her first gloriously, glaringly white mark.

And the next. And the next.

The brush-stroke monotony, up and down, allowed her mind to drift to thoughts of Rory's meltdown, her own running from Tom, Rory's admission that he wished he'd come with her to New York, Val having to persuade their mother to see them, and pausing finally on her mother's affair with Syd.

It was something she hadn't really allowed herself to acknowledge since they'd found the letters. Something she hadn't really allowed to change the way she thought about and remembered her past. The affair existed as something in the background, like the Hoover going when the TV was on. An annoyance to tune out.

But it wasn't something in the background. It was something that would have impacted the day-to-day narrative in which she'd existed, without her knowing.

It occurred to her that she and Val had never been to her mother's house in New York when they had visited. That she must have been living with Syd. She wondered whose choice it was that she met Ava and Val at The Plaza. Was it her mother, loving the subterfuge still – her secret private life – or Syd's, uninterested in her life before him? In Leonard's children.

'So if I come and paint next to you, are you going to run away?' Tom's voice broke her train of thought and she realised she'd been standing still, brush paused on the small square of wall that she'd painted.

She watched him approach, all calm and cool in old black jeans and a navy T-shirt. Earlier, he'd dropped them off home after the internet café and left them to it, despite Rory's protests that he should come in for a coffee, clearly feeling like a spare part. Things between him and Ava just a little awkward.

'No,' she said. 'I won't run away.'

He picked up a spare brush and started to paint near one set of huge French doors.

Ava went back to the patch she'd already started.

Neither of them spoke until Tom said, 'Well I searched my bathroom last night for reasons that might have made you leave, and the best I could come up with were the little spots of mould in the grouting. They're now on my to-do list.'

Ava looked away to hide her smile.

'I mean, come on,' he said, 'there was nothing in there, right?'

She shook her head. 'No, there was nothing in the bathroom.'

'Right. Good. OK.' He nodded to himself, mystery half-resolved.

They worked in silence again for a while, Ava trying to stop herself from glancing to her left at his profile. The chatter from inside the café like caged birds as the old ladies painted the walls and scrubbed the skirting board. Overhead the last of the sun scraped the top of the treeline, haloing light in radar stripes. The waves rolled gently behind them on the beach.

'So, er . . .' Tom said, distracted, edging his brush along the line of one of the big doors. 'Are you going to tell me why you did leave?'

'No.'

He laughed and carried on with what he was doing.

Ava painted some more. Then she found herself saying, 'Rory and I found all these letters from my mum to her producer. A guy, Syd, who she was apparently having an affair with.'

'Uh-huh,' he said, face taut with concentration as he focused on his neat edge.

After a few more minutes, as the sun danced across them in fading ribbons of light, he added, 'And how does it make you feel? This affair?' He did the final flick of his paintbrush along the doorway and looked up, brow raised.

Ava dunked her brush in the paint. 'I don't know. Stupid, I think.'

Tom paused. 'Why?'

'Because everyone seemed to know except me. Because I have lived forever thinking that she left because of her talent, and actually she just left for this bloke. She wasn't this great star that I thought she was. Or she was, but it wasn't for the reasons I thought it was. Oh I don't know.'

Tom glanced down at her brush. 'Try not to get drips on the ground.'

'I'm not!' she said, defensive.

He smiled, face angled back towards the door. She could feel him breathing next to her, concentrating on his next perfect line along the bottom of the wall.

She could see the muscles in his back through his T-shirt, the flex of his arm, the line of his tan.

The wind blew and rustled the leaves of the fig tree, making the air sweet in the last of the sun.

Ava shook her head and went back to her patch of wall. 'Aren't you going to say something?'

'I'm thinking,' he said, kneeling on the floor, eyes still concentrating on his painting. Then he paused and sat up, brush resting on the side of the can. 'I'd have thought maybe it wasn't such a bad thing to have found out.'

'Really?'

'Well,' he shrugged, 'surely it makes her more human. Isn't that quite a relief?'

Ava frowned and went back to her wall. The white lines fat and glossy. She blew a frantic little spider out of the way so he didn't get smothered. Was it a relief? 'I suppose I just don't know what was real. I feel like it changes all my memories. I feel like if she was weaker than I thought she was and I spent so long trying to impress her, where does that leave all those things? I don't know. Let's just paint.' She swirled her brush in the can.

Tom was watching her. Ava looked away at the spots of paint she'd dripped on the ground and tried to wipe them away with her flip flop.

'Ava, your life and her opinion of you have to be separate.'

'I know,' she nodded. 'It's just easier said than done.'

She looked across at him and smiled, and realised for the first time that she didn't see the chocolate-box perfect face as it had been on Louise's pillowcase, she saw just a face, a friend with familiar blue eyes with a few lines of green, a mouth calm and serious, and a groove between his eyebrows that she knew when relaxed was white from lack of suntan.

The door opened, bashing Tom hard on the back. 'Ow!' He turned to see who had thwacked him.

'There is more talking than painting going on out here!' Gabriela was craning her neck round the door.

'You're all chatting inside,' Ava said, her argument voided by Gabriela's unimpressed inspection of her wall.

'And we've got half the place done!' Gabriela said, incredulous. 'If you flirt less and paint more, so would you too,' she drawled, before slamming the door shut.

'Gabriela!' Ava felt herself blush.

Tom was loading up his brush, a smile playing on his lips.

Ava glanced inside and saw Gabriela and all her friends, heads together, giggling.

'She's unbelievable,' said Ava, shaking her head, doing big sweeping strokes with her brush, embarrassed, aware, awkward.

Tom stood up, leaned against the doorframe. 'Come on then, tell me why you left last night.'

Ava paused. She bit her lip, a little sheepish, and could barely meet his eye. 'Because I worried maybe I was with you to impress my mum.'

'Jesus Christ!' Tom laughed in disbelief. 'Are you kidding me?'

She shook her head.

'OK, look Ava, I like you. More than most people I meet, actually. But that's beside the point. It was just gonna be a kiss. You didn't really even have to think about it,' he said, hand pushing his hair back, eyes still laughing.

'No,' she said. 'I know.'

'Do you want to kiss me?' he asked.

She nodded. Without even thinking about it. 'Yes.'

'Right,' he said, and laying their paintbrushes down, he took her hand and led her across the café terrace, over the little path and round the back of the giant leaning fig tree, walking with purpose towards the crumbling wall.

The sun had completely set, leaving just a last shiver of white on the horizon, the branches of the fig twisted in the darkness, the leaves flapping like washing on a line. The collapsing wall bowed under wooden supports, prickly pears and scrubby cactuses growing in the gaps holding the bricks in place.

Ava was frantically checking behind her to make sure no one was watching. Her mouth was taut with excitement, her hands shaking a little, her brain whirring with expectation.

Once in the shadow of the tree, Tom stopped and she careered into him as he turned. Holding her steady with one hand, he leant down and kissed her. Full square on the lips. Smelling of warmth and sun and lighting every synapse in her body that had been on edge, waiting for this moment. She felt herself relax, her shoulders drop, her hands reach up to touch his shoulders, feel the seams of his T-shirt under her palms, the press of his mouth on hers, the clash of their teeth and the sweet heady scent of the fig. And she didn't think once about her mother or The Plaza. The only thought she allowed was a fleeting whisper of a giggle back to her teenage self as she slept soundly on her Thomas King pillowcase.

'Where is everyone?' she heard Flora shout, words cutting through the darkness. 'Ava, Tom? Where have you gone?'

It was all broken too soon. They'd had merely seconds.

'Guys, we're breaking for drinks,' Flora shouted into the nothingness. 'Is that you? What are you doing over there? Is there something wrong with the tree?'

Tom sighed, his arm tightening around Ava's back for a moment before letting her go. 'No,' he shouted, walking back towards the path. 'Nothing wrong with the tree.'

Ava tried to follow all relaxed and as if nothing at all had happened, but she saw the moment of recognition on Flora's face. The intake of breath, then the half-laugh, then, 'Sorry, sorry, I just, urm . . .'

Tom shook his head, pausing to wait for Ava to catch up. 'All totally fine. What are we drinking?'

CHAPTER 29

The drinks had an adverse effect on the painting. Especially when Igor mixed another jug of his infamous super-strength sangria. Gabriela wheeled her pug home to get some music and came back with a whole heap of old flamenco CDs. It transpired that she had been quite the dancer in her younger years and hadn't lost the knack – she even produced a well-worn pair of castanets from her bag and took centre stage with Gael, clearly much more relaxed in his casualwear, dancing with loud, confident claps and energetic foot stomping. At one point Gabriela leaned over the table they were all sitting at and snarled passionately, 'You see? *This* is *el duende*! Now get up here, you useless lot,' and hauled Ava and Tom on to the dance floor.

Max and Emilio giggled into their Coca-Colas. Ava escaped Gabriela's grasp for enough time to whisper something in Flora's ear before she was dragged back again. Flora shook her head. Ava made big eyes at her. Then a few minutes later, Flora stood up, brushed down her paint-splattered old sundress, patted her hair into place and asked Everardo to dance. Everardo, clearly not a dancer, went bright red and refused, so Flora sat down again.

Ava made a sad face and decided that Everardo's shyness was from a lack of dancers on the floor, so beckoned Max and Emilio to their feet along with all the other nattering grannies, while Igor did a marvellous peacocking flamenco with a clearly disappointed Flora.

The room bellowed with haunting melody and bewildered laughter. Rory watched it all from the bar, the camera next to him moving between Gabriela and Gael's majestic dancing and Max and Emilio's exaggerated impressions and wild, crazy twirling and whirling. It was the perfect excuse to stay on the sidelines with his beer.

He watched Ava's matchmaking at work. The floor now busy enough for her to chance Everardo's hand. To introduce herself and refuse to take no for an answer on the question of dancing, cajoling him up next to her. Pointing to Tom who was equally at sea. A quick grab of Flora's hand to make her turn and see Everardo standing, shyly unsure. Rory watched the subtle shift that swapped Ava for Flora. Saw Everardo's hand as it settled self-consciously on Flora's back. Saw Ava step away grinning then be swept round by Tom, and for a moment, in the loud, raucous chaos of it all, he saw her look of complete unadulterated pleasure, and with it a shock of the same effortless magnetism that he remembered from his mother. That made her seem, when she chose to turn it on, larger than life. And in the rare moments he'd glimpsed it in his mum, he had basked in the radiance. Those were the moments he had lived for as a kid.

The party drifted on till the early hours of the morning. Out in the bay, fishing boats tempted curious little anchovies with their bright lights hovering over the water. At dawn the sky started to soften. Max and Emilio fell asleep on pushed-together chairs, and someone, Tom probably, suggested a swim while

Gabriela called for a pedalo. And suddenly, like a herd of stampeding cows, the room cleared as Gabriela, Rosa and Gael led the way to the sea. Fully clothed, they splashed their way into the water, laughing, dripping, soaked to their knees. Gael and Tom pushed a great yellow pedalo out through the sand then helped Gabriela, Rosa and their friends aboard. Flora went in to her waist, skirt billowing in the water like a giant squid, while Everardo floated on his back. Igor had a cigarette in the shallows. Ava and Tom pushed out a paddleboard that they now sat astride, facing one another, chatting quietly, laughing, occasionally steering themselves with the paddle when they got too close to a moored boat.

Rory watched from atop a stack of padlocked sun loungers. His hands behind his head, his body clock all over the place, wide awake from an afternoon spent sleeping off his previous all-nighter.

The rising sun glistened on the water. Behind him the garbage van arrived and left. Someone tipped water on to the pavement. A tiny shoal of fish jumped, but Rory didn't see because his eye had been caught by a figure walking towards him over the sand.

He squinted. It looked like her.

He scrabbled to sit up like an overeager dog and nearly fell off the stack of loungers as she got closer.

'Well, this certainly looks like an emergency,' his wife said, depositing her bag on the sand and pulling off her sunglasses as she stopped next to him.

'Claire? You're here,' Rory said, standing up, straightening his T-shirt, trying to smooth his hair down with his hand.

'I am, Rory,' she said, head cocked, expression a little weary. 'I was told by my son that you'd gone missing.'

'Shit.' Rory put his hand over his mouth. 'Sorry.'

'Yes,' she said, sardonic, looking out at the frolics and fun on the water. 'Don't worry, Ava told me she'd found you. But I thought I should probably come and see what was going on for myself.'

Rory nodded. Felt a little foolish. Like he'd proved he couldn't cope on his own.

Then he looked at her properly, barefoot in the sand, her blue jeans rolled up, sweater round her waist, vest top a little skew-whiff, make-up mostly rubbed away. Underneath the bravado she looked tired and worried.

'Have you come straight from work?' he asked.

'Almost. The earliest flight was midnight. So enough time to chuck some stuff in a bag. I now know who shops at the airport,' she said, holding up her tote stuffed with plastic carrier bags. 'People whose husbands have absconded to internet cafés.'

Rory smiled.

She glanced at the sea then back to him, expression uncertain.

It all felt very polite. Like two acquaintances unsure what to say next.

Rory remembered all his promises to be more open. But in the flesh it was hard.

She tipped her head to one side and studied him.

Rory swallowed, looked down at his tanned toes in the sand. 'Welcome to Spain,' he said in the end, unable to jump the last hurdle, feeling himself close in like a tortoise into its shell.

So it was lucky, he realised, that he had been with Claire for ten years. That she had been in control when she married him. That she knew him better than he knew himself, because she gave him a small punch on the shoulder and then dragged him into a hug. 'Rory Fisher, what am I going to do with you, you complete and utter idiot!'

Rory felt like chocolate melting into her. 'I'm so sorry,' he said into the tendrils of hair that had fallen loose around her neck, smelling the Chanel and the flash shampoo that she'd obviously restocked while he was away, the warmth of her skin. 'I'm so, so sorry.'

She held on a little tighter then pushed him away. 'Let's sit down.'

They sat side by side, cross-legged in the sand.

In the distance the pedalo was heading out to the horizon. Ava and Tom were paddling into shore. He knew that Ava had clocked Claire's arrival but was leaving them to it, hauling the board on to the sand and sitting down in the shallows.

Rory wondered if it was possible for a brain to explode, his packed to bursting with stuff he wanted to tell his wife, yet he seemed unable to say any of it.

'How was the job interview?' he asked.

Claire buried her bare feet in the sand. 'Terrible. They've given it to a twelve-year-old from digital marketing.'

'Oh.'

'Yeah.' She looked at him, disappointed. 'I knew when I walked in I hadn't got it. I got really nervous and messed up my presentation. You'd have been rolling your eyes.'

Rory thought about how previously he would have asked her what went wrong, whether she'd looked at the brief from the right angle, suggested that perhaps the twelve-year-old from the digital marketing department had offered something fresher, and perhaps she should ask for an interview debrief. Instead he said, 'They're arseholes. The interview should have been a formality. You had the most experience.'

Claire looked at him, surprised. Then she laughed. 'I *did* have the most experience. They *are* arseholes.'

Rory buried his feet next to hers. It felt nice to be on the same side.

'I'm sorry about the job,' he said.

'It's OK. Maybe I'll get it in another ten years.'

'Or maybe you should quit and we should come and live here,' Rory said, realising as he said it quite how serious he was.

'Rory, we're not going to move to Spain.'

'You said you'd love to.'

'When?'

'At home, when you were doing the washing up.'

She gave him a look like that was just dreaming.

'Well why not?' he said. 'We've done everything the world has wanted of us corporately. We've done everything the way we were meant to do it. Maybe now we should do it the way we're not meant to do it?' He ran his hand over his face. 'I don't know.'

But Claire was intrigued. 'What would we do?' she asked, tentative, as if not wanting to scare off this new side of Rory.

'I don't know. Honestly, it's a whim. Maybe you could freelance, set up some cool little magazine. Anything. Nothing.' He chucked a handful of sand in the air. Ahead of them the watersports pontoon bobbed on its barrel floats, the skis and paddleboards neatly racked, the lifejackets dripping from their hooks on the wall. 'We could rent the house out, live off that for a bit. Ava's airbnb person is paying her rent. Who'd have thought Ava would sort stuff like that out . . .

We could do that. Let someone else pay the mortgage. Even just for six months. A year. Live off our house.'

'This isn't what I was expecting you to say at all.'

Rory shrugged a shoulder. 'What can I say, I've changed,' he said drily. 'I've watched Max here and he's like a different kid. You know he's been waterskiing every day, he's learning how to drop a ski – he says this, I don't really know what it means, but it sounds good.'

'It does sound good. Not really like Max.'

'No. Not a laptop in sight. If you'd asked me a month ago I'd have said good school first and foremost. That's all that matters. But I went to a good school and I'm looking at my kid out the window, envious.' Rory slung his arms over his knees. After a pause he said, 'I've started cooking, in the café.'

'Really?' Claire smiled down at the sand.

Rory studied the familiarity of her profile. Thought how reassuring it was to have it in his life again. To understand so minutely another person's expressions. 'You knew that, didn't you?'

She nodded. 'Ava's been keeping me updated.'

'She was meant to be digital detoxing.'

'She was. She'd ring me from the café.'

Rory stared out to where Ava was splashing her legs up and down like a synchronised swimmer in the rippling waves. He was quite taken aback at the idea of these two women looking out for him.

'So go on then, tell me what happened this morning,' Claire said, and Rory suddenly found he had the words to explain everything. Everything he felt about their life together, their marriage, about his mother, his father, about his realisation that he had packed their marriage full of things rather than ever telling her what he felt. Then at the end he said, 'And the weirdest thing this morning, Max touched me on the shoulder and said that I was the best dad in the world, and normally I'd think it was because he wanted an ice cream, but in that moment the relief . . .' He puffed out his cheeks. 'It was like you wouldn't believe.'

Rory put his face in his hands for a second then looked up at the view with a deep exhale, as though the air would never stop. Ahead of him the sun was just rising, like a huge fat orange pushing up out of the water. The pedaloers had stopped to stare.

He nudged Claire to watch as well, then studied her profile instead of looking back. Eyeliner slightly smudged, eye shadow faded from the day, she looked beautiful.

'Do you think we're OK?' he asked. 'I know I'm not the best husband in the world but we'll be OK, won't we?'

Claire picked up a handful of sand and let it trickle through her fingers. 'Some things will have to change, you know that, yes?'

Rory nodded.

'You can't be away as much as you have been.'

'No.'

'You can't be on your phone all the time. People only need to read the news once a day, you know?'

He nodded again. 'Yeah, I know,' he laughed. Then he bit down on the corner of his lip as he traced a pattern with his finger in the sand. 'Do you think I'm running away?'

Claire sighed. 'No, Rory, I think you're having a break. A rest. For goodness' sake, go back in five years if you still want to, when this will all just be seen as funny – if it's remembered at all. You can tell people how much you've grown as a result in interviews.' She stared at him matter-of-fact and he nodded. 'But you have to stop trying to get that bloody BAFTA. Because you don't even want it, I don't think. You just think your dad will like it, which he won't. He'll think it's garish.'

Rory snorted a laugh. 'He *will* think it's garish.'

'And you have to accept that you and I are different from your mum and dad.'

Rory buried his toes deeper in the sand. 'Yes,' he said.

'No,' Claire shook her head. 'Don't just say "yes" like that. Believe it.'

Rory swallowed. He stretched his legs out and looked up at the sky.

Claire said, 'I'm not your mum and you are not your dad.'

Rory closed his eyes, coloured jellyfish of light playing on his lids. He breathed out. Feeling like his body was a fraction less heavy. He opened his eyes. The sun had risen, blasting the sky with yellow.

He turned to look at Claire. 'I know I'm not him. And I know you're not her.'

She smiled. 'And that's OK.'

Rory nodded. 'And that's OK.'

Claire shuffled closer to him in the sand. 'We're our own family, Rory, and we'll do it our way. We can buy things, we can not buy things. We can live here, we can live at home. We just have to be. And we have to do that together. I chose you then, Rory, and I choose you now.'

Rory nodded again, turning back to look at the view of the Summerhouse, at the pine trees and the walkers coming round the headland. And then up to the acres and acres of sky. Blue as far as he could see. It felt like the lid had been lifted off the world.

'If you're a dick, I'll leave you,' Claire added. 'But only then.'

Rory laughed and wiggled his toes across so they met hers under the sand. Claire leant over and rested her head on his shoulder. And into the softness of her hair, Rory said, 'I choose you, too.'

CHAPTER 30

Claire's arrival marked a new order in things. A sense of routine, like the wind had changed and everything had settled. They'd all been floating around a little lost, but were now tethered into place.

The next morning, Ava woke up after the best night's sleep of her life to find Tom wrapped in a sheet like a Roman, sprawled at one end of the sofa, and Claire, feet up on the coffee table, sitting opposite him and finding out all the behind the scenes gossip on *Love-Struck High*.

Getting over the shock of them both being there, Ava remembered. She remembered why she had slept so well. Why she had drifted into a nothingness of contentment as he lifted her bare feet up to rest them on his sheet-clad thighs.

Max burst in to sit with his mum, giggling when he looked at Ava and Tom covered only by sheets, doing fake kissing faces when Ava was the only one looking, to which she mouthed the word 'Selena', which shut him up because he didn't want her telling his mum and dad who he fancied.

Rory came back, sweaty from his run, stuck his head into the living room, snorted a laugh at the fact that Ava had slept with Tom and said, 'Five minutes, everyone, café won't paint itself.'

It took two more days of renovations. Claire took over managing the interior design aspect, softening some of the glaring whiteness of Flora's mood board. Suggesting a pale yellow for the far wall and bringing the outside in with a new lemon tree and an old gnarled olive in a terracotta pot that sat in the corner like a baby elephant bedecked in fairy lights. She also panelled over Ricardo's ghastly spotlit bar with big mirror tiles, and almost immediately on entering the bar ordered Gael and Rory to haul up the black rubber floor. Beneath it, to Flora's amazement, were nearly perfect original Spanish tiles that both Rosa and Gabriela suddenly remembered existed and couldn't believe the travesty of covering them up. All their polyester-housecoat-wearing friends took to the task of polishing them up till the floor glowed in intricate patterns of turquoise, red and white.

It was on the second day that Claire asked Ava how much of her grandmother's stuff she was keeping. 'Only sentimental stuff,' Ava said, 'I've started making a pile over there.'

'Not these pictures?' Claire asked.

Ava shook her head.

'Those ornaments?'

Ava made a face.

'Mirrors?'

'No. Why?'

'Can you help me carry them to the café?'

Ava had to stifle a laugh. 'Flora won't be happy.'

'She'll just have to trust me. In the end she'll realise I'm right,' Claire said. And not for the first time Ava understood why she was the perfect woman for her brother.

Flora's jaw dropped when she saw all of Val's junk headed her way. 'No thank you,' she called. 'Not in here.'

Claire just laughed, arms laden with pictures and lamps and a little statue of a poodle. 'I promise, if you don't like it, you can throw it all in the bin.'

The heavy gilt mirror was hung on the wall opposite the bar, above Flora's little table, next to which was placed a black lacquered art deco standard lamp. The painting of the girl with the rose and four others made a higgledy collection on the yellow wall around the kitchen hatch. The little poodle was given a spot guarding the bar, while two big gold candelabras were screwed to the wall on either side of the optics. Each table now had a little antique vase or jug with a sprig of bougainvillea, and some of the more bonkers little ornaments peered secretly out of the orange tree pots – there to be discovered if somebody looked.

The morning of the third day, a man came to replace the awning with a new buttercup yellow one with Café Estrella printed along the front. Rory took his place in the kitchen, sous to the self-appointed head chef Gabriela. Flora took to sashaying about front of house, loving her new space, her freshly painted walls, her little lemon tree, her scrubbed tile floor and most of all her customers, chatting them up with her old *joie de vivre*.

Claire took a satisfied break and spent the rest of her family-emergency time off work sitting at Café Estrella, admiring her interior design skills and sampling her husband's cooking while hiding from the aching heat, or lying under a sun umbrella reading a book. She spent the occasional evening waiting tables in the café, her I-haven't-done-this-since-I-was-sixteen enthusiasm as yet unbroken, or sipping sangria, becoming the type of regular that people sat and told their life story to.

Tom and Ava packed up the house together, dressed in the fewest clothes they could decently wear but still ending the day damp from the cloying, sweaty heat. They packed everything, shoes boxed up and coats folded into bags, photographs removed from frames, papers shredded. Ava realised that the lonely, grey fear that had stopped her when she first arrived was nowhere to be found. Dissipating with another heartbeat to share the job with.

All while Max perfected his mono-skiing and his tan.

It felt like they could live like this forever. Tom and Ava sleeping crammed on the hot velvet sofa, even while there was a huge house up the road that was his. They were a gang. No one wanted to leave.

CHAPTER 31

One morning Ava was returning to the house, trying to balance two take-away espressos and a little cardboard tray of churros, when the front door flew open.

'The grapes are ready,' Tom shouted, racing down the path. 'The grapes are ready,' he said when he got level, holding her shoulders, his whole face grinning. Taking his coffee and a bite of rapidly cooling churro, he added, 'You wanna pick?'

Ava nodded, bemused, the energy and the great white smile infectious.

'Right,' he said, clapping his hands together, almost shaky with excitement, 'let's go and round up the troops.'

The regulars were all crammed into one corner of the café, gnarled hands slicing pastries as they eyed the tourists and beach-goers who now occupied the rest of the space with contempt; on the one hand pleased for Flora, Gabriela and Rosa and thrilled with the addition of the churros, on the other wanting their sprawling breakfast to return. Almost in rebellion, the chess players had edged themselves on to the path, bringing their own little stools and fold-out table. The sun was already burning scalps. The sand frying like it was in the pan. But the old men didn't seem to notice, perched in the dappled shade of an orange tree, hats and waistcoats on.

Claire, Rory and Max were sitting at a round table at the front of the café, all tanned and tousled. Max had been for a ski and insisted that Claire sit in the back of the speedboat videoing his achievements. He was watching himself on playback as he munched through an oil-dripping plate of *pan con tomate*.

Tom strode into the centre of the concourse and bellowed, 'The grapes are ready.'

The tourists glanced over in bemusement.

The regulars stood immediately from their chairs, pastries left half-eaten. The chess players paused mid-checkmate, all of them rising as one.

'They can't be,' Gabriela's hand stilled on the chocolate pot she was filling, 'it's too early.'

Tom pointed to the burning sun. 'It's the heatwave. They're ready.'

Rosa stopped the churros machine. Igor wiped his hands on a tea towel and started to take his apron off.

'I'll make some calls,' said Gabriela, moving towards Flora's café phone.

'Hang on,' said Flora, a tray packed with pastries and juice in her hands, 'you can't all go. It's not like last year. We have customers . . .' She nodded to the heaving forecourt.

Ava watched with interest, unable to believe anyone would want to pick grapes in this heat. She glanced at her brother who looked equally flummoxed.

'You lot coming?' Tom called over to Rory, Max and Claire. 'You get paid in wine,' he said, and suddenly everyone's enthusiasm seemed viable.

'What about me?' Max asked. 'I don't like wine.'

'You I'll pay in cash,' Tom said.

'OK.' Max was on his feet in a second. Waterskiing was a costly hobby.

In the café Flora was trying to pin down her team. She and Rosa would stay until breakfast finished, at which point Igor and Gabriela would return and swap with Rosa. Igor was not happy about missing the evening's picking, while Ava couldn't believe they would still be working that late. Flora made out like she was being really hard done by, but in the end said, 'OK Igor, I'll give Everardo a call, see if he can help me this afternoon,' and sashayed off, clearly quite delighted with the excuse.

'OK team!' Tom rubbed his hands together, standing on the step of his tractor, face lit up with excitement, cap pulled low.

It was no more than half an hour after the first call had been given for the grapes, and amassed in the searing heat of the vineyard were maybe forty people. Along with all the regulars from the café, Ava recognised some of the faces in the group from her grandmother's funeral; there was a similar low buzz of nattering gossip, phone calls, handshakes and cigar smoking.

'First rule: be gentle with the grapes,' Tom shouted above the chatter, voice serious. 'Hands are kinder than machines, remember that.'

The group nodded as one. Ava looked dubious as she felt the sun scorch the back of her neck. Beside her Rory was nodding eagerly. She glanced at him in his running shorts, hair almost completely blond, skin gold, arm slung over Claire's shoulders, hand on Max's head. She remembered after the funeral saying that there was still time to ace his life. He seemed almost unrecognisable from that person; the thing about Rory was that, consciously or not, he could never turn down a challenge.

Up ahead, Tom introduced a huge bear-like man with a black bushy beard and the palest blue eyes

Ava had ever seen: Matías, the vineyard manager. While Tom rattled through the rest of the instructions, Matías wove his way through the crowd handing out bottles of water, pairs of little secateurs and head torches. Ava snorted at the head torch; surely it was wishful thinking to believe this lot would be here past sunset. She gazed over at the rows of grapes. It wasn't a massive vineyard. She reckoned they'd be home by cocktail hour.

CHAPTER 32

'How are you doing, Ava?' Tom asked, as she tipped her bucket of grapes into the back of the tractor. The sun was unrelenting. Bees buzzing on the crates of fruit.

'I'm dying,' she said, without looking up past the brim of her hat. Face pink, muscles burning, brain screaming as she trudged back to her row of vines.

She heard Tom's chuckle as he drove away, top off, hair slick with sweat, tractor bumping over the rough terrain beneath him.

It was two o'clock. The air was sticky with heat and mosquitos. Ava's back felt like she was hefting a gorilla around, her posture now more comfortable when stooped. And she had never realised the relationship one could form with one's water bottle. It was a thing of reverence. When she dropped it once and it started to roll away down the hillside she almost cried. Rory had stopped it with his foot.

No one complained though. Every person Ava reached, she was ready for a good old bitch about how horrendous the process was, to show them how cut and swollen her hands were, the scratches on her arms, to moan about the stickiness of the grapes or the annoyance of the bees. But no one was biting. Rosa and her pals just seemed to glide from one vine to the next, gossiping without seeming to pause for breath. Their chat as constant as the cicada hum.

Rory had said the word 'invigorated' more than once. Ava was almost wishing the old Rory back. Max was barely pausing to wipe the sweat off his brow; spurred on by the promise of cold hard cash, he and Emilio were practically racing up the aisles.

Claire was the only one to nod sympathetically when Ava showed her the trail of mosquito bites on her leg. But then she'd shown her own leg and seemed to have a million more, yet remained uncomplaining. Ava had sloped away.

She stopped at the furthest point of the vineyard with her black bucket on the floor beside her. Bees buzzing by her hands. She was hot and tired and everything hurt and she was not enjoying herself. She took a moment to sit down on a rock. The sun chuckled overhead. Sweat streamed down her temples. She looked up to see Tom striding towards her, T-shirt slung over his shoulder, cap stuffed in his pocket, boots half-undone and shorts covered in grape juice.

She didn't want to see him. She didn't have the energy to pretend she was enjoying herself.

'That doesn't look like working,' he shouted, teeth sparkling as he grinned.

Ava shielded her eyes with her hands. 'I'm slacking,' she shouted back. 'Go away.'

He came closer. She could see him trying not to pity-laugh.

When his shadow blocked the sun she shuffled over so he could share her rock. They sat together for a moment, Ava pretending to enjoy the view as Tom gulped from his water bottle.

'You need any more water?' he asked, wiping his mouth with the back of his hand.

She shook her head. 'No thanks, I'm fine.'

He nodded, drank some more.

'I don't think I get it,' Ava said, ashamed of her failure, scratching the bites that dotted her legs.

'No?' he said.

She dabbed the corners of her eyes. She was so tired. 'No.'

He frowned, his forehead crinkling in lines, his expression perplexed. 'That's OK. It's definitely not something to cry about,' he said, handing her his T-shirt in lieu of a tissue.

'I'm not crying,' she sniffed, wiping her eyes, smelling his sweat and soap and suntan lotion.

'Just have a break. Enjoy the view.' He pointed towards the light catching on the leaves and the twisted trunks, the big stone house, the acres of fir trees in the distance, the epic blue sky.

Ava nodded. Then after a second or so of watching everyone hard at work, she said, 'I can't look at any more vines.'

'Well look the other way,' he said, pointing between a couple of old almond trees at the sea.

From this vantage point it looked like the land just dropped into the sea, the cliff edge within walking distance, seabirds floating lazily on the warm air, in the far distance white boats cut through glassy water like models on a boating lake.

'That is better,' she said.

Tom tipped his head. 'I'm glad you approve.'

They sat side by side until Matías called him back; there was a problem with the tractor. Tom waved a hand to say he'd be there in two seconds. He stood up and slicked his hair back, pulling his cap on. He drank the last of his water before saying, 'Ava, this isn't a test, you know. You don't have to like it because I like it.

I don't care if you like it. Go back if you want, Flora's there. Go and have some sherry.' He looked down at her, his smile splitting his face in two, eyes eager with his absolute love for what he was doing. Backing away a couple of paces he added, 'I'm not crazy about antiques. Call it even.' Then with a wink he strode off, hand tapping the occasional vine leaf, back to where the tractor needed seeing to, the bees like fog over the sweating grapes.

CHAPTER 33

Igor loaned Ava his moped to go back to the beach. He was set in for the duration and assured her he'd catch a lift back in the morning. Ava pootled back, completely unable to grasp everyone else's enthusiasm. It felt like a club to which she'd been refused entry. She wanted to understand it. Going back she felt like a failure, sloping away, admitting defeat.

She parked the moped in the car park just before the path down to the beach, not wanting to explain her presence to Flora, and nipped unseen along a back road that led her out into the cobbled square and the cocoon of her grandmother's house.

Restless and annoyed with herself, she had a shower, washed her hair and dowsed her legs with Afterbite. Then she paced the hallway, the kitchen, the veranda, pausing to sit and drink some water, but then stood up again, seeing in her mind only the people still at the vineyard.

She felt like her mother. Positioned slightly to the side at family events. Watching. Kept satisfied like a tiger in case she suddenly gnashed. Her drink always topped up. Her chair always in the shade. Her book forgotten: '*Ava, run and get it, there's a good girl.*'

Leaving the veranda, Ava walked through the kitchen and up to her grandmother's bedroom. It was strange how when she'd first arrived, walking in had seemed too nerve-wracking, too emotionally powerful, yet now she just marched through as if it were an airport corridor, a non-descript passageway whose purpose was purely the departure gate.

She felt her heart start to race as she opened the door to the little ante-room. She hadn't stepped in since they'd found the letters so was surprised to find a shelf had collapsed, the wooden support snapped. Some of the fallen contents had been haphazardly bundled away, but half of it still lay discarded on the floor like shimmering puddles.

Ava knelt down and started to organise the mess, folding sequinned couture dresses into a glossy shopping bag, gathering handbags and purses together and sliding them neatly underneath the rail of clothes.

It was beneath the furs that she found the other box.

More letters, different handwriting. This scrawl she recognised. The same sparrow-like scratch that was on the writing bureau in the living room, that signed her Christmas cards 'Valentina Brown. (Grandmother)'.

The airmail envelopes were blue. They smelt of old books and citrus and juniper cologne. Ava wasn't sure if she wanted to open them or not. She went downstairs to get a glass of water.

Glancing out the window at the end of the hall she saw the café in full swing. Flora guffawing delightedly with customers. Everardo gracefully stealth-like in the background serving drinks. Resisting the pull of that familiar reality, she turned and headed back up to the stuffy little room.

Sitting down, cross-legged on the floor, she took out the first envelope.

Isabel, sweetheart, we've booked our tickets, you have to be there. I specifically told you 3rd – 8th December and you promised you were free. You're just going to have to tell that Syd to go

without you to LA, I'm sure the man can last a
weekend without you, and you him! Honestly
darling, I'm sure I brought you up with more
backbone than this. Tell him you must stay. Poor
Ava's so excited. Please don't do this.
And, aside from that, I'm not flying all the way to
New York to see the understudy.
Weather here glorious. Very mild and sea warm.
I've bought a wonderful new swimming costume.

All my love
Mother

Ava folded her arms across her chest, the letter tight
between her fingers. She shut her eyes for a second. She
would turn time back and not read it if she could, just
to save her younger self the humiliation of having been
excited. She lay back on the hard wooden floor and
stared up at the bare bulb and cracks in the ceiling, her
neck bent up against the unbroken shelf strut. Letting
the letter drop to the floor she pulled out the next one.

Isabel, sweetheart, wonderful news about Carmen –
one of my favourites. Congratulations, darling.
We will be there!
Ava and Rory have just been to stay for the
summer. Oh, they are such marvellous company.
We swam every morning, Rory's started running at
some ungodly hour. He made us take out a pedalo –
I warned him of the boring tedium of the pedalo
but he refused to listen (wonder where that comes
from!) until we were right round the peninsula and
they finally got it. Ava managed to convince lovely
Lucas from the watersports centre to tow us back.

She has all the charm of youth. Had us in stitches later about a cheeky little kiss they had and an orange falling on her head from the tree.

Isabel, they're such lovely children. Not so much children any more I know but a lovely pair to have around. Rory bossing us about like he owns the place. Just delightful. I actually cried a little tear when they left.

A credit to you, sweetheart. You should come back more often (I know, I know, I can't help myself).

All my love
Mother

Ava sat up. Re-read the letter with the paper really close to her face, felt a bubble of hope teetering inside herself, not quite given the go-ahead to inflate.

She pulled out another letter. A quick skim. Then another.

Ava is doing marvellously in Art. Apparently not quite so well at Maths. Her father has got her a tutor but as far as I can tell the woman's so young that they just gossip about television programmes for half an hour – a girl after my own heart. Rory is straight As but a little too serious on the telephone. I've mailed him a joke book.

Then another.

I bought Rory a camcorder. Expensive but worth it. His father isn't going to encourage him. Too many tutors in my opinion. He posted me a film of some squirrels and magpies fighting in the garden. I

*think he wants to be like that famous man that I've
forgotten the name of. Battenberg?*
*I've asked Gabriela. She says David Attenborough.
I'd have never got that on my own.*
*Did I tell you? Poor Gabriela's husband died last
month, Felipe, remember him? It was terrible. She's
bought a puppy which is most unlike her – said
she wanted another heartbeat in the house. I said,
get a cat. It's a ridiculous dog, can't even breathe
properly, face all squished in and ugly as sin.*
*Ava has developed a passion for car boot sales.
Her father apparently fears for a lot of old junk
in the house like Val's! The cheek of it! I think it's
wonderful.*
Please, Isabel, you have a telephone, use it.

All my love
Mother

They went on like this. All little updates. All casual
snippets of Ava and Rory's lives. Their achievements,
their tantrums, the funny little things they'd done or
said. Information. Updates.

The minutiae of life that Ava had never dared bore
her mother with. But someone had. Someone had
told her. And whether her mother cared or not it
didn't matter. What mattered was that she knew. The
information had been logged somewhere in her brain.
Forced to take precedence, even for mere minutes, over
the things Isabel Fisher had ranked higher in her life.

Lying on her back, Ava stared up at the dresses.
Sequins shimmering like fish scales. Gold lamé
winking in the light. Beady eyes of dead fox stoles
staring back.

She sat up and pulled the gold lamé skirt off the hanger. She scrunched the material in her palms, remembered the feeling of the scratchy fabric.

She was standing in the wings of the theatre. Nine years old. Too old to sing out of tune now. Too old for bobbing dance moves. Hair still curled in little ringlets, cheeks rouged like a doll. Body shaking so violently with nerves that the gold material started flapping and the wooden floorboards creaked.

'I can't.'

'Get on,' hissed her mother, pointing to the stage.

'No.'

'You're embarrassing me.'

All the assistants hovering in the wings.

'I can't.'

The slap. The shock of it making her wet her pants. Standing rigid, paralysed with shame. Cheek stinging. The gold lamé skirt hiding the trickle of pee down her leg, soaking into the white frilly sock.

'Get out there now.'

A shove to her back. A wide bright stage. A million eyes staring in the darkness. And Ava standing, wide-eyed, mouth open. Words forgotten. The music starting but no noise would come out.

She remembered the look in her mother's eyes as she knelt to give her a great hug on the stage before an assistant came on and ushered Ava away – the venom.

Now, sitting in that little room, skirt scrunched in her hand, Ava fumed at the idea of her mother being angry with her. The audience weren't there to see her sing terribly. Why couldn't they have just said she was ill? That it would be just Isabel Fisher that night? And every night.

Because . . . why?

Ava sat up.

Because her mother didn't have the courage yet? Because she needed a crutch? First Ava, then Syd. Always someone else making her famous so she never had to stand up and do it on her own.

Ava had stood in the wings of the theatre for the whole set in her pee-soaked socks, going from gasping tears to red-puffed face, waiting for her mother to finish.

And when it had ended, backed by the cacophony of applause that proved Ava was no longer necessary, she had bobbed in front of Isabel, reaching for her hand, saying, 'Mummy, I'm sorry,' but her mother had marched past without even a look.

She remembered the agent – *'Someone take the kid home.'* She remembered being handed from person to person. Left to wait in a chair. Ushered down a corridor. The half-empty rooms, a man's hand stroking her hair. The nervous fear. The dry cigarette breath. A woman in a headset clicking her fingers. More corridors. The foyer. 'Wait here.' Suddenly out front, alone. Black sky. Bustling people. Never daring to ask someone to call her father – he'd be so mad. So mad with their mother. And who had come to her rescue in the end? The infamous Syd, who smelt of coffee and cigars. He'd stuffed a Trebor Extra Strong Mint into her hand, told her a terrible joke and packed her into a taxi. If her mother knew where she'd gone, Ava had no idea. She just sat alone in the cab, wiping away tears with non-absorbent gold lamé, clutching the dusty mint in her hand, all the while despising her previous self for not having had the courage to sing.

Back in the present, alone in the little room, Ava found herself once again dabbing her eyes with gold lamé. This secret shameful memory. She imagined someone treating little Max the same way and felt a rising fury inside her.

Yet she had spent her life trying to simultaneously bury the moment and make up for it.

She remembered telling her dad when he answered the door that she'd been ill, weaving a whole story about her mother missing the first part of the set to walk with her to the kerbside to hail a cab.

And of course her mother had never come home again after that night.

And of course Ava had never told anyone what had happened, too gobbled up with worry for letting her mother down.

And of course Ava had never realised that she had left them for Syd. Syd of the extra strong mints and the unfunny jokes.

She balled the gold skirt up in her fist, biting down on the urge to shout out loud, then chucked it into the back of the cupboard and wiped her eyes with her hands. She sat for a bit, looking round at all the stuff, suddenly garish in its splendour, and reached over for the last letter in the box.

Isabel, sweetheart, you have to rest! This is ridiculous. Your voice is straining because you are tired. You looked worn out the whole time Ava and I were there. You need to calm down and for goodness, sake, stop checking on blasted Syd all the time! One thing I can tell you about men is the tighter you try and hold them the more they struggle. Like fish.
But when have you ever listened to me?
Just get some rest. Your voice is too precious to waste on a man.

All my love
Mother

Ava saw herself much older in New York, her mother getting bored and annoyed at The Plaza, calling over the maître d' to complain about the table, taking a phone call midway through, make-up thick and eyes jittery, refusing to eat anything then standing up and walking away before Ava and her grandmother had even finished the sandwiches. They sat politely waiting for her to come back, both ashamed that she never did, neither speaking of it. Her grandmother fumbling to pay the extortionate bill. Then the two of them walking arm in arm to Central Park zoo, where they stared at the majestic cats restlessly prowling and foolishly romanticised the whole afternoon by nicknaming a beautiful snow leopard Isabel.

Ava realised she had spent all that time trying to be enough for one person, when another had adored her without her even trying. Had laughed at her jokes, rubbed suntan lotion on her back, prescribed bizarre remedies for her ailments, delighted at her achievements. Had marvelled over the perfect little sandwiches at The Plaza while her mother had waved them away with disdain.

Someone had loved her, well and truly and completely. Had deemed her enough.

While the other, by the end, barely deemed her anything.

CHAPTER 34

In the suffocating heat of the afternoon sun, Ava stripped all her mother's dresses from their hangers – velvet with a nipped-in waist, big gold roses, red and ruched, Pan collar, leopard print, turquoise, a green one covered in zebras, the gold lamé skirt – and folded them into a huge paper carrier bag. She walked them downstairs, out through the soupy heat and across the concourse to Café Estrella where Flora was having a coffee at her little table during the pause before evening service.

'I have something for you,' Ava said.

Flora looked up. 'What's that?'

Ava put the bag on the floor and opened it.

Flora peered down, looked back up at Ava, frowning. When Ava stared, resolute, Flora reached down and pulled out the green silk number with the zebras. 'Is this Versace?'

Ava nodded.

Flora held it up against her. The cinched-in waist, the sweetheart neckline, the kick-pleat skirt, all perfect for her figure. She looked cautiously at Ava like a kid on the brink of Christmas Day. 'Are you serious?'

Ava nodded. It was weird to see the dresses with someone else. Immediately transforming into Flora from their mother. Suddenly the zebra dress was fun and flouncy rather than slick and showy.

'I really like this one,' Ava said, reaching into the bag and pulling out a fitted yellow dress with big pockets, buttons down the front and a white Peter Pan collar. 'It goes with your mood board,' she said.

Flora checked the label. Chanel. 'Ava, this is thousands of pounds' worth of clothes.'

'I know,' she said. 'Just don't tell Rory they're worth anything.'

Flora shook her head. 'You should sell them,' she said, picking up the bag and thrusting it in Ava's direction.

'No,' Ava said, raising her hands so she couldn't take it. 'I don't want the money. I don't want someone who can afford them to have them. I want someone who will make good out of them to have them. And you will make good out of them,' she laughed. 'If that's even a phrase.'

Flora took a moment to look at Ava, her eyes narrowing to see that she was certain, then she held the bag close to her chest and said, 'I will make good out of them, I promise.'

'Good,' said Ava, feeling instantly lighter.

Flora picked the green zebra dress out of the bag again and held it up against herself. 'I might even wear this on my date,' she said with a raise of her brows.

'You have a date!' Ava gasped. 'With Everardo?'

'With Everardo.' Flora's cheeks pinked.

'Oh that's so exciting. I'm so pleased.' Ava did a little excited clap.

'Well, it's just a little date, probably nothing will happen.'

'Or everything might happen,' Ava replied.

'We'll see.' Flora looked a touch more vulnerable as she folded the dress up.

'It'll be good.'

'And what about you?' Flora said with a knowing look. 'You and Tom seem inseparable.'

Ava waved the comment away. 'It's just a holiday thing.'

Flora looked surprised. 'Really?'

'Of course,' said Ava.

'Does he know that?' Flora asked, more serious.

'Yes Flora, we both know that,' Ava said, shifting her weight from foot to foot, suddenly keen to get away. 'I'm going back to the grapes now.'

'To be honest, I'm quite pleased I managed to get out of it this year.' Flora shook her head. 'It's a bloody nightmare!'

'It is,' Ava agreed, 'but I'm determined to enjoy it.'

Flora laughed. 'And you say it's just a holiday fling . . .'

'It is a holiday fling,' Ava insisted. 'The grapes are for me.'

'Right,' said Flora, in a voice that made Ava scrunch up her face even though she knew she was being wound up.

CHAPTER 35

At the vineyard it was as though time had stood still. Everyone was still bent over, snipping their little bunches off the vine.

'You're back?' Tom stopped the tractor as he met her on the path, wiping the sweat from his face with his T-shirt as he jumped down to stand opposite her.

'Yes,' Ava said, hands on hips, shoulders back. 'And I'm going to need a head torch.'

Tom laughed as he pulled his own torch out of his pocket and chucked it at her. 'You're here for the duration?'

'I am indeed.'

'Glad to hear it,' he said, hauling himself back up into the tractor seat and driving away with a grinning salute.

Dowsed in mosquito repellent, Val's wide-brimmed straw hat on her head, huge bottle of water in her hand, Ava stalked determinedly back to her vine. As she walked she felt stronger. Taller, even. She hadn't expected to feel changed by a few letters but her step was definitely lighter. Her self less doubting, less fearful. Angrier. But in a good way; the best way. An anger that led only to confidence and change. To acceptance.

Surrounded by bees and the glaring late-afternoon sunshine, she glanced around her at the people chatting, pausing, sipping, looking, laughing, and was suddenly struck by the line in her dad's letter to her mother: *A person invested with the ability to find interest and adventure in the everyday things of life has a much more enjoyable time than a person who is always seeking to be amused.*

And by the time the church bells chimed midnight, Ava wasn't necessarily enjoying it as such, but she was beginning to understand it. She was beginning to feel the urgency, the togetherness, to enjoy the pain, to enjoy the fact that her brain zoned out and she'd find she'd been picking for an hour without realising, to relish the pause for sandwiches – serrano ham, manchego cheese and a drizzle of olive oil never tasted so good – and the hipflask brandy, and the collective turn like sunflower heads as they stopped to watch the sun set. She'd been cursing it for most of the afternoon but now, as it hovered big and bold and red in front of her, she could start to forgive it. Her burning skin cooling in the dusk.

On occasion she found herself chuckling as she picked. The lightness inside her escaping, like she knew a secret. A realisation that the past had been completely out of her control and as a result she could live a little freer. She tipped her head back and stared into the darkness at the million dots of light in the sky, she popped the odd little sour fruit into her mouth, she watched with satisfaction as her bucket filled up with fat, ripe bunches, and she made her peace with the last remaining bees.

At two a.m. Max was sent inside for a nap, but came back half an hour later with the camera and marched up and down the vines filming the workers in the moonlight.

Tom came to stand next to Ava, offering his battered hipflask. 'Loving it?' he asked.

Moths flickered around her head torch.

'It's bearable,' she said, masking the tiniest of smiles with a brandy sip.

Tom nudged her on the shoulder. 'I knew you'd come round to it.'

'No, you didn't.'

'I so did!' he laughed, and before she could counter, his hand was pressing warm between her shoulder blades, pulling her close, tight, and with the self-assurance of someone a bit drunk on brandy and high on grape-picking he bent down and kissed her hard on the lips, the heat of the night searing between them. The moment ruined only by a little cringe when she heard Max wolf-whistle and realised everyone had stopped picking to watch.

CHAPTER 36

They finished at seven o'clock the next morning. At five the sky had changed from black to blue to peach as the sun creaked its way above the horizon, the vineyard bathed in a morning mist that swirled around them like snow. It felt to Ava like magic.

Walking with her last bucket of grapes, legs cement heavy, eyes closing as she walked, skin chapped and burned and bitten, hands scratched, she felt a tired satisfaction fill her whole being, a sense of being alive that she wasn't sure she'd ever felt before. She saw Gabriela and Rosa ambling slowly, arm in arm, to Gael's Renault and realised that she too would want to do this every year. Would suddenly be the first in the queue, just to experience the feeling when it was over: the completeness, the memories.

They piled into Tom's Jeep. Max, who'd gone to bed at four, gently snoring on Rory's shoulder. Wrapped in a contented peace, no one said anything. Just trundled along down the hillside road, Tom glancing at Ava every now and then, tired eyes smiling.

Then into the nothingness came the sound of a phone ringing. Ava felt a creep of shame as she reached into her bag and pulled out her mobile.

Tom shook his head, incredulous. 'Do you know what detox means?' he asked, as she fumbled to answer.

'I got it when Rory went missing. Hello?'

It was work.

'Just a quick question,' she heard Hugo drawl. 'Nothing to worry about. Just wanted to clarify a price you'd quoted the Jamesons on the Murano chandelier. Bit of a pickle. They said you said five thou. Peregrine says that's lower than cost. Any idea?' he asked.

'Hugo. The five thousand for the chandelier is if they take the pink marble console table as well. It was a deal, they know that. It's all in my notes.'

'Yes, yes, no, don't worry, darling,' he said. Ava could visualise his face puckered tight as he feigned listening like a *Made in Chelsea* extra. 'Just wanted to double check. That's exactly what I thought.'

'Hugo,' she said, uncertain, 'have you looked at my notes?'

'Absolutely. Never look away. They're my Bible.'

He hung up.

Ava was about to put her phone back in her bag when it rang again. 'Ava, darling!' This time it was Peregrine.

She glanced around the Jeep. Rory was looking out the window, Claire had her eyes shut, Tom was concentrating on the road. It felt like she'd welcomed in a beast.

Peregrine was talking. 'So basically it's all a complete disaster and I'm about three grand out of pocket. We're up the proverbial without a paddle and I think you're just going to have to come back. Provided you've found yourself, of course,' he laughed, deep and jolly but glib enough to make it clear that the holiday was over.

Ava swallowed. 'Yes,' she said. 'Yes, absolutely, all present and correct. I'll be back beginning of next week.' She glanced round when she heard Tom sigh, but he appeared to be focused on the road, no obvious sign that he'd made a noise at all. In the rearview mirror she saw Rory open one eye and close it again.

'Just what I wanted to hear,' Peregrine drawled, and she imagined him reclining in his chair, twirling his fountain pen. 'Right, I'd better go and sort out this fiasco. *Ciao ciao*.'

Ava sat with the phone in her lap. She couldn't even muster what would once have been colossal delight for being proved indispensable. The car was quiet. Tom had pulled up by the café and turned the engine off.

After an awkward second or two, Rory made a show of yawning and said, 'Righto, better go and get some sleep.' Claire came round to help him with Max.

'That was a great day, thanks Tom.' Rory reached into the Jeep window to shake Tom's hand as sleeping Max resettled himself on his shoulder.

Tom nodded.

Ava toyed with her phone.

The beach was starting to fill up. Sun loungers bagsyed with towels, toddlers waving spades about while teenagers basked in the sun, sleeping off the night before.

Tom's hands were resting on the steering wheel. 'So you're going back Monday?' he said, watching the view for a second before turning Ava's way.

She swallowed. 'Yeah, looks like it. They're in a mess.'

Tom sucked in his bottom lip. Then he said, 'I hate that phone.'

Ava chucked it in her bag. 'Me too.'

The seconds on the clock counted on.

'We're really tired,' Ava said, opening her door. 'We should go and get some sleep.'

Tom turned the key in the ignition.

Ava had been expecting him to come with her. 'You're not coming?'

'I've got work to do.'

'You're kidding. We've been up all night.'

'Not loads, but still some work.'

She wasn't sure if she believed him, but she shut the door and stood by the open window.

'So just to check, with us, that's it?' he said, one hand on the steering wheel, as if it were some simple off-the-cuff remark.

Ava sighed. 'I don't know. I guess so. I think it has to be.'

Tom nodded.

'You belong here. I belong there,' she said.

'No one belongs anywhere,' he said, rubbing his eyes and staring at her, face impassive.

'Come into the house with me,' she said.

He shook his head. 'I can't. I really do have work to do.'

Ava pressed her fingers into the corners of her eyes, tiredness encroaching, making her suddenly want to cry.

Tom tilted his head as he studied her. Ava could hear her heart beating in her ears. He reached his hand out the window and touched her cheek for a second. 'OK,' he said, putting the Jeep in gear. 'I'll see you later.' And with a quick salute, he drove away, the throaty roar of the old exhaust like a rocket taking off.

CHAPTER 37

Rory finally understood the expression 'slept like the dead'. At home he slept lightly, the blackout blinds not quite obscuring the streetlight outside. The noise of the planes thundering over at four a.m. It was his belief that he'd never quite recovered from Max's baby years, sleeping in short, sharp two-hour bursts, lying in his bed desperate for the wave to carry him from one to the next because if he missed he was up for good, whatever time of night.

The day after the grape-picking, however, he sank into a trance of oblivion. The world could have imploded and he wouldn't have known. Shut in his little room with his wife and son, it felt like he'd bedded down in the most perfect cocoon. When he woke up he could have sworn he'd retreated to a younger form of himself, his eyes felt wider, his muscles lighter.

'It's all that sea air,' Claire said, yawning and rolling over to go back to sleep.

But it wasn't, he knew it wasn't, it was more than that. It was contentment.

He went into the hallway expecting to find the house in silence but was surprised to find the living room empty and Ava already up.

He found her sitting on their grandmother's bed, feet just touching the floor, a pile of possessions next to her on the satin quilt, the dusty air shimmering gold in the sunlight.

'You alright?' he asked, mid-yawn, trying to flatten his hair after catching sight of himself in the hallway mirror.

Ava glanced up at him. She looked worn out. From the dark circles under her eyes, he presumed she had not had such a luxurious sleeping experience as his. 'I'm going to take these things. That OK?'

Rory walked over and examined the little pile next to her. A gold ring. A black silk dress with a green stripe. A pair of red dancing shoes.

'Fine,' he said, sitting down next to her on the bed, rubbing the sleep from his face. 'So you are leaving then?'

She nodded.

'Did you know there's a party tonight?' he said. 'At the café. Apparently there always is after the grape harvest.'

'Yeah, I know.'

'I think we might stay,' Rory said, lifting up one of the shoes and tapping it on the quilt.

'For the party?'

'No, in Spain.'

'What do you mean, stay?' Ava asked, frowning.

'As in – stay.' Rory leant back on his elbows. He'd never felt so relaxed in his life. 'There's a fairly decent international school half an hour away. Claire will freelance for a bit, set up her own thing maybe. I don't know, actually, if you can believe that. Might do your airbnb.'

'You know it's not my airbnb, don't you? It's a massive international company!'

Rory snorted. 'Whatever, I'm pretty confident the rent will cover our mortgage.' He held his hands wide.

'So. Who knows. Give it a try for a year and see what happens.'

'Hang on a minute, where are you going to stay?' Ava asked, eyes narrowing slightly.

Rory swallowed. 'Here,' he said a little sheepish. 'At the Summerhouse.'

'Oh it's the Summerhouse now, is it?' Ava said. 'You never call it the Summerhouse.'

Rory shrugged, trying to seem nonchalant, knowing that not so long ago he'd refused to let Ava even contemplate the idea of not selling the house. 'I've fallen for its charms.'

Ava raised a brow.

Rory scratched his head. 'It's not definite. I mean, we'd only stay if it's OK with you. I know before I was a bit, you know . . .'

He watched Ava's lips quirk up in a half-smile as he stumbled over his words.

'It's OK with me, Rory,' she said. 'I've never wanted to sell this place.' Then after a pause she added, 'You're really lucky I'm not you, you know that?'

Rory grinned. 'I know.'

'I can't believe you're going to stay,' she said.

Rory laughed. 'I know. Amazing, isn't it? Completely unlike me.' He sat up and looked over into the little ante-room. 'I broke the shelf in there by the way,' he said, standing up to go and have a look. 'By accident,' he added.

When he opened the door he saw that everything had been neatly folded away into boxes, the shelf hammered back into place. 'Did you fix this?' he asked, turning to look at Ava.

She nodded.

He crouched down and had a flick through some of the packed-away stuff: the million pairs of sunglasses, the collection of spangly brooches all pinned to a square of black velvet.

Ava came over and knelt down beside him. She pulled a shoebox off the shelf and handed it to him. 'These letters are interesting,' she said. 'They're nice. I read them yesterday and they made me feel—' she paused.

'Feel what?' he asked.

'I don't know.' She shook her head.

Rory knew that look. He knew that vulnerability. He'd spent half his life telling that look that everything would be OK. 'You do know.'

She skimmed her fingers over the letters like a xylophone. 'I suppose they made me feel good enough about myself. You know, like Flora said in the bar about Ricardo, *You spend your whole time thinking: why wasn't I good enough?*'

'Did she say that?'

'God, Rory, do you not listen to anything?'

'I listen to the stuff that interests me,' he half-joked, while inside he was thinking that this shouldn't have been how she had felt. That she should never have had cause to doubt that she was good enough, and the fact that she had meant that he and his father had failed in their attempts to protect her.

He sat down, leaning against the doorframe, and watched as she folded and refolded a silky-looking blouse, tucking it in neatly with the other stuff.

'I should have told you about Syd,' he said. 'We should have talked about it all more. I'm sorry about that.'

Ava sat down opposite him, leaning against the shelves. 'That's OK,' she shrugged. 'I don't know how much I would have listened anyway.' She pulled her hair away from the back of her neck and fanned herself with a theatre programme.

It was quite satisfying, Rory thought, to see the glossy booklet treated with so much less reverence than earlier in the holiday.

When the air was a fraction cooler, Ava stopped fanning and looked at the front cover picture of their mother in the red dress. 'I suppose,' she said, 'I mainly just wish that I had accepted a few more of her weaknesses. Maybe if I'd known more I wouldn't have filled in all the gaps with her greatness. I don't know. Who knows?' she smiled, her face softening, then she put the programme back on the pile. 'I wish I'd tried less hard to impress her.'

He nodded. 'You should stay.'

Ava shook her head. 'No. I'm not staying. I like my life.'

'I thought you came out here to change your life?'

'And I have changed my life,' she said, closing the lid on the first of the boxes. 'I will be going home with much less FOMO,' she laughed, 'and I will find amusement in the things around me. I'm reformed.'

Rory took over with the box as Ava struggled to get the flaps to slot into place to prevent it reopening. 'What about Tom?' he asked.

Ava sat down against the wall again. 'It's not real. I have a life at home. A job. Friends. A life. An existence.'

'You're crazy,' Rory said, the box satisfyingly shut. 'I'll tell you who's not real – that bloody Peregrine.'

Ava laughed. 'He's OK.'

'He's a charlatan. He always has been. And your friends, well, you watch.' Rory started work on the next box. 'They're all getting married, having babies and they won't be there on a Friday and Saturday night to go out with you, Ava.'

She rolled her eyes. 'I think you're not giving my friends enough credit.'

'Maybe not. But I'll tell you something, they will be out much more rarely. Try adding forty-quid babysitting to every meal out. And they won't want a raging hangover with a six-month-old at home.'

Ava stood up and went back over to sit on their grandmother's bed, gathering her little pile of stuff together again. 'You're painting a very bleak picture of parenthood, Rory.'

'No, I'm trying to make you see that you are at an age where the lives of the people around you are changing and you can't make everything stand still.' Box closed, he stood up and turned the light in the little room off. 'Don't go back in search of what you had, Ava. That's all I'm saying.'

'I'm not trying to make everything stand still. I'm just becoming a realist,' she said.

'There's not that much joy in realism, you know,' Rory said, walking over to have a peer out the window. The café was getting ready for the party, the terrace all dolled up with fairy lights. He turned back and, seeing Ava sitting all prim and small on the bed, threw his hands up in the air and added, 'And why at the crucial time do you lose the bloody annoying part of you that would do something like stay!'

'Hang on, I thought you'd be pleased,' Ava said, stunned by his change of heart.

'I know,' he said, plonking himself down on the bed. 'I guess maybe I was wrong.'

'I'm sorry, what was that?' She leant forwards as if she'd gone deaf.

Rory laughed. 'I was wrong.'

After a minute or two of sitting side by side, staring at the closed door to the room of their mother's stuff, Ava stood up and went down to the hall, coming back up with her bag.

Rory watched as she got her battered pink purse out and unzipped a compartment in the middle. He was still contemplating how she managed to exist with all those receipts and cards bulging out of her wallet when she handed him five folded-up ten-pound notes.

'You know you asked me what I'd done with that money Dad gave us. You know when you got your trainers? I didn't put it in my piggy bank. I put it in a book by my bed. And every night I put it under my pillow. For years.' She shook her head at the thought, like she was crazy to have done it. 'And when I stopped putting it under my pillow, I put it in my purse.'

Rory sat up straighter, his eyes widening with surprise. His fingers almost unable to believe they were holding the notes.

'I kept it because I think I thought if I didn't buy anything she might come back.'

'Nothing we did would have kept her.' Rory looked across at her. 'It was never about us, Ava. It was about her.'

'I know.' She nodded. 'I know it was. Or I know now that it was.' Ava rubbed her eyes. Then she said, 'Tom said I need to make sure that my life and her opinion of me are separate.'

'That was very astute of him,' Rory said.

'Don't sound so surprised.'

'Well, he's an actor.'

'Rory!'

Rory snorted to himself. 'Go on then,' he said.

'What?'

'Separate them.'

'How?'

'I don't know.' Rory shrugged. 'Maybe say it out loud? Shout it.'

Ava looked away from him to the faded rug on the floor, then lifting her chin shouted at the top of her voice, 'I don't care what you think of me!'

'Jesus Christ, Ava, you're going to wake the house up!'

'You said to do it.'

'I didn't think you would.'

She did it again. Shouting at the top of her voice. Then smiling said, 'You do it.'

'No way.'

'Go on. I feel *much* better.'

Rory ran his tongue over his top lip. Looked at Ava. Her cheeks did actually look like they were slightly glowing. He too stared down at the floor, then before his brain could stop him shouted, 'I don't care what you think of me!', aimed more at his father than his mother. Then he laughed, taking himself quite by surprise. 'Blimey, that was actually quite liberating.'

From downstairs he heard Claire's voice call, 'What's going on?'

'Nothing,' he shouted back. 'All fine here. Sorry.'

They sat for a second, the room seeming lighter, brighter, before Ava said, 'Shall we get something to eat?'

Rory nodded, standing up and handing her the folded tenners.

'No, keep it,' she said. 'Give it to Max for water-skiing.'

'Ava, it's not legal tender any more, you idiot.'

'Oh,' she inspected Charles Dickens on the old ten-pound note. 'Really?'

Rory left the room, shaking his head, incredulous, but with the small hope that she hadn't changed as much as she thought.

CHAPTER 38

The party at Café Estrella spilled right out on to the beach, fairy lights twinkling, people dancing barefoot in the sand, sloshing glasses of blood red sangria.

Next door at Nino's, guests lounged on white sofas as torch candles flamed in the sand and waiters served oyster shots and beef carpaccio rolled into roses. It was a picture of contentment, but Rory saw the covert glances, all of them just a little jealous of the fun.

Tom arrived late with a crate of last year's vintage and a leg of the finest acorn-fed Ibérico ham. Flora swished about the place dressed in a green silk dress with zebras on it that Rory was sure he'd seen before but wasn't sure where. Gabriela was marching in and out of the kitchen with plates of fresh, piping hot tapas, refusing to listen when Flora told her to stop and sit down, while Everardo seemed quite at home behind the bar, expertly slicing the ham Tom had brought.

Rory took a moment to stare at his wife on the pretext of filming. She was so tanned, relaxed and happy, Rory could barely recognise her as the woman who had basically chucked him out of the house a few weeks previously. His sister on the other hand seemed on edge. Overbright. She was wearing the black silk dress with the green stripe of their grandmother's and looked stunning, the material wafting about the place as she walked, all golden limbs and crazy curls, but the worry was still there in her eyes when she smiled, like she was struggling with the uncomfortable weight of uncertainty.

In retrospect he wished he'd gone over to her at that point, checked everything was OK, maybe made sure that she stuck with him and Claire, or at the very least got her a drink so she relaxed.

But he didn't. He actually forgot about her. He got caught up slow dancing with Claire. He was called to the kitchen by Flora to force Gabriela into taking a break. He munched some little fried anchovies and sampled the chorizo and chickpeas. He partook in the sangria-downing competition and found himself at the microphone for some impromptu karaoke with Gael, Rosa and Gabriela, who clutched her little dog as she sang. All of it, he noted with pride, captured on film by his son.

That was until all of Max's friends bundled in under a cloud of glitter hairspray and Lynx deodorant, a boisterous clique, half of them ignoring each other while the other half were draped all over one another. The camera was unceremoniously thrust back in Rory's direction as Max, cool and cocky, started casually chatting-up a girl with a 'Selena' necklace and silver stars in her hair.

It was only when Rory took a turn round the room to film that he saw the bikini-clad blonde sitting with Tom. Lithe and sinewy, legs up to her armpits and eyes like a cat. Tom looked like he had the first time Rory had met him: cocksure, louche, like there was no way you'd want him shagging your sister.

Ava saw him at the same time Rory did. She was walking up from the darkened beach, the hem of her skirt damp from the sea. She paused. Tom looked up like he barely knew her.

Rory slowly put the camera down on the table. Over by the bar he saw Flora and Claire stop chatting and pause to take in the scene.

Ava's eyes narrowed just a touch, but were quickly wide again with false brightness. He knew she was trying to work out how best to handle the situation. He watched as her step didn't falter. She carried on past Tom like he wasn't there. And just as she swept past his chair, she said, voice casual and uncaring, 'Didn't take long.'

Rory felt his whole self deflate as he realised she had been right. That this wasn't real. It made a sudden mockery of his now-flighty-seeming decision to stay. He felt like a fool. Not only had he failed to see behind the veil, he had dragged his son and wife through with him. It *was* just a hollow holiday town. His tumbling Twitter feed was more real than this.

He couldn't meet Ava's eye, so looked down at the floor at the intricate twists of the newly revealed Spanish tiles, scoffed at their mocking authenticity, and in so doing missed the moment when Tom's hand shot out and grabbed Ava by the wrist.

Rory glanced up when he heard her say, 'Ow, what are you doing?'

Tom didn't let go, just stood up and pointed to the woman sitting next to him. 'Lola. This is Ava. Ava, this is my daughter, Lola.'

Ava's whole stance changed in an instant. Rory watched her attempt to cover up her mistake. Her hand over her mouth. 'I'm so sorry. God, I'm such a cliché. I can't believe it, I'm so sorry. You look really grown up,' she said to Lola, who could easily pass for a good five years older than sixteen. 'You had brown hair in the photograph,' she added, scrabbling for a viable excuse.

Lola reached up to self-consciously run her hand through her peroxide crop. 'It's new,' she said.

'And it looks fabulous. You look stunning,' Ava gushed, all the while completely avoiding eye contact with Tom. She put a hand on Lola's arm. 'I really am so sorry. I thought you were your dad's date. Ridiculous.' She shook her head, then held her hands in the air and said, 'I am ridiculous.'

Lola giggled.

And Rory's opinion of the world instantly resumed to its original state. He strolled over to stand next to his wife, arm resting casually over her shoulder as, together with Flora, they silently chuckled, cringing at Ava's faux-pas.

CHAPTER 39

The karaoke was in full swing behind Ava, Igor belting out Elvis Presley, sangria sloshing on the floor.

She could see Rory's camera trained on her, Flora pretending not to eavesdrop behind the bar. She extricated herself from her embarrassment with Lola by introducing her to Max and promptly running off to talk to anyone she could, all the while avoiding eye contact with Tom at every opportunity.

Her inner turmoil, she noted, was now personified in Max, who, having been introduced to Lola, could barely speak, Selena et al forgotten as his crush changed immediate allegiance and she heard him stutter out, 'I can mono-ski.'

Ava managed to flit about the party for about fifteen minutes before Tom cornered her by the olive tree and bundled her out through the kitchen and into the pitch dark vegetable garden.

'What is going on?' he asked, standing hands on his hips, legs apart like he was getting ready to wrestle.

'Nothing.' Ava kicked a stone out of the way with her sandal.

'Come on, Ava. Why are you being so completely weird?'

'Because I'm leaving,' she said, looking up at him for the first time since she'd been hauled into the garden. The only light from the kitchen window. The music flooding what should have been quiet darkness.

'You want to leave,' he said, unmoving.

She paced the broken path, confused. '*I know*. I just don't know if I do or not.'

Tom held his hands out wide. 'So stay,' he said.

'No.'

'So why don't you want to leave?'

'I don't know.' It was sticky in the garden, the humid night heat close, pressing against her skin. She walked past him to sit on the rickety old bench. 'You, a bit,' she said, trying to tuck her hair behind her ears but the curls popping back into place.

'Me?' Tom looked chuffed.

'Don't look like that. I can't stay for this.'

Tom frowned and came over to sit down next to her, far enough away that no part of them was touching, close enough that she could feel all the fibres of her being try to stretch across the gap like tentacles. 'You want me to move back to the UK?' he asked, like he was offering to pay for groceries.

'No!'

Tom shrugged. 'I can move back. Winters here aren't anything to write home about. I'll come back to London, we can get to know each other better.' He was warming to the idea. 'Fly out on weekends to see Lola. Fly her out to see me. No problem.'

'No, no, no. No one is moving anywhere. No one's moving for anyone. It's too much. It's stupid. I don't want anyone to have to give anything up for anyone.' Ava shook her head. 'And anyway, you said you didn't even want a relationship.'

He shrugged and rested his head back against the kitchen wall. 'Well I didn't.'

'And now you do?'

'Well I know you now. I mean, please, forgive me for not being *that* eager when it comes to new relationships.'

Ava looked blankly at him.

'My daughter? The injunction? Royally screwed by my ex?'

'Oh,' she said.

'Oh,' he agreed.

The shadows of the peach tree leaves looked like monsters on the ground. Ava stared out at the sickly tomato plants, the huge plate-like leaves of the courgettes. She thought for a second that she would like to see this in bloom, see it fixed and healthy and abundant again.

She sat forwards on the bench, cupping her cheeks with her hands. She felt Tom's hand rest lightly on her back and it made her want to cry. When he had mentioned coming back to England with her, her immediate feeling had been that he would realise it was a mistake, that she wouldn't be enough to make him stay. It was a belief so familiar to her that she clutched on to it without even thinking – the belief that she wasn't worth staying for.

She thought of all those relationships she had fled before the other person could leave. All that time wasted. Habits were hard to shake.

'So why don't you want to stay?' Tom asked, tone intrigued rather than questioning.

'Because it feels weak. It feels weak to be the one making the sacrifice.'

'But didn't I say that I would leave?'

'Yeah, but you've clearly got the better life.' She had to laugh at her own logic.

Tom shook his head, bemused.

'I just don't know if I can leave my life. My job. My flat. My friends . . . It's my life.'

'I can see that,' he agreed. 'Me, I have nothing to lose, I've essentially lived all the hassles in my life. I've had my fresh start.'

Ava didn't reply. After a pause, still focused on sacrifices, she said, 'And there's my pride, I suppose. My respect. The fact that I've only just worked out how to be me, and I'm running into the arms of the first guy I meet.'

Tom blew out a breath. 'Thanks a lot.'

'You know what I mean.'

He made a face like he wasn't completely sure.

'I've just learnt to be alone, I can't stay for the possibility of a relationship.'

Tom nodded.

There was whooping and cheering inside. Ava sat back, knowing his arm was draped along the back of the seat. His hand slipped down, warm on her shoulder. She shut her eyes for a second.

Inside someone called Tom and Ava's names.

'We'd better go.' He pulled her close into his side for a second and, kissing the top of her head, said, 'Ava, things aren't weak if they feel right.'

Untangling herself from his hold, Ava sat up, turned to look at him and, shaking her head, said, 'You're so self-righteous.'

His smirk was just about visible in the darkness of the garden.

Back inside, Rory, Claire and Flora were all poised at the karaoke. Fairy lights glinted in the warm, humid air. As Tom and Ava strolled back in they shouted, 'Come on! Come over here, we're waiting for you.'

Flora was holding out two mics.

Everyone was watching, except for the teenagers who were milling about out the front, Max hovering adoringly round Lola.

'This is not my thing,' Tom groaned, as he was handed a microphone, shaking his head but willing to be dragged up to the stage area.

'Ava, get up here,' Rory shouted.

Ava stood where she was.

Tom was laughing, beckoning her up with a wave of his hand.

Flora leant forwards and thrust the microphone at her. 'Come on Ava, darling!'

Ava stared at the proffered mic.

She thought about whether it might cure her – to stand up and sing on her own terms. But she realised she didn't need curing. So instead she said simply, 'No thank you,' and walked away to stand by the bar.

There followed further cajoling attempts that Ava politely dismissed, but the crowd started to get restless so in the end the music started and the motley crew belted out the most terrible rendition of Sinatra's 'My Way'.

And Ava watched, sangria in hand, smile on her face, content to enjoy the view from where she was sitting.

CHAPTER 40

Rory lay in bed unable to sleep. The luxury of his new-found heavenly slumber gone. The embers of the party at the café still burning outside.

'Ava's so annoying,' he said, nudging Claire to wake up. 'What can I do to make her stay?'

Claire yawned. 'I don't know, Rory.'

'That's no help.'

'Maybe do what she did for you,' she said, snuggling down under the sheet.

'What's that?' he asked, thinking this was no time for riddles.

Claire sat up and replumped her pillow, then lay down again to go back to sleep. 'Think about what Ava needs to hear,' she said, as she closed her eyes.

Rory stared down at his wife, her breathing immediately slow with sleep. He stared at the familiarity of her face. Her features softened as she gently snored, her hair tangled on the pillow. He felt the comforting reassurance of her hand resting on his arm. And he thought how it didn't matter any more who had chosen what ten years ago, whether they married for the baby or because they'd found The One. What mattered was that they were The One now. That they had grown together, irreplaceably. That life itself had made each of them the other's One. And if he was able to see his life played back, he would see that it was fuller, happier, kinder with her in it.

Rory got straight out of bed and went rummaging around in Claire's bag for her laptop, then he sat in front of the blue glow for hours until finally he had earned the luxury of deep, exquisite sleep.

CHAPTER 41

Ava woke up with the sunrise and lay on the sofa, her eyes open. She understood suddenly the meaning of solitude.

She was OK here. Lying staring at the ceiling. The heat was still stifling, but she was calm enough to enjoy the feeling of being hot. To bask.

She had been OK, she thought, before she had stepped out in front of a bus. She had been OK. She had just needed to believe it.

Her phone pinged with a new email. She dug down the side of the sofa to find it. The email was from: Rory.fisher@gmail.com.

Dear Ava,

This is what I would have said if indeed you had lost your life to a bus.

I'd have said you were kind. And funny. And that you always think of other people. And I'd say that you were almost the sum total of my family and that I was truly gutted you had gone, but that I was proud of the person you had become.

I would have said that I loved you very much.

And I would have said that you were most definitely, without a shadow of a doubt, good enough.

Rory

Ava had to dab her eye with the corner of her sheet. Then, when that wasn't enough, she had to sit with her fingers pressed into her eye sockets.

She almost didn't see the little P.S. that said: *Café Estrella, 10 o'clock.*

CHAPTER 42

Everyone was a little the worse for wear at breakfast. Gabriela arrived in huge purple diamanté sunglasses, having overdone the sangria the night before, the pug wheeled behind her a touch slower than usual. Rosa was struggling to summon the energy for the churros. Rory had skipped his six a.m. run for the second time that holiday and the second time in fifteen years. Every new arrival registered the same shock at there being no croissants, Everardo having never made it home.

Ava sat sipping her coffee, watching as he and Flora giggled in the kitchen like truants. She looked at her watch. It was nine fifty. Rory had said ten o'clock and was currently busy doing something behind the bar. She sat and waited.

She watched as people shuffled in, as the chess games started, as the wet-haired swimmers took their seats. She'd seen Lola cycle down to the beach earlier, where she was currently stretched out like a cat in the sun, but there was no sign of Tom. She'd sort of pinned her hopes on a last breakfast together.

'OK,' Rory shouted. And Ava watched as Flora and Everardo started laying out rows of seats inside the café. 'Up you come.'

All the regulars had clearly been informed of the event and were straight up there to bagsy the best seats. Max and Emilio had dragged themselves away from the gang on the beach and were sitting on bar stools, Max glancing back repeatedly to where Lola was flirting with the older brother of one of the English boys, and Selena and the other of Emilio's sister's friends were laughing hysterically at something on YouTube. His attention was clearly divided.

Ava winked at Max as she picked up her coffee and walked to the front. He gave her a look as if to say life was very complicated.

Rory clapped his hands for them all to hurry up.

'Welcome, ladies and gentlemen,' he said. 'Thanks for coming to the screening. I've no doubt you're all here to watch an expert film-maker at work, not to try and catch a glimpse of yourselves on the TV,' he laughed.

Everyone tittered.

Ava frowned. He was going to show his film? How had he had time to do his film?

'As you all know,' Rory went on, 'my sister is leaving tomorrow.'

There was a collective ahhh, fully orchestrated by Rory. Ava blushed and sank down into her chair.

'And I didn't want her to go without a viewing of my – and my son Max's – latest masterpiece,' he grinned. Max beamed, taking a bow from his seat.

Ava was intrigued. She leant forwards, elbow on her knee, chin resting in her hand.

'So without further ado, I give you: *Café Estrella – A Star is Reborn*,' he said, pressing play on the laptop and the image springing to life on the TV.

Ava didn't know what she'd been expecting. A wobbly documentary charting the café's refurbishment, with some poignant chats with Flora. Not this. Not a film about all of them. All the bits from when no one thought they were filming. Ava put her hand over her mouth when the opening scene was her doing some stupid funny walk to make Max laugh, the camera wobbling as he snorted with giggles. Flora flouncing her hair and complaining of the camera angle while dropping a pearl of wisdom into the mix. Then a montage of people laughing, big belly laughs. Gael, with his walrus moustache, falling off his seat. Gabriela bashing Rory on the bum to make him gyrate his hips. Someone, probably Emilio, filming Max doing Gangnam Style in the sand. Tom lying back in a chair, eyes shut, waking himself up with a snore and opening one eye to check no one was watching. Igor measuring brandy for the sangria, winking at the camera as he chucked in another slug. The dead tomatoes. The pug on wheels. Max holding up some dubious knitting and making a face. Gabriela giving a thumbs up about Everardo. The unearthing of the churros machine. Ava's hand on Rosa's. Flora flirting with Everardo. The ugly bull stencil disappearing beneath white paint. Ava and Tom chatting outside when they were meant to be painting, caught through the window, him looking at her like she lit up the world; Ava, no make-up, face freckled and tanned, red top splattered with paint, looking the happiest she'd ever looked in her life.

Ava watched with her hand pressed over her mouth. The queues for Rosa's churros. Rory and Gabriela sweating in the kitchen. Ava on her bicycle. Max learning to drop a ski. The flamenco. Claire. The grapes. The sunset. The party.

Gabriela and co. out on a pedalo, Igor smoking in the shallows, and Ava and Tom lying on their backs in the surf, a big beaming toothy smile just visible on her face. And then the final shot. Max's little hand writing in shells on the beach: *Our Café Estrella*.

Ava looked up and caught Rory's eye. He winked.

She wanted to watch the film again and again.

This was her life, here.

Everyone was clapping, Rory simultaneously batting away and lapping up praise at the front.

'You should put it on YouTube,' Flora shouted.

'That's the last thing I need,' Rory called back. 'Right now, I've accepted the position as Flora's sous chef. Or should I say, Gabriela's sous chef.'

Flora rolled her eyes.

There was another great cheer.

Ava felt extraordinarily proud.

Then, all serious, Rory added, 'Except, yes, I will some day show the film to the wider public. Of course. It's a bit of fun, but it's also a part of my portfolio.'

And Ava sniggered to herself in the back row as he waffled on about his career as a film-maker. She watched Max blow bubbles in his Coca-Cola, Claire hold in a smile as Rory started to give a more technical breakdown, Flora flirt covertly with Everardo, Gabriela glance at the kitchen then at the clock.

Ava watched and realised that if she did stay, she would be staying for this. She wouldn't be staying for a man or a relationship, she would be staying for them. She would be staying for this life. This happiness. This freedom.

Rory took a bow, Max and Claire giving him an exuberant standing ovation.

She would be staying for her family, she thought. For more than Christmas and birthdays. To see Max grow up. To have a second chance at the type of family that tries to persuade you to stay because you are good enough for them. And they are good enough for you.

She looked at Rory as he donned his apron, chivvied by Gabriela into the kitchen, leaning back to shake congratulatory hands with Gael and the others.

This would be their chance, Ava realised, the bubble rising inside her, to break their mother's legacy. To show that it hadn't broken them.

CHAPTER 43

Ava sat there for an hour. She had eaten her *pan con tomate*, the toast yesterday's bread. She had drunk two coffees and sipped her orange juice by the time Tom arrived. She heard the Jeep come down the hill.

Pushing her chair back, she left the café and jogged up to the car park where she stood waiting in his spot.

Tom was not looking at the road in front of him as he swung the Jeep round in a manoeuvre that he did every day, his eyes looking towards the café.

'Jesus Christ, STOP!' Ava shouted, too late to move from where she was standing.

Tom's head shot round and he slammed on the brakes. Gravel spat. A cloud of dust mushroomed. The Jeep stopped inches away from her. 'What the hell are you doing?' he shouted, jumping down from the car.

'I was waiting for you! I didn't think you were going to run me over.'

'Why were you standing in my spot?' His arms were raised, his voice incredulous.

'Because I thought it would be cool,' she shouted back. 'Now I see that it was less cool than it was meant to be.'

'No kidding. You could have died.'

'Yes. OK.' Ava straightened her top and brushed her hair from her face. 'Can we just ignore that bit?'

Tom shook his head. 'You're a vehicle liability.'

'Can we move on?' she asked.

He strode over, clearly still annoyed, and leant against the front of his truck. 'What can I do for you?'

Ava straightened her top again, nervous. She cleared her throat. 'I have a business proposition for you.'

'You do?'

She took a step forwards. 'It's actually just a proposition. The business part is mine.'

'What is it?'

'Well, businesswise, I think I might set up on my own. I've spoken to Peregrine. I'm going to buy and source for him initially, but also build up my own clients. I've got the contacts, so,' she felt her voice stammer slightly with nerves at the prospect of such change, 'it should work. I hope. I should have done it years ago. But to do it I'm going to have to travel. And I may need a passenger, you know, at times.'

Tom pushed himself off the Jeep, his eyes suddenly narrowing with interest. 'You might?'

'Yes,' Ava nodded. 'And a base, but that could be anywhere really. Even maybe here in Spain.'

'Really?'

'Maybe.'

Tom put his hands in his pockets. 'So this proposition, it means you might stay?' he asked, expression still uncertain.

'Well,' Ava started to smile, 'the staying bit does have some strings attached because, in reality, a beach town is not necessarily the ideal base for setting up this business, but if the other factors were in place, then I think I could make it work.'

'And those other factors,' Tom asked, 'I take it they are human factors?'

'They are.'

Ava was conscious that more people were moving to sit on the side of the café that overlooked the car park. She could see Max's little face resting on the metal railing as he watched. She shifted from one foot to the other, felt the sun warming her skin. She looked at Tom, jaw dark with stubble, eyes like he hadn't slept much in a couple of days.

'And what would those factors have to do?' Tom asked.

'They would have to see that while they had played a part in this decision, they must be aware that they were not the whole part and so must not in any way take the decision for granted or at any point feel or act like they had won.'

Tom shook his head in disbelief. 'Is this human factor actually your brother?'

'No!' Ava said, close enough now that she could bash him on the arm. 'No, it's not my brother.'

She watched as he bit down on the smile spreading across his face, as he glanced away towards the sea and then back to look at her, blue eyes dancing. 'Well, suppose the human factor was me, and I'm just taking a gamble here in thinking it might be. I would definitely feel that I had won,' he said. Then he smiled. 'But not in the sense you're thinking.'

'You would?' Ava found herself on the verge of giggling.

'Definitely.'

'That's good to know,' she said. 'If indeed the human factor did turn out to be you.'

Tom looked down at the ground, scuffed the dirt with his foot, then glanced up again. 'I actually can't stop myself from smiling.'

Ava stepped forwards, put her arms round his neck, as close as she could get, and kissed him right on his smile. And as she did, as she felt his hands crush against her back, the dust in the air, the fierce red sun on her skin, the whole café launched into applause, making her life feel like the encore to the movie.

**The ovens are pre-heating, the Prosecco is chilling...
and *The Sunshine and Biscotti Club* is
nearly ready to open its doors.**

But the guests have other things on their minds...

Libby: The Blogger

Life is Instagram-perfect for food blogger Libby...until she catches her husband cheating just weeks before her Italian cooking club's grand opening.

Evie: The Mum

Eve's marriage isn't working, but she's not dared admit it until now. A trip to Italy to help Libby open The Sunshine and Biscotti Club might be the perfect escape...

Jessica: In Love with her Best Friend

Jessica has thrown herself into her work to shut out the memory of the man who never loved her back. The same man who's just turned up in Tuscany...

Welcome to Tuscany's newest baking school – where your biscotti is served with a side of love, laughter and ice-cold limoncello!

HQ
One Place. Many Stories

The home of bold, innovative
and empowering publishing.

Follow us online

 @HQStories

 @HQStories

 HQStories

 HQ Stories

HQMusic